MW00587174

SACRIFICIAL ANIMALS

SACRIFICIAL ANIMALS

A Novel

KAILEE PEDERSEN

ST. MARTIN'S PRESS
NEW YORK

This is a work of fiction. All of the characters, organizations, and events portrayed in this novel are either products of the author's imagination or are used fictitiously.

First published in the United States by St. Martin's Press, an imprint of St. Martin's Publishing Group

For information, address St. Martin's Publishing Group, 120 Broadway, New York, NY 10271.

www.stmartins.com

Library of Congress Cataloging-in-Publication Data

Names: Pedersen, Kailee, author.
Title: Sacrificial animals : a novel / Kailee Pedersen.
Description: First edition. | New York : St. Martin's Press, 2024.
Identifiers: LCCN 2024003331 | ISBN 9781250328243 (hardcover) | ISBN 9781250328250 (ebook)
Subjects: LCGFT: Horror fiction. | Novels.
Classification: LCC PS3616.E2935 S23 2024 | DDC 813/.6—dc23/eng/20240202
LC record available at https://lccn.loc.gov/2024003331

First Edition: 2024

10 9 8 7 6 5 4 3 2 1

SACRIFICIAL ANIMALS

I.

THEN

Moonlight slashes open the boy's face like a luminous wound. He puts on his brother's goose down jacket, still too large for him, but the spring cold is crisp and bitter and there will be nothing to warm him outside the house. Through the screen door he can see one of his father's favorite greyhounds lying half-asleep in the tall grass. Westerly comes a sharp wind that wakes the animal and sets it running up the gravel road leading to the entrance of the family manse past the glass-eyed buck's head welded to the curlicued front gates. The people from town call it Stag's Crossing after this vulgar display of taxidermy. One thousand acres of rich loam atop the Ogallala Aquifer but only one man there calls himself master of the house with the ornate staircase and milk-white facade. Carlyle Morrow paterfamilias and patriarch. Tall and angular in a peculiar way his face marked by the heat and silt of his childhood in South Carolina. His eyes sharp and green as cut emerald his hair going an early gray. His gait slightly bent to one side like a limping animal though he is strong as any of the summer farmhands he hires to thresh the wheat and husk corn. He drives his white Ford into town every weekend to play pool and drink and stand at the bar and look out the window like he is scrying his own future.

Married only once: his wife French-Oklahoman, a heathen wildness in her gaze dead now for several years having given birth to a monstrous child that in its dying killed her in turn. At the funeral the pastor spoke of the two boys she had left behind though now that she is buried they have forgotten her entirely. Motherless as though Carlyle had cut them from his own flesh. As God made man from a fistful of dust.

Nicholas and Joshua he calls them, the younger and the elder. Whistles to them like a pair of hunting dogs. The older boy Joshua blond like corn silk and the younger one Nick walnut-colored in hair and eye. Like two young bucks they have jousted for dominance in their youthful and garish splendor though Joshua as heir apparent has always been the fated victor. With no women in the house they turn against each other easily with the characteristic cruelty of young boys bereft of civilization. Leaping over the shallow creek and racing through the woods south of the house one pursuing the other until there is no distinction between the courser and the game.

At thirteen Nick is whelped of mother's milk, his walnut hair grown darker with age to a raw hazelnut. He goes out of the house with his father's hunting rifle like an angel sent by God to do his killing work. Had he any sense he would have killed his father with it long ago but he has not. Patricide is the least of his concerns. His father says some beast has been laying its tracks around the house and is in need of a good killing so he paces outside the house that night with the gun to reestablish man's dominion over the animals like his father's dominion over his children. Carlyle possessing like his own father did before him a violence keen and beautiful as the silver curve of a fishhook. Nick gentler and perhaps even fawn-like, strange somehow. Fashioned in the image of his mother—even more than that he is the last evidence of her presence at Stag's Crossing, the singular inheritor of her most feminine and sibylline qualities that fill his father with unease.

Having come round the eastern side of the house and found nothing he joins his father in the driveway where Carlyle stands surveying his vast demesne. The Ford idling out front like a waiting hearse.

Didn't see anything out back, Nick says.

Then look harder, Carlyle says. He points to tracks in the soft soil. Nick squints. Whatever animal has left these behind is swift of foot and light upon the earth. One of his father's greyhounds comes up behind him, sniffing his hands. He recalls their restlessness, their alacrity. Drawn tight as a bowstring they might at one moment sleep soundlessly in the driveway as peaceful as children only to awaken and overtake a hare with a perfect, savage brutality.

Might be one of the dogs, Nick says.

You ought to know better than that, Carlyle says, lightly cuffing Nick's ear. Nick sways on his feet; he is lucky it is not a harder blow. Look at the toes.

Fox, Nick says, at last. Probably here for our chickens.

His father nods.

Should I get Joshua? Nick asks.

No, Carlyle says. He draws his heel over the track, burying it in a furrow of upturned dirt. As though its very existence offends him. Joshua's going to college in a few months. You need to learn to handle things without him.

I can handle things without him.

No, you can't, Carlyle says. Get in the car. I'm teaching you.

A few of the greyhounds have gathered round them now, crowding into the back of the truck. Nick climbs into the passenger's seat and his father slowly pulls them out onto the main road, past the gates of Stag's Crossing.

Only a short drive, Carlyle says. Just need to get to the other side of the woods. We'll make a stealthy approach.

It's late.

Not for foxes.

After negotiating the turn west of the house that points toward the woods, Carlyle says, You ever seen a foxhunt?

In a book I read. There was a picture.

Glossy, bright colors. A fox set upon by a group of sight hounds and torn to pieces. A gnawing anxiety growing within him as he turned the page to a picture of the hacked-off vulpine head, the tail, the paws. Kept by the hunting party as trophies. He took no pleasure in these images; he has always known that his particular viciousness is not the viciousness of his father, who meets all things with a violent contempt so total there is almost no need for the cruelty that inevitably follows it.

In a *book,* Carlyle scoffs. God willing, you'll see the real thing tonight.

At the edge of the woods Carlyle parks the Ford and gets out.

Come on, he says. He has already grabbed another rifle from the back. Two hounds leaping from the truck bed to trail behind him, their ears flattened in submission. Like Nick they were bred to serve.

Nick adjusts the rifle strap and follows his father through the woods. Carlyle muttering to himself as they walk. His voice too low to discern what he is saying though Nick knows exactly what he means. Forced to witness the unending catalogue of his own failures, formed imprecisely as he has been in the furnace of his father's ambition.

The dogs yelp and cavort in the shadow of the trees. The dappled branches menacing overhead as Nick trails behind his father, whose face is partially shrouded in darkness. Most of his father's dogs are pure-blood greyhounds that hunt by sight alone, but from one crossbred litter he had begotten some bloodhound mixture, a monstrous and beguiling lurcher with a broad black snout. The dogs have no names, instead they are many-named: Rover, Fido, Rex, whatever capricious mood has caught Carlyle in the moment of calling out to them. Now the lurcher takes the lead, face pressed to the dirt, intent on flushing out its prey.

A peculiar trembling fills the air. Nick feels almost outside of himself, like he is observing this scene from afar. Knowing his father's true designs he disdains them; he prefers the slow agony of fishing to the garish violence of hunting with the dogs. Watching as they course down any number of animals, returning, always, with the smug satisfaction that befits them. If Carlyle could have had dogs for sons he would have been a happy man; but when has a Morrow man ever been happy? No thousand acres, no grand inheritance can ever be enough to postpone their destinies. Nick will die as bitter as he came into the world. He knows this just as well at thirteen as he will in thirty years.

Peering into the darkness of the forest where hardly anything can be seen except what is pierced by the moonlight Nick catches a glimpse of the fox. A pair of pointed ears in the distance. He looks down the sights of his rifle, straight at it. His finger hovering over the trigger.

That's my boy, Carlyle says.

One of the dogs startles, takes off running in pursuit. The fox darts away, a red smear in the landscape. A loud shriek resounds through the trees, a haunting cry like the scream of a woman, distorted somehow, a melody in the wrong key. Vanishing into a thicket like it was never there. Two of the hounds stop dead in the clearing, unable to pursue their quarry any farther. They return with their heads hanging, dismay in their eyes.

Carlyle grabs Nick by the collar of his hunting jacket. You missed the shot, he says. It was clean.

I had it, Nick mumbles. One of the dogs—

Did I ask for your excuses?

Nick shakes his head. His father releases his grip. Leaving no more of a mark on him than he usually does.

Looked too small to be a dog-fox, Nick says, finally. Must be a female. Could be a den nearby.

Carlyle steps forward into the clearing. There the dogs have begun pacing in an anxious circle. The lurcher perks his head up and barks once, twice. Lifting his paw and sticking his tail straight out it points directly at a half-fallen tree, hollow, already covered in moss and rotting away.

Carlyle gestures for Nick to come closer. At the base of the tree is an opening into which the lurcher peers with slavering intent. He brushes away the cover of dried leaves and sees two fox pups slumbering within.

She's only got two of em. Still young too, Carlyle says. They are bright orange-red and just about the size of Nick's outstretched hand. No tod in sight—elsewhere, maybe, or already hunted down by the dogs in a delightful afternoon game.

Pick one up, Carlyle orders.

Nick hesitantly puts his hand out and picks one up by the scruff. It is practically helpless, making only a pitiful noise that falls just short of a shriek. Nothing like the piercing woman's wail of its mother.

Go on then, Carlyle says, gesturing toward the dogs gathered round. The pup dangles in Nick's hand. He is unable to move his body, unable to understand what his father desires of him.

After a few moments of standing in silence, Carlyle says, Give me that. Seizing the pup from Nick's arms so violently that Nick is left with tufts of fur in his hands. Instead of throwing it to the dogs to be torn apart he takes it by the neck and wrings it with a sharp crack. The head sags, lifeless. Carlyle grabs it by the ears and pulls it off completely, detaching the head from the body in a grotesque motion. Ignoring the spray of blood that hits Nick in the face and arm he tosses both pieces to the dogs. They feed on what remains, without malice, knowing only the profane thrill of teeth against bone.

Nick peers inside the den. The last cub lies sleeping. With a trembling hand he picks it up and pulls it out from the hollow tree. The dogs are sent into a frenzy of eager barking—or perhaps he only imagines them barking in his nightmares, years later. He closes his eyes and throws the pup, still alive, into their midst. He cannot force himself to witness this wild omophagia, weeping uncontrollably as he does this, wiping his face, blood and fur crusting his hands.

Stop that, Carlyle says. Nick feels as though he is being harmed by an outside force, a physical injury piercing him though his father has not laid a hand on him. He doubles over, shuddering in pain, before finally the attack subsides and he straightens himself upright. His face swollen and tinged red.

Are you finished? Carlyle says.

I'm finished, Nick says.

They trudge back to the car in silence. Nick looking down at his feet, unable to meet his father's gaze. Once they reach the Ford before he sullies his father's car with his stained hands he wipes them hastily on his pants. He will have to wash them later, hunched over his sink reciting his pathetic jeremiads to no one in particular. The dirt smearing his hands, the stain that will never leave him. With the dogs and guns piled high in the truck bed they begin their languorous drive to Stag's Crossing. A place to which Nick can only turn back, looking over his shoulder at a fragment of the past.

On the dirt road east of the house his father slows the Ford down slightly, looking through the passenger-side window at the sloped ditch, the stretch of meadow covered in bloomless vetch. In the distance is the shadow of Stag's Crossing, the charnel house that looms. The last gasp of spring almost upon them. He watches his father unlock the car and pull the silver interior handle of the passenger-side door. The gust of wind that enters nearly throwing him from his seat. Two of the dogs have leapt from the truck bed and are now gamboling freely in the shallow ditch next to the dirt road.

You'll walk the rest of the way, Carlyle says. He puts his hand on Nick's shoulder and he is shoved violently forward, tumbling out of the car and onto the rocky soil. He lands on his shoulder and winces at the sharp crunch of pain. Lifting his head from where he has fallen he can see his father's Ford rounding the corner just ahead. His father has never been one to look back. Carlyle Morrow has never turned back in his life, not toward his children nor toward the city of Sodom that might burn so brightly in the flat plains outside Omaha.

In twenty, thirty years his father will ask Nick to stop reliving the past, for Carlyle has no understanding of it, this childhood that could scourge and wound with violence. Nick's face blooming with a fresh bruise as he crawls on his hands and knees in the grass. A few of the dogs crowding around him, licking at his face and hands with wild abandon.

Overhead the birds swarm in agony, screeching and muttering to themselves. If this is a warning Nick cannot interpret it. He thinks about the animals he has just killed, their sacrifices without meaning. The feeling he had of killing that his father had attempted to impart the pleasure of, only to fail miserably. The softness of the fur he had grasped, understanding why they would be skinned for their pelts and hung in his mother's old closet with the rest of her furs.

Through the yellow grass he crawls. Unable to stand up until he can no longer hear the relentless hum of the engine, can no longer smell the exhaust in the cloying air. Finally at the edge of the road he gets to his feet and pulls his jacket tight around his shoulders. Beginning the long walk back to Stag's Crossing. The ground beneath him still treacherous in places, slippery and choked with mud. Only a few wretched dogs to keep him company.

As he passes through the veil of branches that heralds his return from the world of beasts into proper civilization he sees himself at last, clearly, reflected in the dew on the leaves. Joshua's unlikeness, the impending cataclysm of his house. In all manner of ways he is marked by death; he stinks of it; like the third brother that tore open his mother on the way out.

li.

NOW

At forty-three Nick has emptied himself of all nostalgia. His childhood a strange illness from which he will never recover. Out of necessity he has learned to feign the appearance of an ordinary man with an ordinary boyhood. Always ready with an amusing anecdote, a bland characterization of his father as *strict*. He might even believe himself, forger and plagiarist that he is, that the strike of his father's hand slapping his broad and shining face was not unlike love. Perhaps not quite the same but close enough—just as he is close enough to the man he would like to be. His coldness, his fits of depression only apparent in the bleakest of winters. The trees hemorrhaging their leaves as promptly as he discards the trappings of civilization. With a voracious and bestial appetite he has consumed all his lovers, publicly savaging his acquaintances with eloquent condescension. Turning upon them knife in hand. Blood of his father blood of his brother cascading through him ceaseless as summer rain.

He has long vowed to be unlike Carlyle—named by his mother after the patron saint of children and thieves. Yet as time passes inexorably he grows more and more into his father's cruel likeness seen through a cracked windowpane. None of the same handsomeness that afflicts his brother. His eyes have grayed and his hair has darkened to a still-vibrant mahogany but the jagged lines on his cheekbones are entirely his father's. Second son of a second son.

Still his mind is cutting as ever. Having applied his vicious and mangling intelligence to literary criticism he is unfailingly erudite. After two decades set loose upon the world he has learned to affect the banal hostility of an East Coast intellectual. Sawing off all trace of a Midwestern accent from his anodyne English he is exacting in his deception; he refuses the moniker of *America's heartland* and jeers at any hint of the provincial. No sense about him that he could unload and clean a hunting rifle in the dark without shooting his finger off nor that he has hunted geese knee-deep in brackish water a shorthaired pointer crashing into the lake after him. No sense at all that he has known the thrill of an apex predator vanquishing all manner of animal before him. Greyhounds with no table manners bloodying the foyer of his grand house with gore.

That was the Nick of his childhood. Now he is a different man, an impostor. Were he to return to Nebraska he would be a stranger at Stag's Crossing. Prodigal son returning. Would he kneel before his father's magnificence and eat oats from his hand like a wayward steer? Would he see his brother in all his glory like a young Christ in the house of his father?

Unrecognized he would come as a guest in his own home. His brother would embrace him and all would be well in that place where time has no dominion and memory is a mere recursion of the past. Where the edges of Stag's Crossing might have been the edges of the known world and its centerpiece a two-story magnificence built by hand. His father intended them to be born and die there, as with all princes and their castles.

If only Joshua had not done the unforgivable. Married an unacceptable woman from an unacceptable family. If only Carlyle had not chased him from the house like an uninvited guest. Crowing: How dare you. I can't believe it. You brought that bitch into this house. Have her as your mistress, do what you want. It's all the same to me. But your wife! Your *wife*!

Nick watched from his bedroom window. His father's rage shaking the floorboards of the house. Waking the spring cardinals and setting the sparrows to flight. Joshua turned back to his car where his wife waited for him and Nick saw her—saw the curve of her neck and the delicate parting of her hair.

Joshua said, Emilia, we're leaving.

Emilia! O Emilia! Dark and burnished with dread falls that name upon the ear! He must cast her from his mind or else he will die; he must disdain them both. Awakening each day with the absence of his brother curdling within him like the wheat that rots on the stalk. To survive is to flee from the errant ways of his heart which goes where it pleases. But he could never defy the man who terrifies him more than God.

Unlike God his father will die one day. He takes pleasure in this fact. He hates his father so much he could die from it; he is almost sick with it. Yet each Saturday at midnight exactly he picks up the phone to hear Carlyle's lamentations; castigations; a litany of his excruciating failures as a son. Carlyle's voice on the phone an aged and conciliatory baritone. He apologizes and then forgets he has apologized. Sometimes he calls Nick a liar, a fantasist. You've got a great imagination, he says. No wonder you grew up to be a writer. Made up all those things you say I did but didn't. Never beat you with a belt but my pops used to do that. Taught me right from wrong.

Having vindicated himself thus he might rage endlessly against the tyranny of old age—the Jews—the Viet Cong. The miasma of his hatred like a fog that obscures both vision and language.

Remember them? Slit-eyed, yellow as ochre.

Dad, Nick says. He is lying in bed with the receiver pressed against his ear. In an hour he might sleep or else he will lie awake all night thinking of Stag's Crossing. His childhood bedroom. The smell of oak, pine, fresh loam. Crawling on his hands and knees from a roadside ditch, his coat spattered with blood. Out back with the dogs he would tumble, tangled between the long-reaching roots of a willow tree. Writhing in the arms of another boy, not so young now, never so young as they once were—

Remember how I once loved your brother just as much as I love you now.

I know, Dad.

Can you remember the last time you came back and visited your old man? Must've been years. Course I'll be dead soon.

The last time he had visited his father, Carlyle had spent the entire visit complaining that Joshua never called. Nick felt it unwise to point out that being disowned tends to put a damper on family reunions and left after three awkward days.

You always say that.

My hip's been giving me some trouble. I even fell last week almost went right down the stairs. Busted up the side real bad. Hurts to walk and get up sometimes so I went to the doctor and got a scan. It's cancer.

You're kidding.

No real treatment. Got a couple of months.

Nick says nothing in response to this. Debating whether or not he might half believe his father's lunatic assertions. The constant proclamations of his impending death. Yet what Carlyle says seems true enough. In all his decades of brutality, Carlyle has never outright lied to him.

I want to die at home. If I get too sick promise you'll put me down like a dog.

Come on.

Like a dog, Nick.

All right, he says. Turning the geometry of his infernal obsession over in his mind. His heart leaping with mad pleasure. He dares to think of the bastard wasting away, outlived at last. Perhaps his father will go the same way he came into the world; angry and angrier still. Or else it will be the thunderous passage of an era where men were once men and wielded their violence with an ancient and primeval ecstasy.

I've been thinking, Carlyle says. I've got no brothers or sisters back in South Carolina. They're all long gone. Maybe I made a mistake with your brother. Family's supposed to be the most important thing.

I don't know what you mean, Nick says.

Call Joshua. Tell him he needs to come home. To bury me.

And his wife?

He can bring her too. After all these years, I forgot what I disliked so much about her. Maybe she was too arrogant for me.

It was not her arrogance that led him to drive the newly minted Emilia Morrow from the doorstep of Stag's Crossing and they both know this. Nick lets it pass without comment. *Slit-eyed, yellow as ochre.* Carlyle has always feared an outsider at Stag's Crossing since the death of his wife, whom he never mentions though his neurosis has been irrevocably altered by her painful absence. When the doctor from out of town said there was nothing to be done for her or the baby Carlyle would never again admit strangers into the house; he would stand in the doorway with a shotgun in hand the moment even the milkman opened the gate. Seeing in every newcomer the face of an intruder, an invader that must be repelled.

With the years Carlyle's intimations have grown darker and more foreboding—in every blighted crop, every patchwork sale of unused land, he sees long-delayed retribution. His punishment for cutting down half of the woods to make a home for himself and his two disappointing sons. How many birds and rabbits and little foxes did he cut down likewise so that his children might have a future on those thousand acres of land. Now after all this he must accept Emilia Morrow at the doorstep of his home, this woman who portends ruin, who in another era more amenable to men like Carlyle they might have burned for sorcery. So decisive was her entry into the family. Even more decisive was her removal of Joshua from the fold, an uncanny and otherworldly act of seduction. Carlyle's dread and resignation over the course of these events, inevitable and enraging, clear to Nick even through the telephone.

I'll let him know.

Good. Don't come earlier than Sunday. Have to clean the house first.

Yes, Nick says. He already knows which suitcase he will use, which shirt and ties he will pack. All his life he has been waiting for this, the graceful denouement. Standing at his father's deathbed. The faces of the bereaved at the funeral. The long and endless afterward.

He dares not think of Emilia. Having looked upon her face once before he knows to recall her is a venture that will bring only disquiet to his carefully hermetic disposition. In the right-hand drawer of his writing desk he has stored all the letters she has sent him over the years. She was a painter before she married Joshua, or so she says; she sends him drawings. Whatever she can fit in a standard envelope. Charcoal and pastel studies of animals. Multicolored birds, dogs, a fox chasing a hare. On occasion she sends him a painting in the Chinese style. The colors muted, the brushstrokes superb and delicate. So thinly laid onto the paper they seem almost to shift before his eyes. Once she sent him a portrait of a woman in an Oriental robe, ordinary like any other, except for the nine bristling tails that grew from her backside. The woman's face obscured by her long hair, her visage unrecognizable. The painting filled him with such unease he put it face down at the bottom of the drawer and did not look at it again.

He tries now to conjure an image of his brother whom he has not seen in twenty years. Joshua must be as marvelous as he was in his youth. His beauty is not the kind that listens to age. A face so handsome it borders on obscenity.

With a vain quirk of his mouth he could be mistaken for another Narcissus; yet his recklessness and disobedience mark him as a rebellious child of God. Eschewing the Morrow fortune, the bloody masterwork of his father for what Joshua might have called love but surely must be closer to hypnotic possession. How else to explain it? As he once set fire to Nick's books he has now set fire to his family. His desire akin to self-annihilation.

lii.

THEN

The killing of a fox is one thing. The killing of its children, another entirely. Such a crime, once committed, can never be undone. That night Nick climbs the spiral staircase to the second floor of the house and scrubs himself raw in the bathtub. The stain of it lingering. He hardly eats for three days. Remembering the silent huffing of the dogs, the cracking of the bones as they chewed. The bruise on his face as he rose from the ditch. The little foxes, so small in his hands.

After a late supper he readies himself for bed with the most perfunctory of gestures. Combing his hair as his mother had taught him, when he once sat beside her at her vanity. Looking at her, at her reflection in the large mirror as she carefully parted his hair and combed it out for him. His father in the background, fixing his tie: Now,

now, don't give that boy any ideas. Don't want him growing up like a woman.

Lying awake in his small bed beneath the slanted ceiling he pushes the image of his mother from his mind; she is long dead though he still feels a part of her perhaps remains present in the house. It is not something his father or brother could ever perceive or understand. Her voice in the wind, the soft touch of her hand in his hand when he is drifting off to sleep. These apparitions are not meant for them, they are Nick's inheritance alone, cursed forever to bear her memory within him. The penitence of a mourner.

One of the dogs slinks up the stairs, nudging open the door to his bedroom. Pressing its wet snout into his hands. Insistent on something, though what exactly it is, Nick cannot tell. With the window open he can hear a few of the hounds taking off into a run toward the back of the house, letting forth a furious storm of howling. Unusual, for Carlyle bred his dogs to be seen and not heard, much like children.

Downstairs he fetches his boots, his jacket, the hunting rifle. Leaving quickly through the back door. The gun loose in his hands as he walks through the tall grass past the stalks of alfalfa and the bowed willow toward the chicken coop. He and his brother hammered it together a few summers ago when his father said if they wanted to eat deviled eggs every Fourth of July like they had when their mother was still alive they could raise the chickens themselves. With the moon bright and guileless he can see a part of the chicken wire is torn at the bottom where some animal has pushed through. Blood staining the wire. He goes round the back of the coop and sees eggs scattered and crushed in the dirt. A hen lying grotesque and headless on the ground. He gets on his hands and knees to look for the other half of it but cannot find it, only dried blood and feathers. Whatever animal came down to feast has already thoroughly enjoyed its nighttime aperitif and left. The firmament bearing the deep gashes of its claw marks, its shameless violence.

He bends the chicken wire back in place. Later he will come back and glue it down more firmly. Maybe put up a little fence around the coop if he has time after school. Not enough flesh left on the chicken for the dogs so he kicks some dirt over the corpse until he can come back with a shovel in the morning. Already half an hour past midnight and the stars are still brilliant as ever. Joshua once taught him some of their names but none of them come to mind now.

He walks back with the rifle tucked under his arm. If he were not Carlyle Morrow's youngest and most serious son he might resemble a carefree farm boy in some bucolic Winslow Homer painting though his father has always favored the charcoal work of Goya. In the doorway he takes off his muddy boots and hangs up his brother's coat. Unloads the rifle and hangs it on the wall next to the coat by its leather strap. The screen door falls closed behind him and he makes sure to latch it.

Swiftly and violently as a gunshot a scream pierces the sloped fields lying open and fallow behind the house. Sounding like a woman being murdered in the way he has seen it on television where her agony is drawn out over several breathless and voyeuristic minutes until he changes the channel. Yet he knows it is not a woman but some unnamable beast of the forest come to bewitch and maim. A mother despondent, in all her devastated keening—the fox whose children now reside in the stomachs of the hounds at Stag's Crossing has finally returned.

He hastily locks the inner door as well but even that does not quiet the unholy calling that pursues him past the foyer and deeper into the house. In the fox's wailing he recognizes the lamentations of the bereaved; with its children dead, it is an expression of grief without end. He knows he will only be safe in his bedroom under his three blankets where he can sleep with the lights on like a child. Up the spiral balustrade that snakes to the top floor he sees his father turn on the light and emerge barefoot in his long maroon bathrobe. He is unshaven and his guttural baritone is hoarse from sleep.

God damn it, Nick, he says, what'd you chase up back there?

A fox, Nick says.

A sliver of light escapes from beneath Joshua's doorway—he is awake now too. He sticks his head outside gazing down at his brother with an imperious frown. Young princeling, seventeen and anointed successor his thick blanket wrapped around him like a royal doublet. Even having just awoken unkempt he is preternaturally handsome. His hair the color of sand struck by lightning. In ten years he will be lithe as one of the dogs and burn with the delicious pleasure of his attraction.

Fox? Joshua says.

Eating the hens, Nick says.

There's a boy out in Blair who's real good at hunting

foxes, Joshua says. Could call him up and ask him to come out sometime. Goes by the name of Will Skog.

You think I'd let some nobody from Blair come here and intrude on our land? Carlyle says. His hostility flaring like the roar of the fireplace, stoked to a fierce blaze.

I can do it, Nick says.

Already had it right in your sights and you let it go. It'll come right back. Once a fox finds a fat henhouse it'll never leave.

I said I can do it.

Then kill it, Carlyle says. Kill it and be done with it. And let me sleep.

Nick says nothing. Without the gun he has no power in this house. His father could strike him dead where he stands. In some sense he has already been struck down, made to heel like an unruly cur fed and disciplined by the same decisive hand. When his father retreats into the blackness of the master bedroom he walks up the narrow stairs and to the small child's bedroom with the slanted roof at the end of the hallway. The hallowed and forbidden place he will return to so often in his dreams.

He fixes the mosquito screen against his window and crawls into bed not having changed into his pajamas. Marveling at the garden strangely silent and smelling of fresh grass. The verdant scent of wealth pervading the house and the land that surrounds it. Watered by the blood of their family this apocryphal lineage carved into the Morrow name and resonating like thunder through each successive generation. He is Southern moneyed, Midwestern moneyed. Seeping into the earth and making an abattoir of his childhood stained now and forever by his birthright.

He lies awake listening to the terrible groaning of the house. As though Stag's Crossing itself might grieve alongside the wilderness that surrounds it, the bowed willow, the black soil that swallows the fox-bones, the last remnants of what he has done. Years from now, when he is man enough to stand taller than his father, the garden will not rise to bloom again; it will lie fallow and barren as their family tree. Their line destined to end here, with him.

That night he weeps to think of his brother whose handsomeness has now begun to approach the sublime. Weeps to think of him running through the fields blood on his knuckles blood spattering the rye. Behind him comes Nick with his hunting rifle. Behind him comes the vivid premonition that one day when they are old enough to be called grown men Nick will usurp his brother and in this unholy annexation he will rise again as someone strange and new.

His regicide is imminent; ambition grows within him like a strangling vine. Second son, second born: Jacob above Esau, Isaac above Ishmael. Pretender to the throne.

IV.

NOW

At his desk he ruminates without mercy. Scratching anxious lines into his face with slim fingers he is seized by a familiar and seductive neurosis. Like Daniel interpreting the will of God at Belshazzar's table he must decipher his father's edict. Summon Joshua back to Stag's Crossing. Bury his father and with him the rage that has tormented Nick for decades. A rage that has disfigured him in body and mind. Has set him apart from others who in their anodyne lives cannot understand how deep and tumultuous this anger runs. Splintering him open like a fault line. When a man standing naked in his bathroom shaving says, Well, I've got a father hang-up too, Nick nods and says nothing. Steam from the shower shrouding his face, his expression of frank disgust.

Only his brother could understand these things: Carlyle

and his whims, his insults, his strange genius. They are both forever unable to escape that place wherein lies the terrible essence of their childhood. Disgraced by their history that marks them indelibly as Carlyle's sons. Returning to their father once more. He who has forgiven the transgression of Joshua's youth in his magnanimous old age.

Nick, you know I'm a man of mercy, he says. A man of God.

He whose hands have beaten and baptized. He who has reckoned with idolaters and struck them down with his divine and inexorable will.

Have I ever wronged you? he asks.

No, Nick says. You haven't.

What will Nick say to his brother, his brother's wife? He has not seen them for twenty years. Each time they move—Minneapolis, Boston, Seattle, San Francisco—Emilia writes him an elegant letter enclosing their new address and phone number. Her lovely regards.

Joshua, of course, does not write.

He takes out the latest envelope dated September 1994 from the right-hand drawer of his writing desk. The letter and its envelope a delicate eggshell-and-cream color. Copies down the phone number inside with a madman's scrawl onto a pad of paper and then rips the envelope in two and rips the letter in two as well. He cannot bear to read more than a sentence of *Dear Nick, I hope this reaches you well*—as though each word foretells some imminent disaster. His days of prophecy are over; he can no longer see what was, what is, what will be. What calls him back to Stag's Crossing is not the providence of priests but something much more heretical. The exquisite euphoria of his envy and rage.

Sent as the unfortunate messenger of Carlyle's benediction he has come to bring Joshua back into the fold like a wayward lamb. Long have they both wandered in the wilderness far from the demesne of their father. Now he and Joshua must return to Stag's Crossing. Return to that grand two-story house where as children they were left alone for hours at a time savaging each other like wild dogs.

Between the two of them there is nothing left to say. It is too late for hesitation; twenty years too late. He dials the number without looking at the keypad and with each subsequent ring he is like a young man in the woods again. Stalking ever closer to a group of ducks flushing them from the water as he appears from out of the darkness and takes aim as they retreat to the skies. The vicious crack of the shotgun. The death squall of a gadwall as it plummets from the air. Barest hint of red mottling its tawny feathers. Nick dashing into the lake to grab it by the neck—

Hi, this is Emilia Morrow.

Hi Emilia, it's Nick.

Oh—Nick—how nice to hear from you, she says. The way she says it indicates that she is lying and wants him to know that she is lying. Deliberate in the sharp neutrality of her voice. Her voice, as he achingly remembers, is so pleasant to the ear. Voice of soubrette or nightingale. A slender needle in the throat.

At times he is unsure if she hates him or loves him, in the manner only family can hate or love. Either way he would not be surprised; he has once witnessed the cold brilliance of her scorn. Emilia looking at his father like she could kill him as he chases her husband from the house, cursing her infernal presence. Carlyle without his rifle but with the air that he knows exactly where he left it—he could go back into the house and fetch it if he wanted to, if he wanted to hurt them in the same way Joshua has transgressed and committed this act of patricide. Defied Carlyle and spit in his face as though he has been taught nothing. Nothing about the proper order of the world. God's dominion over man and man's dominion over animals. Such a disruption of their family can only be fixed by death—death of the father or death of the son.

I need to talk to Joshua.

Why so? she asks.

It's about Carlyle.

She pauses for a moment. Is something wrong?

He's dying, he says. Bone cancer.

Will it be painful?

Most likely.

Then why not let him die? she asks. There is no anger, no hatred in her voice. Only the question—why not allow the world to turn, the seasons to change, without Carlyle in their lives? Why disrupt the equilibrium they have built so carefully? Joshua, the eldest in exile. Nick, the hapless go-between.

He imagines her waiting by the phone listening with a bitter cunning in her gaze. Yet quickly as this vision comes to him it vanishes—he is unable to grasp her true nature. Her outline in his memory scraped over like a palimpsest.

In the background he can hear a man's voice saying something indiscernible. A television tuned to static or else some meaningless commercial. No voices of children, no background cacophony of dogs or cats or otherwise. Only the sound of the street: the sound of cars going by and the rattling of blinds against the windowsill.

Hang on, she says. Passing the phone over he hears the scraping of her nails against the receiver.

Nick? Joshua says. Sounding like the voice of a young god as he might have spoken to a mortal supplicant eons ago.

Joshua.

It's been a while.

Yes, it really has. I'm calling to let you know about Dad.

What about Dad?

He says he's got bone cancer.

Is he in the hospital?

No but he only has a few months left.

That's a shame to hear.

He wants you back at Stag's Crossing.

Does he plan to kill me? Joshua laughs a bit without humor.

God no. He's serious.

Surely he's lying.

Didn't sound like it.

You know I can't do that. Emilia—

He says bring Emilia.

No he didn't.

Says he doesn't care anymore.

Yes I'm sure my racist father has magically changed his mind about my Asian wife.

It's what he said.

For God's sake, Joshua says. You must really be naïve.

You don't want to find out?

He doesn't want to see me. He's going senile.

You think so?

You brought that bitch into this house, Joshua says. An uncanny imitation. Deep and murderous as his father two decades ago. Such an excellent mimicry that the familiar childhood dread rises in Nick's throat and is forced down again like bile.

Family's family.

Emilia is my family.

That's not what I mean.

That's exactly what you mean.

No.

Liar.

Don't say that, Nick says. I'll be there on Sunday. See you then.

Get away from me. And stay away from my wife.

Nick listens for several seconds to the empty blare of the disconnect tone and then hangs up. He has no doubt that he will be seeing his brother shortly for the irrational has always triumphed over reason in their family. A commandment from their father is not one to be disobeyed. Tangled in their vertiginous madness they are woven together thick as a crown of thorns. Wreath of white yarrow.

He walks into his bedroom, sparsely decorated. Pulling his small suitcase out from where it is stored underneath his modest twin-sized bed. The sheets neatly made every morning, just as he did when he was a child. Folding his clothes as meticulously as his father taught him he picks out his best shirts and pants. Without thinking he goes to the right-hand drawer of his desk and rummages in it for the little Chinese painting Emilia sent him. At the bottom of the stack it remains there, face down. He turns it over and realizes that whatever uncanny power it held over him now has dissipated; he finds it almost charming. A strange relic of another culture, another era. It bears no artist's signature. He tucks it inside his suitcase and thinks he might ask Emilia to sign it for him.

In another hour Nick will call his editor. Set aside his papers and finish packing for the journey westward. Forty miles outside Omaha lie his father's thousand acres in the desiccated heart of the country. Where Carlyle Morrow forged his progeny from steel, glass, flesh. Where as a boy Nick once lay silent and still for an entire evening amongst the wheat golden as his brother's hair. The long shadow of the house cradling him in its motherless embrace.

V.

THEN

Nick sits at the edge of the dry creek with his father's rifle slung over his shoulder. His face in shadow he is a mystery even to himself. With very precise movements he takes the rifle off his shoulder and puts his finger on the trigger. He slides the safety forward, just like he has done a thousand times before. He points it at the trees, the famished creek, and finally props the rifle against a rock and looks straight down the barrel. The sky above him white with clouds. Then he slides the safety back into place and carries the rifle in his arms pointing downward like his father showed him when he first gave it to him, as though nothing at all has happened. The self-annihilating impulse leaving him just as quickly as it came.

Resting his chin in his hands he watches a few ants, undeterred by the cold wind, as they carry frozen blades of grass back to their colony. Crossing over the creek on their makeshift bridge, a sapling that was felled during a lightning storm two years ago. A whole line of them marching along with enviable determination. Sometimes he feels as small and insignificant as they are, leading a meaningless life just as God put insects on this Earth for the sole purpose of being crushed underfoot. Similarly he feels doomed to this anodyne existence forever with the only respite being death itself. Certain days, good days, he vows to leave Stag's Crossing once and for all and make his fortune east or west of here, far from the world his father has carved out for him and his secondary place in it.

Other days, he is beset not by a childish misery but a cultivated sense of despair that marks his passage into manhood and will pursue him until his last moments. On a day like this, he wakes mute, melancholic, and spends the hours drifting aimlessly in his thoughts. Obsessing over his myriad inadequacies, how he is neither made in Joshua's image nor his equal. Second-born in all the ways that matter, and in some that do not. At night he feels as though he is being burned alive in a vague and unreachable sense. The sensation inflicting itself upon him at a distance, on skin that is not his own.

Carlyle left for town that morning with Joshua, saying very little. They would return whenever Carlyle decided to leave off from his infinite business deals, wreathed in cigar smoke—endeavors that could last anywhere between several hours or several days.

This morning Nick watched from the front window of the house as the Ford peeled away. Then he went into the

Quonset and fetched a hunting rifle. Carrying it with him now as he paces the outline of Stag's Crossing, not knowing what it means or what he might do with it, only that it gives him pleasure to possess one of the grand instruments of his father's destruction.

He thinks he might venture deeper into the woods and look for some of the bluebirds that nest in the trees. Hiding in the deepest cavities where the wood is smoothed over and polished by the wind and Nick can put his whole arm into that hollow place all the way up to his shoulder before touching a nest. When he was with his brother Joshua would tell him to break the eggs for no reason but Nick would always put them back. Thinking it was pointless to be so cruel.

In time, he will understand. Cruelty is its own justification.

He stands up and leaps onto the fallen sapling. Balancing on one foot with boyish, effusive pleasure, then picking up a branch that has fallen onto the ground and sweeping away the dirt in his path. The ants scattering as he stomps on them without a further thought. He goes back and forth a few times, pretending he is doing a high-wire act, before deciding it is too cold to stay out much longer. His father and brother could return at any moment—late afternoon is Carlyle's favorite time of day to prowl Stag's Crossing with the exacting neurosis of a once-caged tiger, now unleashed on these unsuspecting thousand acres.

As Nick walks up the hill toward the coop, the house with its striking outline in the distance, his mind drifts to darker conceits. The further contemplation of patricide might occur to him only rarely, though when it does the thought is delicious and intense—last Thursday he heard on the radio of a gruesome killing somewhere just south of Crete, in one of those many nameless towns that the state seems to have collected by accident, as a beachcomber amasses an assortment of misshapen shells. It had been an only child, an only son—something Carlyle would have found intolerable, to have no replacement in the event of Joshua's death or disownment—who had killed his father with a shotgun and left the body for his mother to find. When questioned, the boy had said, I don't know what came over me. Like someone else had done it. Some other force guiding the strike of his murderous hand.

He is halfway to the house when he hears the warbling bark of neither dog nor bird ring out in the frigid air and turns around. At the edge of the woods he can make out a treacherous streak of red through the trees. Immediately his hand is on the rifle; he brandishes it without thinking. Kneeling down he struggles to steady his aim. The fox's blurry image barely visible. He imagines killing it from such a distance. A single bullet through the skull. A crack shot, his father would call him. With his shoulders rigid he feels the weight of the gun in his hands, the cartridges he had loaded earlier that day in anticipation of violence, though in what form he had not known at the time.

He recalls, unwillingly, the specter of his grand crime: two pups. Dark brown. So small they might be no larger than his hand. The smell of the blood on his face, the howling of the dogs. His incorrigible weeping. The root of his despair.

His finger is still on the trigger. Yet he does not move. Would it not be a mercy, to end its wretched life after the deaths of its children? The memory of his mother coming to him, unbidden, her lifeless hand in his as he stood next to her deathbed with a loyalty so undying only the hounds can understand it.

A bird, perched overhead, cries out. The fox dives straight into the narrow underbrush. He swears quietly to himself, watching it disappear into the woods unblooded. A part of him wanting to cut the vixen's throat and skin it as it lies dying in the grass, to carry the torn fox-fur back to the house, triumphant with his spoils of war. Another part of him, the softness that lies beneath, taking no pleasure in this brutal imagining. He is an aspirant to violence, a pupil of his father, one who has not learned his true lesson. He could end this now, this strange dance of death. Had he the mettle, the firing arm. But he does not. He is too weak to enact his will upon the animals of Stag's Crossing that trample underfoot; he will never be called the master of this domain and will die as pathetic as he came into the world.

A fox who has found a fat henhouse will not give up its blood sport so easily. Not until all the hens are dead.

Deeper into the woods he pursues the fox. Past the fallen trees that lie blackened and dead at the border between the forest and the clearing, Carlyle's domain and the world beyond it that he can never control, that riles his obsessive anger like nothing else. Carefully he steps over treacherous bramble, scattered branches, following the tracks it has made in the soft and yielding soil.

The tracks stop at the foot of a hollow tree trunk. Kneeling down Nick looks inside; it is empty. A lone beetle gnawing at the bark. He scoops out the soft leaves, the tangled greenery, searching for answers. He finds nothing. Not even a single fox-hair shed from its glorious claret pelt.

Slowly, watchfully, he circles round the trunk. On the other side there is a single print pressed into the ground. Neither fox nor dog nor coyote. Nick squints; the shape is blurry, indistinct. Too small to be a bear. With his finger he traces its outline. The length of it, the lack of claws is all wrong for an animal, he realizes. It is a human footprint, delicately made. Placed there in the dirt like a warning.

What manner of stranger comes to Stag's Crossing? Carlyle Morrow has no friends that might visit; he has subordinates, farmhands, men he treats no better than lackeys. None of them would walk barefoot here, where the ground is slippery and wet with spring rain. The very presence of the uninvited makes a mockery of Carlyle's fierce disdain for all things foreign to him.

Through the trees comes the sound of a vehicle slowly making its way up the road. What can only be the Ford. Nick quickly stands up and adjusts the rifle strap. Breaking into a breathless run. Though he has never been much of an athlete he can run like the Devil is chasing him, with all the gracelessness that implies. As he bursts through the trees into the clearing one of the greyhounds sees him running and joins him, its long-legged strides almost a gentle mockery as he rounds the coop and throws open the back door of the house, hanging up the rifle and unlacing his boots with shaking hands just as the Ford pulls into the driveway and Carlyle opens the front doors of the house.

Behind him comes Joshua. They talk among themselves in a shared dialect that Nick cannot, will not ever understand. Standing in the kitchen Nick strains to overhear pieces of the conversation—the spring has not gone as planned, corn prices are absurd, how many acres will they plant this year—Carlyle predicts a bad yield, the ground deader than the wife and third son he buried years ago at Stag's Crossing.

Bad luck, says Joshua. A bad year.

No, Carlyle says, his voice louder and clearer now. Someone's got something against me. I can feel it.

His footsteps reverberate against the wood floors. He is pacing now, like a caged animal.

Crops don't just die off like that. There was ergot in the rye. Now that I can't explain. And that boy at the market selling seed with his father, he had a funny look about him—wouldn't be surprised if he was a Jew, they're everywhere these days—

Nick goes into the hallway. Against his better judgment, he says, Why not rent the land. It'll still grow grass. The Rasmussens could use it for grazing.

Carlyle turns on him, furious. What did I tell you about eavesdropping? If I wanted to hear your opinion, I would've asked for it.

Okay, Nick mumbles. His father approaches and Nick backs away into one of the tall bookshelves lining the hallway. Shrinking to make himself as small as possible, almost on instinct, and despising himself for it.

You feed the dogs? Carlyle says. Joshua is silent, watching them.

Yes, Dad.

He steps closer. Why did you take one of my rifles from the Quonset?

Nick shrugs. Went looking for the fox.

And did you find it?

No. Just tracks. Human ones too.

You see? Carlyle says to Joshua. Vermin in our midst. Spirits. You let the woods get too big and the place starts to have its own ideas.

Come on, Dad, Joshua says. Putting his hand on Carlyle's shoulder. It's probably just one of the Rasmussen kids.

We'll see about that, Carlyle says. Turning back to Nick, he says, What're you doing just standing around? Either find something to do or go upstairs and finish your homework.

Nick retreats upstairs, his head spinning. In his little bed beneath the sloped roof he lies face down on the comforter. The beating of his frantic heart like a metronome.

Despite his opulent fantasies he knows he cannot raise a hand against his father. Not now, maybe not ever. These are merely seeds sown in parched soil that like Nick himself will never sprout nor bear fruit; diseased and barren remains the landscape of his mind, the innermost chambers of his desolate heart.

VI.

NOW

How strange it is, to hear his brother's voice again. Muffled and distorted by the telephone line, but Joshua's voice nonetheless. Deeper than Nick's heedless and occasionally reedy tenor—time has smoothed over its graveled undertones, leaving behind a voice as handsome as the man who wields it.

The last time he and his brother had spoken was at Joshua's wedding. Nick had driven all the way out east, to a small Lutheran church in the New York suburbs. Their father had long made his position clear in a letter delivered that autumn. The words slashed into the page by an angry, frenzied hand. All of Carlyle's unkind regards, now shredded to pieces—*if you marry this woman—disowned—how dare you—might as well spit on my grave—after all I've done for you.* Joshua had shown Nick the letter, asked him if he thought this would be the end of it.

Probably, Nick had said. Knowing the depth of his father's anger, perhaps this was foolish to say. Carlyle's memory was long, though life might prove to be longer yet.

The sidewalk was covered in wet leaves. He was early, too early—he had the time wrong by an entire hour. Stepping inside he found the place occupied only by silence. The nave full of candles, burning happily. The pews empty of all onlookers. Joshua had asked nothing of him, not even a toast, and Nick had not offered. He was to wear his second-best suit and smile appropriately during the ceremony. Afterward, he would hand over his small gift of middling cutlery and leave.

He crossed to the front of the pews and looked at the altar, which held no power over him any longer. Where his father was a man of faith but not shackled by it Nick was and is a man without convictions. Chained, painfully, to his memories of the past.

Standing before the grand church organ Nick remembered how his father had once told him of his third-grade teacher, who had cried upon hearing him sing a hymn. In those days he possessed a real boy soprano, tremulous and fine as a strand of silk. She had suggested singing lessons. A spot in the school choir. Carlyle had laughed at this, laughed telling Nick on the phone about this foolish old woman who had never married, spending her evenings playing piano at the church.

She thought you were so talented, Carlyle had sneered.

His quotations precise with derision. *Such a natural musician.* She thought I'd waste my money on that nonsense for you. And what, so my boy can turn into some fruit?

Nick had not sung since. But then again, what is there to sing about at Stag's Crossing? The tuneful whistle of the whip-poor-will is melody enough. Lying in the dirt as Joshua slaps the life out of him he hears the thrumming of his blood vibrant and moving as any symphony.

From the eastern side of the church came the distant hint of music. A directionless, haunting echo. He stepped out of the nave and into a narrow hallway. The doors on his right were closed to him, all except one at the end of the hall. He walked to it, as if drawn not by his own power but the gleaming of a feathered lure dragged through shallow, muddy water.

Inside he found Emilia Morrow. Combing her hair, long and dark as ever. Her face turned toward the window, which reflected nothing. The skirt of her wedding dress was so expansive it seemed to almost swallow her up, a sea of white fabric that spilled onto the vanity, the floor. He stood politely outside, unsure of what to do with his hands.

Finally, she turned to him. Only the slightest tilt of her neck, elegant as a swan's. She squinted briefly, as if studying him.

I've never seen you here before. Do you work here?

It's me, he said. Nick.

He was unnerved by the discovery that upon closer inspection she was just as attractive as he had expected. Even worse, it was the unsubtle, conspicuous beauty that Joshua also possessed—a self-evident magnetism that drew the eye with its assuredness. She looked even younger than he was, and lovelier besides. A delicately proportioned face. The softness of her features almost endearing. Yet beneath such attractiveness lay an unfocused, humming dread. There was something profoundly unnatural about her. Disconcerting and entrancing in equal measure. The sense that she was almost—and still not quite—the likeness of a perfect woman. Elegantly shaped, sculpted with such artistry so as to be almost unmistakable from the real thing.

A single look at her served to annihilate such thoughts from his mind. Before this, she had been merely an image to him, blurred by memory. Seen from a second-story window as she sat in his brother's convertible with the top down, her face angled slightly away from him. A dark curtain of hair obscuring her from view. Now, having glimpsed her at last, he was unable to look away. His attraction immediate and all-consuming.

He struggled to free himself, like a man slowly sinking into quicksand. To organize his thoughts in a rational manner.

Nick! she said. I hardly recognized you.

Well, we've never really met.

No, we haven't.

I'm so glad you were able to come. Joshua's told me a lot about you.

Has he?

Of course. His beloved little brother.

She put down the comb and gestured toward the box in his hands. What's that with you?

Oh. This? Just a gift.

How charming, she said. She reached to take the box from him. Their fingers touched, gently.

What is it? she said.

Nick tried to focus. The faint hiss of static entered his mind. Since he arrived at the church he had felt it lingering there, in the shaded alcoves. The presence of something strange and unknowable, which he had attributed to what remained of his religious belief. Yet maybe it was something else, hidden behind the veil of ambiguity that often accompanied both weddings and funerals.

He seemed unable to move, to let go of the box of silverware, to look Emilia directly in the eye. Perhaps all these things were unrelated; merely the nerves of meeting another person for the first time. His brother's soon-to-be wife, looking at him with expectation. Expectation of what, he could not discern.

Silverware, he said, at last. Handing the box over to her. She took it from him with an enviable gracefulness to her movements, neatly tucking it beneath the vanity next to what appeared to be her shoes for the wedding. High heels in a tasteful cream color.

How wonderful, she said. Up close he caught a glimpse of her left hand, crisscrossed with a lattice of scars, before she quickly hid it beneath the skirt of her wedding dress. Just what we needed. He expected her to be sarcastic, but nothing in her expression betrayed anything except a shameless honesty.

As she brushed some of her hair away from her face, one of the pins fell to the ground. Almost against his will Nick found himself bending down to pick it up. A gesture made as though his hand was not his own, as though he was no longer the maker of his own design. Holding the small piece of metal to the light he heard Emilia—her voice coming at a distance—saying, No, let me—

He had seen his mother doing it many times in front of the large mirror in the second-floor bathroom. Getting herself ready for her husband. For Carlyle Morrow himself.

Emilia's hand came up to grasp his wrist. Lightly looping her index and thumb around his arm as he carefully brushed the strand of hair behind her ear and slowly pushed the pin deeper.

Nick, Joshua said.

He jerked his hand away. Emilia moved just as quickly, turning her face back to the window with a studied casualness. Her hand falling back to her lap, as though it had never left it. The smile on her face immovable—thought perhaps it dimmed slightly as Joshua approached. His hands in his pockets, walking with the nervous swagger of a man about to married.

You made it, Joshua said. Dad unchained your leash for once?

You're the one that's getting disowned, not me.

Ha-ha. Funny kid, this one, he said. Clapping Nick on the shoulder just a little too hard as he passed.

Isn't it bad luck to see the bride before the ceremony? Emilia asked. Receiving Joshua's peck on the cheek with a sly smile.

I couldn't help myself.

Well, at least tell your brother thank you for the gift.

What'd you get?

Silverware, Nick said.

Joshua said, My God. We'll have a mountain of it by the end of this.

Joshua. Be nice.

As this charmingly domestic scene unfolded Nick watched his brother's gaze remain transfixed, powerlessly, on Emilia's upturned visage—an open doorway that might welcome any manner of guest. A silent conversation occurring between the two of them that he could not understand. Something he might one day grasp when he is married—though he knew, even then, he would never be married. Destined for a fatal and incomprehensible loneliness.

Come on, Joshua said, putting his hand on Nick's shoulder. Help me get set up for the ceremony.

Back in the nave, Nick stopped in front of the first row of pews. Joshua followed behind him. They knew each other far too well and Nick could tell by the pattern of his footsteps that Joshua was itching for a fight. The thundering stride that signaled their father approaching was now the inheritance of his brother, about to be scratched out of the will without so much as a further mention.

What was that? Joshua hissed.

What?

He could feel Joshua's temper flaring, wild as any unbroken stallion. You putting your hands on my wife.

Nick regarded him coolly. Don't be absurd. We've literally just met. Her bobby pin fell out.

And she couldn't put it back herself?

You think it's a good idea to be this paranoid on your wedding day? If you ask me, you shouldn't marry her anyway.

Because Dad doesn't approve?

He shrugged. I just don't think this will end well.

He had known as soon as he had set foot in the little church below the hill. The infernal buzzing in his head could only be one of his headaches that had practically split him open as a child. An omen, a bad one. Joshua had brought an outsider to Stag's Crossing—and they would be paying the price for his foolishness for years to come.

I'm parked out front; we can leave anytime.

Funny, Joshua said. Examining him closely. Like he saw something in Nick that even Nick himself could not perceive. I always took you for a fairy.

Such a blow did not come unexpectedly. It would have stung a decade ago, when Nick was still tender-eyed and knew little of the world. It was too late now; the young man who so often occupied his thoughts in childhood was long departed, and with him what remained of Nick's capacity for shame.

Have it your way, he replied. He was too tall now for Joshua to strike him down with a single right hook, too old for these games that had ceased to hold any meaning for him. It's clear I'm not welcome here. Enjoy your gift. Give my regards to the new Mrs. Morrow.

Outside the sun was shining. A listless rain fell. He found his car parked at the edge of the lot, spattered in bird shit and blood. He swore, seeing a hawk's leftovers indelicately deposited onto his hood. A lifeless sparrow with its head torn clear off. He had seen such a scene before. A hazy memory, quickly pushed aside.

Nimbly extracting the corpse from his windshield he held its dead body in his hand. It barely fit in his palm, a small and pathetic thing. A trickle of liquid came out of its neck, like blood but darker, almost black. Staining the tips of his fingers. He dropped it onto the asphalt and entered his car. Looking for a napkin to wipe his fingers on, he dirtied the glove box with black fingerprints. Already the rain had begun to pour down, washing away any evidence of this encounter. The untamed suddenness of death lingering in the humid air.

He had just pulled onto the highway when he realized with only mild alarm that he was not driving in the direction of Stag's Crossing. Instead he was going north, back to his sad apartment near the graduate school, that held all manner of books yet suggested no intimacy with literature. He knew then that he would call his father and tell him he was going to stay out east after all. That terrible foreign country that represented every pernicious corruption and intellectual posturing that Carlyle despised.

And now here they both are. Summoned, for the final time, to the foyer of Stag's Crossing. He takes no pleasure in the thought of seeing his brother again. Of seeing Emilia again. He has been good, he tells himself. A good boy, in the Lutheran sense. Not thinking of her often since then, though she has sent him letters that burn all too easily, a furtive correspondence to which he does not know how to reply. Then there is a phone ringing, perpetually ringing in his tiny shoebox of an apartment. Sometimes he answers; they speak, briefly. He will tell her, You shouldn't be calling me. And she will say—as if taunting him—Say you don't want to hear from me again. *Say it.*

But he never does. She has never asked why he left her

wedding early, or why he thought she and Joshua were ill-matched. She does not have to; in the intervening years, they have said all they needed to each other. Everything else has been merely digression.

VII.

THEN

All afternoon the dogs have harried him. Begging for scraps from his breakfast of two eggs and a piece of sausage that Joshua had burned on one side. Leisurely they frolic in the grass as Nick sprays them down with a garden hose. They nudge at him with their wet noses, childishly, sniffing for food in his pockets. Their leader as of late has been a dark red specimen, Carlyle's new favorite, a bitch standing nearly twenty-nine inches at the shoulders. He saw his father feeding her from his own plate at dinner once, a privilege experienced by very few. She is just as bloodthirsty as he is, and that is what Carlyle loves most in a dog—the swift and merciless kill, the sight of a hound with a hare in its mouth coming up over the hillside.

Nick has not seen her for some time now. Surmising she

might have been bred already and found a shaded nook to hide herself in, somewhere hidden within the mysterious and vast confines of Stag's Crossing. She might return in a few weeks with a few puppies trailing behind her. Carlyle would examine them, one by one, picking the best to keep and sending the others away. A pity he could not do the same with his sons.

He goes up to the porch where one greyhound lies on its back, sunning itself with the grand imperiousness that is natural to all the animals and men born and raised at Stag's Crossing. Sitting next to it Nick surveys the sloped driveway before him. Beneath these thousand acres of bucolic idyll seethes his father's relentless ambition; the land into which Carlyle has carved the foundation of the house. Through the open window drifts the sound of his father and brother reviewing paperwork in the study, a strange ritual Nick has never been allowed to understand. Seed prices, crop sales. His dead mother's oil fields, overflowing.

All at once, the three dogs lazing in the gravel-laden driveway leap to attention, as if spurred to hunt. In terrifying unison they make a mad dash down the sloped path, toward the gate that stands closed, as it always does; Stag's Crossing has admitted no visitors since the death and burial of Nick's mother and brother on that selfsame ground.

He follows them. One greyhound begins to yelp and leap at the gate, though it knows it cannot cross over the boundary that separates Stag's Crossing from the outside world, so thoroughly has Carlyle segregated the world of strangers from the civilized world of men.

Come on, he says. Leaning against the gate and looking at the empty road that runs just outside Stag's Crossing. There's nothing here.

The dogs prick up their ears, shuffling nervously from side to side. On his left coming up the bend in the road is Peggy Rasmussen though his father only calls her *the neighbor girl* in his dismissive way. Peggy's father has made his fortune in cattle ranching and has bought up most of the land east and west of Stag's Crossing, a fact that irritates Carlyle to no end.

She walks up the road with what looks like a stole dangling from her fist. As she approaches Nick can see that it is the pelt of a fox. Hacked inelegantly from the animal it bears no resemblance and is instead rendered into a long strip of red fur.

Hello Peggy, he says, shyly. He is unpracticed in the art of talking—to girls, especially. Unlike the mystery novels he buys for fifty cents and hides beneath his bed he has realized that women do not contain easy nor logical solutions. Stag's Crossing having been so long empty of women since the departure of his mother that to see a girl at the front gate is a distinct and self-conscious pleasure.

Nick, she says. She is thirteen and petulant as ever. Wearing a dark blue ribbon in her hair. His eye is drawn to it, tied in a bow around her ponytail.

How're things?

Good.

How're the horses?

Good, she says, like she would rather be doing anything other than speaking to him. A certain lazy Midwestern drawl sneaking its way into her vowels, utterly charming.

You've got quite the stole with you.

Not a stole. My dad ran it over. He told me to bring it back to the house and see if my mom wants it.

Oh.

She hoists it to eye level. Here. You feel that? Still soft.

He touches the pelt with his fingertips, very gently. The sheen on the fur dulled in death but still the same brilliant carmine. Yet he knows from the shape of the skull, the intact sex organs, that this is not the fox he has searched for in vain. Not the creature that birthed the kits in the hollow that he destroyed like the unfeeling hand of God in a Bible story his father might have read him as a child. There is a story woven in the soft fur that he traces with his fingers: this is the father of those unfortunate progeny, now dead and hacked to pieces with tire tracks imprinted on the spine.

Yeah, it's really soft, he says, letting go of it.

I've gotta get back, she says. She fiddles with a strand of her hair. As she turns to leave, the ribbon comes loose and falls to the ground. He watches it slip from her ponytail and into the dirt where he picks it up, feeling the soft material between his fingers. Real silk. A dark and luminous blue.

You forgot your ribbon, he says, handing it to her.

Thanks, she says. Their hands touch, briefly. An image of her father enters his mind: Andrew Rasmussen tenderly tying the ribbon in place, helping her pack her schoolbag, telling her, *Be good at school today, Daddy loves you.* Such gentleness is completely foreign to him; he cannot imagine Carlyle speaking to him in this way any more than he can imagine his mother alive once more. Striding down the halls of Stag's Crossing. Holding his face in her hands, telling him that he has a real gift for understanding people that comes from her and her line of women—a mysterious, vatic power his father disdains and will never acknowledge.

He watches Peggy walk down the road until she disappears over the horizon. Then he turns around and goes up to the front porch where his father and brother sit, eating sandwiches. A big pitcher of lemonade set out.

Who was that? Carlyle asks.

Peggy Rasmussen, Nick says. He watches his father and brother eat. Taking nothing for himself.

You fixing to find yourself a little girlfriend? You could do better than that thing. Skinny as a reed and none too bright. Her father will have a hell of a time trying to marry her off.

Nick shakes his head. The feeling of the silk ribbon in his hand lingering. The sensation, the memory of it, a moment he cannot forget.

Nick's never going to get married, Joshua says. Just you wait.

There is truth in his words and Nick knows it. There is something terribly broken inside him. A boy of splintered glass and spare parts. Not even fit for the trash heap piled in the corner of the Quonset. He is destined for loneliness; all the myriad futures he envisions end with him, alone. Stag's Crossing aflame. The fields, the house. A thousand acres laid to waste. The foxes and their bones, laid to rest in shattered soil.

That night Nick lies in his corner room with the slanted roof. Moonlight creeps across the floor, illuminating his discarded socks, his folded shirts in a half-open drawer. A tremor of anticipation lances through him, sharp as electric current. He feels it beneath his skin before he hears it—the lonesome shriek of the fox. Devastated, desolate. Sounding almost like a widow-wail, the tearful cries of the women he remembers crowding around his mother's coffin and tearing at their hair. Seductive and inescapable in their sorrow. The premonition of a greater loss still yet to come.

viii.

NOW

And what is Stag's Crossing without Carlyle Morrow? Surely without the man of the house himself all two stories of his grand design might fall into treacherous ruin. A shapeless, formless wreck just an hour west of Omaha. Neither of his sons fit to rule after him. Nick knows this as well as anyone—he has grown brilliant and dreamy, with a certain softness around his eyes. Thin as a bulrush and sharper besides. Eminently unsuitable for the broad-handed work of reaping and threshing. Deep in the cornfield where the stalks grow so high you can hardly see the horizon.

Nick imagines his father with the long spiraling wire of the telephone looped in his hand, sitting outside on the porch. Announcing to his son the news of his impending death. There on the steps that Carlyle had measured himself, by hand, when he was a far younger man. Far younger than Nick is now, newly arrived in this strange and hallowed place.

He has heard the story dozens of times over the years: that summer evening when Carlyle had finally told his father he was leaving South Carolina forever. A year into his exile from the magnificent plantation that had once seemed to encompass the entire world and he had already made his plans to seek his fortune elsewhere.

His own father, a Carlyle among Carlyles, whose Christian name was Edward, had lit his cigar and smoked it thoughtfully. Listening to Carlyle's grand speech of a future that would come to pass: the unblemished land west of the Appalachians. His new wife, freshly yoked to him and more pregnant by the day. Carlyle demanded a son, knew it would be a son as soon as he put his ear to her stomach. Already scheming how he might have another. Each of them in his perfect and destructive imitation.

Edward had said, Then you're going.

Yes sir.

Edward had leaned close then. As though he were imparting some secret and ancient knowledge onto his second son, which he would not heed.

Out there it's not the same as it is here. You'll be a foreigner to everyone you meet. They won't welcome you.

If they leave me alone it'll be better than how I'm received here.

You remember the rest of the families that used to live around here? Birch, Estes. All gone now. Yet we still remain. And why is that? Both of James Birch's sons died in the war. That boy he took in, his cousin's son? Ran the place into the ground. Isabella Estes went half-mad after her husband died and she took a new man. Some traveling salesman from Idaho, the sad wretch. If you're going to make a name for yourself—and I have my doubts—remember this. You can't bring a stranger into your house and expect any good to come of it.

That's all?

Well I'm certainly not giving you any money if that's what you're asking.

I'm not.

Good.

Edward had stood and clapped Carlyle on the back, which meant he should leave. At the end of the path to the house he had turned around to gaze upon this mammoth work for the last time. Knowing he would not return to South Carolina. The newness of his destiny taking shape before him.

In the succeeding years Carlyle would turn over this proclamation in his mind. Allowing it—like a wound—to weep, to fester. Wondering what his father could have meant by this. What terrible form this oracular prediction might take.

Then came the matter of his third son. He had done everything right: bought a thousand acres and reforged them into his design. Purchased four greyhounds and raised them with the same elegant and brutal upbringing that he would later bestow upon his children like an unwanted gift. Sired two boys in quick succession. Each born at home, in the master bedroom on the second floor. A local doctor, well-respected, came in his Plymouth sedan and attended to Carlyle's wife with quiet efficiency. Two simple, uneventful births.

How overjoyed he was, to know his third child would be another son. Would have named him Christopher. Right before the birth his wife had a dream about Christopher and said she had dreamed of another blond cherubim just like Joshua. In that moment he knew he loved her like never before, this woman who read her prayer book every night and was destined to return to him threefold what he so desired from her. He had never even struck her, not a single time though he knew how to do it from watching his father—knew exactly how it felt from having borne these blows himself, with the burning anger of a bullwhipped steer.

They were sitting in the dining room, talking of nothing, when she began to convulse with labor pain. Too early, too early by far. The pallor of her face a sickly color that Carlyle will never forget. He told Joshua to take his mother upstairs and have her lie on the bed. To Nick he gave no instructions at all. He went to the phone in his study and dialed the doctor's office. The secretary said he was in Crete. There was another doctor, his colleague, who would come. He was highly recommended—he had gone to medical school in Connecticut.

Carlyle went down to the gate to open it. The man who came did not come up the driveway in his car but instead parked and walked up the gravel path with him carrying his bag in hand. He wore round glasses that made his eyes look larger than they actually were. When he spoke it was with an accent that Carlyle had never heard before in his life.

Have you been here long? Carlyle asked, as they came up to the porch.

Not long at all, no.

But your family's from here?

No, they're all back east.

He felt the doctor's eyes on him, a strangely distant gaze, as they walked through the front doors and went upstairs into the bedroom. Nick and Joshua were there, standing obediently by the bed.

Out, Carlyle said.

Nick did not move, still holding on to his mother's hand.

Get out, you two.

The boys ran out the door and back into their bedrooms, the sound of their little footsteps fading down the hall.

His wife lay on the bed. She was very pale. There was already blood on the comforter, which he would need to wash later. He knelt and held her face in his hands while the doctor washed up and began to poke at her with his instruments. Eventually his wife began to breathe faster and faster and the doctor said they should call an ambulance, which would not arrive quickly enough, though Carlyle called for it anyway. She was delirious by then, speaking of things that had no meaning. She had always been like that, touched by an otherworldly hand. Perceiving things he at times could not comprehend, God-fearing man that he remained—a woman's intuition, perhaps, or something more mystical still. An uncanny insight she would pass down to Nick, who would inherit what little of her that remained.

He looked down at her as she clutched at his shirt-sleeve. A pathetic desperation in her eyes.

Carlyle, she whispered. Her voice a pitiful sigh. Who is this man?

The doctor.

He doesn't belong here. Wild and frantic, she clawed at him. Please. Get him out.

He'll be leaving soon.

Is the baby coming? When is the baby coming?

He looked at her belly, swollen as a ripe peach.

It'll be here. Just lie back and rest.

When the baby came, it was dead. There was not much blood at all, in the end. He was outside waiting for the ambulance when the doctor came to him and told him his wife had also passed away. A most unexpected occurrence. The gate was open and Carlyle could see the long black hearse coming up the road already. What passed for an ambulance in those times, so far from the city.

He went back upstairs and found Nick had snuck out of his room. Still standing by the bed, gripping his mother's hand with childish ferocity.

In his innumerable retellings, Carlyle does not mention this detail. But Nick remembers everything Carlyle has long forgotten: the limp curl of her auburn hair, the cold stiffness of her fingertips. Slipping from his grasp as his father picked him up and took him back to his room.

On the eve of his mother's death his father will sometimes call him and remind him of the moral to this sad tale. How Carlyle had once let a stranger into Stag's Crossing—a fatal error. That doctor with his fancy degrees that had killed his wife and son. The last woman at Stag's Crossing now sacrificed at the altar of its prosperity—how high, how tall grew the alfalfa once her blood had nourished it. The seed of Edward Morrow's admonition flowering into a paranoia that has gripped Carlyle since.

To grieve is to rot from the inside out. The gate to Stag's Crossing would remain closed for years afterward. The milkman hardly allowed past the edge of the porch. Carlyle in the master bedroom, watching from the window. Like a snare, the noose has tightened over the years; Carlyle's unease grows ever broader. Threatening to swallow up the entire world that exists outside of Stag's Crossing. He alternates between a clear-eyed lucidity and a crushing, vile suspicion of every man both like and unlike himself. For much of Nick's childhood the locus of Carlyle's ire were the Black yardmen who had infested North Omaha, the Jap strikebreakers—nowadays it is the Jew bankers who funnel money out of his accounts and Emilia Morrow herself. Having appeared, as if conjured, to take Joshua away from him and threaten all he holds dear. Her power over him something altogether greater and more enduring than mortal attraction, what Carlyle might describe as closer to diablerie.

Nick packs, thinking of Joshua's sharp reply: *You brought that bitch into this house.* Yet Joshua like Nick himself will be powerless to refuse. Like dogs they will come when they are called, the Morrow boys. Twenty years has changed nothing. Inside them remains a dark and dangerous longing to see their father. In the vain hope that he who has unmade them might make them again, in his image. Rendering them good and whole again. A real family at last.

IX.

THEN

Late summer they make their annual pilgrimage to Halsey. North-northwest more than three hours from Stag's Crossing lie endless acres of pure forest all the way up to the Sandhills where the auburn grass grows high amongst the dunes. Joshua and Nick sitting in the truck bed with the deer rifles though their father favors the bow and arrow. That year it is a rich and extravagant season for deer hunting, half-summer half-autumn, Carlyle somehow having stolen or swindled an early permit. They go like good Christians to their yearly worship. The place filled with the inimitable temptation of leaping venison. Lined with rich fat they might grill or smoke. The aroma like French cologne wafting through the house.

As his father's ugly white Ford cleaves through the landscape Nick beholds all manner of fish and fowl: belted kingfisher, largemouth bass, sauger, and walleye. If he puts his torn magazine over his eyes just right the sunlight will scald him less but he can still half read his *Field & Stream*. Since sunup his pallor has been that of a dead man drifting from delirium to delirium. Nausea overtakes him; the ascent of a singular summertime mania. A dread so all-encompassing he is rendered helpless by it. The dew on the grass the tremors of the gravel road beneath the truck.

Joshua sees him lying down next to him perfectly still. Breathing through his nose softly like a newborn foal.

Are you okay? Joshua says.

No, Nick murmurs. His voice white and dry as though coming from someone far away. Joshua gives him lemonade to drink fans him a little with his hand until the color comes back to his skin. Like a mother bird tending to her young. Such tenderness in the gesture Nick cannot say anything about it. Will remember the pristine and holy silence between them until he dies. The face of his brother shaped by gentle concern. This silence only interrupted by the sinister appearance of mosquitoes looking to feed. Together they slap the mosquitoes away from each other before they begin to slap each other until Carlyle yells at them to stop.

Boys, he grouses. But there is pride in his complaint. Their violence inexorable. Their desire to crush to mangle to maim thrilling them with electric pleasure. Nick has broken his wrist against this desire. Like a cardsharp he plays only for the joy of winning. Seeing another boy stagger back blood streaming from his nose. Calling him names in the unknown language of young men set loose upon each other primeval and wild. Nick—son of a bitch—I'll kill you. The same marvelous pugilism of his father put to work for a divine purpose wrought by a merciful hand. He puts his fists up puts his arm into it just as his father says, *Fight me, boy,* until Nick untethers himself from his body with the same perfunctory violence. Slitting open the belly of a downed buck to peel the skin from the meat. Joshua cutting off the forelegs so the hide goes in a single fell motion. Guiding his hand to take the bone saw and rip through the spine.

The last few seasons have been flush with the russet bodies of slain deer. Nick sometimes has premonitions, headaches, the pains of a seer. He has a strange knowingness that this year will be no different. Joshua will sight the buck and pierce it through the skull with a single bullet. No use damaging the backstrap with a shot through the shoulder. Joshua is the best shot by far so he will take the lead. Best to leave no room for error—fifteen seconds or less for the animal to stagger then fall to its knees. Nick ready with the knife. Slit clear up the midline. Exposing the rich scarlet flesh beneath.

Perhaps unsated by this killing they might pack the meat with ice and fish for a few hours looping over to the lake on the way back. Rainbow trout in perfect season. Fishing is Nick's métier more so than deer; the calculations of the bobber the hooking of the earthworm's thick and tantalizing gut. With his slender and agile fingers he is like a violinist with the rod. As if in parody he will affix grilled cheese to the hook, all manner of foolish bait, but still the fish leap and plunge to their deaths. Still Nick finds himself stringing fish after fish onto a hooked chain and throwing them back into the water while Joshua struggles to hook even the smallest alevin. Therein lies the difference—the fisherman's language is deception and deliberation while the deer hunter has only his forthright violence. The savage brilliance of his weaponry.

Nick lies back down and examines the contortions of the clouds. Daydreams of long and beautiful coils of fishing line stretching out before him like the landscape itself. Joshua hunches next to him sweating even with his linen shirt. Rubs his arm against his forehead and then asks to get into the passenger's seat.

You've lasted seventeen years in this damn heat, Carlyle says. Two more hours won't kill you. Won't be back until after college anyway.

I'll be here over the summer and at Christmas, Joshua says.

No, you won't.

Joshua looks like he might say something but doesn't. His palm salty with sweat becomes a fist then opens again gentle as a daylily. Nick wants to tell him that it is no use—Christ cannot raise a hand to his father. They are the same in being and essence though Joshua's physical resemblance to Carlyle is a strange sort of likeness, one best perceived in the half-light of a fading afternoon. Certainly he is more handsome than his father—a generation has smoothed out the crooked Morrow nose, the uneven smile. Yet his wrath is a perfect imitation. Carlyle in all ways.

Joshua puts his hat on and lies down next to Nick. Such an anger emanating from him. What son does not hate his brother, his father, his own flesh? Yet here they are like twins joined in the womb. Joshua growing strong and supple while Nick has the svelte and angular look of one of his father's prized greyhounds. Fowler, courser, chaser of game.

Lying upon his metal palanquin Nick dreams of leaping deer their eyes black with hatred. A magnificent stag dead by his hand. Joshua helping him pull the hide away from the body sorting the entrails. The head hangs straight down from the bent spine the antlers scraping the floor. Blankly staring from a place beyond death. Yet something has become strange about its face—writhing its hooves scraping the ground it transforms into a monstrous eidolon. Shade, shadow, visage, another.

Fight me, boy, the deer rages. Froths at the mouth and shakes upon the hook. Its hide torn and bleeding. The metal gambrel swaying pendulum-like inside the dark Quonset. Smell of blood and dust. The frenetic hum of bluebottles droning ceaselessly as he raises his arm with the knife pointed vertically downward puts his elbow into it. Ferocious as a scythe upon the chaff.

Nick, Joshua says shaking him awake. Come on, let's go. The Ford has stopped near a ravine off the dirt road and already Joshua has gathered up the rifles unfolding his canvas hunting jacket with the too-long arms. Nick crawls to the edge of the truck bed to put on his jacket too, once his brother's and still smelling of him.

The white door of the truck swings open with a metal screech. Out steps his father his hair tarnished silver by the afternoon sun. His sons turn to look at him and then turn away burned as they are by his noonday glory; starry huntsman he is, luminescent as one of the constellations.

Ready? he says.

Nick nods.

Good. He takes the best hunting rifle and inspects it. Savage Model 99 meant for elk or antelope or man. Hands it wordlessly to Joshua then sets off down the ravine into the forest. Like men to the gallows they go in single file. If Nick looks back at the perfect moment he might see a flash of vermilion come out from behind the white Ford tall and lean or else on all fours like an animal. But when he does it is too late. Nothing there at all except the white Ford and the gap in the brush through which they have come. Summer grass flecked with golden light. Cicadas singing their midsummer dirge high and plaintive as the tuning of a symphony.

X.

NOW

He is halfway to the airport when his brother calls. He takes his phone from his briefcase and listens carefully. Detecting a resigned edge to Joshua's voice that stings even over the phone.

Glad I managed to catch you before you boarded, Joshua says. Emilia said this was the best number to reach you at. When are you landing in Omaha?

Changed your mind, did you? Nick says.

I didn't. Emilia insisted.

Well, that's surprising.

Her parents died in a car accident when she was in college.

That's even more surprising.

I know. We had a long talk about this last night, and

she thinks it's important that I have the chance to say goodbye.

Are you coming this evening?

No—I've got a meeting. I'll be there tomorrow afternoon. But she's landing today, five o'clock Nebraska time.

Why isn't she flying with you?

My flight's too early, she likes to sleep in. It's all the same to me, we'll end up in the same place anyway.

Makes sense.

I was wondering if you could drive her to meet Dad. She doesn't want to go alone. I'll pay for the rental car, if you want.

I land at six Central. Are you sure she won't wander off into traffic by then?

You'd be doing me a favor, Nick.

Last week you were telling me to leave you alone.

Are you going to continue holding this over my head, or are you going to actually help me?

Fine. What does she look like?

What do you mean what does she look like. You've seen her before.

That was twenty years ago. I don't even know what you look like now. Just give me a general description.

Joshua sighs. She's tall and has long black hair.

Thanks, Keats. I'll be on the lookout.

Just try to get her back to the house in one piece. And make sure Dad doesn't poison her or something.

Something tells me your wife would poison him first.

You're probably right, Joshua says, and hangs up.

Stag's Crossing: more than destination it is merely destiny. Even with his eyes gouged out like Oedipus

Nick would know the way. The final resting place of his heart.

At the ticket counter he says to the woman, One round trip to Omaha, please.

Departure date?

Today.

Going on vacation?

Nebraska's not really a resort hot spot, he says.

In the waiting area he folds the ticket over and over until it is like a crumpled piece of origami. Each edge of the paper now ridged like a mountain range. When he hands the ticket to the flight attendant he is sure that she has immediately and irrevocably diagnosed him as a high-functioning neurotic. His expression the expression of a man midway to drowning. Having boarded and taken his seat and latched his seat belt with shaking hands he is no calmer—he falls into a sort of half sleep alternated by periods of unbearable nausea. Returning again in his mind to the threshold of his childhood home the threshold of his childhood itself that exists forever in a place beyond the past. The locus of his violent and half-dead dreaming.

In the dining room of Stag's Crossing Nick and his brother will be set against each other in eternal strife. Like civilized men they will sit across from each other at the table brandishing their forks with the politeness of medieval torturers. But their faces will not be the faces of men but beasts of the woods and the lakes—boar and stag, wolf and eel. Meat eaters all. Tearing into their steak before they put down their utensils and tear into each other instead. His father's dominance sudden and fierce as a thunderbolt. His brother opening his wide and lascivious mouth to reveal his fatally sharpened teeth.

As a boy he used to strike himself in the face repeatedly; beating himself as he was once beaten by his father. The relentless fury of the surf throwing itself against the rocks in the bay. Having outgrown such childish things he has not done this for many years. But he feels it. Parts of him hardened and scarred over from the continued injuries of fate.

Get up, Joshua says after one of their many sparring matches. Nick lying motionless on the ground. Breathing hard through his nose. His eyes unblinking dewed with tears. At eleven he is developing into a brilliant strategist but is matchless against his taller and stronger brother who possesses the skill and foreknowledge of some ancient fighter. He blocks Nick at every turn ignoring his feints until Nick is felled easy as an amateur. His face pushed into the dirt. His bloodied cheek caked with soil.

I can't, he says.

Then why are you even fighting.

I don't know, he says. He tries to get up on his elbows and collapses again.

Stop crying, you idiot.

I'm not crying. He wipes his muddy face and tries to put his fists up again but finds he cannot. His knees are torn up and his nose is bleeding. He turns around and starts to limp back to the house like a broken-legged dog. Hoping to find a place to lie down and die there amongst the rich clover that grows near the front of the house where his mother's garden still grows. He spends the rest of the morning hidden and unmoving beneath the shadow of the Quonset. When the sun is at high noon the metal siding is hot as a cattle brand and Nick relishes touching it until his entire body goes numb. Until his skin has no more room left for sensation.

Joshua finds him sleeping there just after five o'clock. As though seeking forgiveness he suggests they get ready for supper and says he will debone the trout. Nick fetches the garbage bin for the bones and wipes down the plates. One of the greyhounds comes to the kitchen to beg for scraps and Nick chases him away.

You're a good fisherman, Joshua says. You could teach me a few new tricks.

Nick remains silent. Remembering how his brother had been the one to instruct him on the subtle art of ice fishing, though those days of amicable brotherhood have long passed. Instead he imagines Joshua pierced through the mouth with a hook. Imagining him flopping uselessly on the bank of the river. Gutted and laid out sloppily on a cutting board then fried in leftover bread crumbs and butter.

You've got dirt on your face, Joshua says.

Nick turns to look at him. The kitchen light illuminating the strange sadness of his face which is no longer that of a child but merely childlike. An imitation of what used to be.

Real beat-up right there.

And who did that.

Joshua says, You've got to learn somehow.

Nick remembers this; will remember forever the destruction his education has wrought upon him. When the neighbor boy Eli Martindale comes up to him after school and calls him a sissy and his mother a dead whore at first he says nothing. Not because he does not want to fight but because he wants Eli to come closer. The gap between them narrowing until Eli is right up next to him. The boy's breath smelling like tobacco. Vulgarities and spittle clinging to the shell of Nick's ear.

Swiftly Nick turns and punches Eli in the throat. Eli stumbles and Nick wrestles him to the ground. They struggle like that for several seconds until Nick grabs hold of Eli's hair and yanks so hard Eli begins to whimper like a dog and finally begs piteously for Nick to let him go. Satisfied by this savage beating Nick releases him. Watching him limp home with anxious pleasure.

Afterward he washes up for supper careful to clean his face and hands with a fresh rag. Letting the water cleanse his face like a baptism. He can hear his father and brother downstairs setting the table and pulling up the chairs. Mashed potatoes and green beans by the smell of it.

Nick goes downstairs and sits at the table. He fidgets; cracks his knuckles.

Joshua, why don't you say grace, Carlyle says.

Thank you, Heavenly Father, for this bounty, Joshua says. Amen.

Amen, says Nick. He reaches for his spoon.

No elbows on the table, Carlyle says.

Sorry, Dad. Nick moves his arm to avoid touching the table and Carlyle sees the dirt on his sleeve the seam split open in two places. A fresh scab on Nick's elbow.

What happened to your shirt?

Got into a fight, Nick says.

Did you win?

Yeah.

Carlyle raises his hand and for a moment Nick thinks he is about to strike him across the face. Yet his touch is soft. Gentle as stroking the mane of his favorite mare he pats Nick on the head.

That's my boy, he says.

Xi.

THEN

For Carlyle all the questions asked of a man in his lifetime can be answered with the barrel of a gun. To this end he has shaped the violence of his sons with force and precision—Joshua an excellent shot and Nick a master with the lure. When they are not tilling and sowing they spend their afternoons fly fishing, watching television. The boys chasing each other down the shallow ravine east of the house. Carlyle himself farms only for personal enjoyment—his late wife's money can pay for anything so long as the oil wells keep pumping. Black gold from Oklahoma pouring forth from the earth thick and rich as maple syrup.

Carlyle comes from harsher blood than his father-in-law who never worked a day in the oil fields himself—Scottish and English tradesmen so the story goes. Above all he is a South Carolinian who at twenty-five found himself thrown out of his father's palatial plantation home for all manner of licentious offenses—poaching, thieving, rakish behavior. Third of five children he was the runt of the litter. Expected to go into business or perhaps the clergy.

How wrong they were. His ambition fomenting malevolent and maniacal. First he went to the capital seeking a wife. His body was strong and handsome and women looked at him often. In church he did not worship but instead considered his grand plan. A family, a house. Neighbors who would know his name know him by sight. Know him by reputation. His children attentive and obedient. His legacy assured.

Outside the church painted a blinding dove-white he saw his wife for the first time. Her auburn hair slightly ashen; her gray eyes bright with dew. As she walked arm in arm with her sister he saw the face of a woman who had always been loved. Had never tasted the goad nor the bridle of father or husband. He sensed she had never raised a hand to anyone for that viciousness must be taught at a young age. Her family unstained by casual brutality.

He knew then that he would court her, elegantly so, with serenades and clandestine letters passed between church pews. Perhaps he loved her in his own way; a love unflinching and untender. They married in that same church a year later. Her father displeased that the bridegroom was nearly penniless but Carlyle's stock ran pure and true. His lineage the unerring marker of his destiny.

Westward then. Westward until he could go no farther. Cheap land for the taking in Kansas, Nebraska, Iowa. He brought a suitcase full of church clothes and money. His wife in her plaid sundress already pregnant with a beatific glow.

In the car they argued. She had wanted to go somewhere picturesque and warm like California. Here there were blistering winters so cold the ground became caked with frost. The land flat and unyielding.

If you want to go to California so much why don't you go on your own, he said.

But I've got the baby.

He doesn't even have a name.

Yes he does. It's Joshua. He told me.

Carlyle said, Fine. Do what you want. I'll build the house and you can stay in it or you can leave.

Some old man gone back to Omaha to die sold them what was left of his farm. Carlyle and his wife's ownership of the land is under false pretenses but this is shrouded by the veil of history. Before it was called Stag's Crossing it was a thousand acres of nameless land in eastern Nebraska with an ugly Sears catalogue farmhouse and a distinct lack of imagination. Carlyle bulldozed the house and watched with satisfaction as the laborers carried away the broken entrails. In its place he envisioned a house as arresting as his father's. Crafted in dreamy half duplication of the sublime southeastern plantations he had marveled at as a boy. In Nebraska they could not be imitated by any man other than himself for the specific architecture of the South was foreign to them. The taste of his neighbors pedestrian and insignificant. How they mocked him. How they stared. Watching as the very soil denied him. He built the place atop bedrock that wept at his approach, that refused to yield to his inescapable will as he made great gaping wounds in the ground, his shovel pressed beneath his heel. Driving his truck from Omaha each day laden with lumber and brick. Stag's Crossing rising slowly from the ground as if of its own irresistible accord.

Now they must bear witness to his gaunt and neoclassical manor with tall windows, a grand and perfectly helical staircase, bedrooms of mahogany and pine—not so large on the inside nor the outside but possessing an immensity whether of madness or mastery it could not be said—but this sylvan grandeur gives it the sense of timelessness and subjugation. Like a wedding veil a sense of dominion gossamers over it. Forcing the submission of the kingdom of the animals the land itself. The willow trees bowing like footmen and the calves of the surrounding farms sullen as young maids. The susurrations of the creek falling upon the ear with the gentleness of a motherly lullaby though Carlyle Morrow has no brethren known to man and was not born so much as he is his own grotesque invention. Speaking and talking and listening with the waiting air of a pit viper. His voice taking on a feverish and manic cadence, the voice of a salesman or prophet. Voice of the Devil himself.

Even his deer calls are otherworldly. More like the sounding of a trumpet than a true deer grunt. He cups his hands against his mouth and his boys watch him with apprehension. They are deep in the forest now. Barely any sound coming through the trees except the fluttering of birds. Having walked for at least an hour they have still not seen any deer.

Joshua tries his own call which ends in a pathetic squawk. Nick examines his map and compass useless as they are. His father has been here so many times he has no need of them. Could navigate solely by the sun or stars.

Stalking his prey of choice perhaps Carlyle has some oblique premonition that one of his sons will betray him. It will not be Joshua—could not be Joshua. The destroyer in the family photo. The Judas at the dinner table. Staining his family forever with the gravity of his transgression. Yet for now it is merely a faint vision that hovers just beyond his perception—one of his sons will prove to be the son that denies him, a betrayal so great he cannot even imagine it.

Should've brought a dog, Carlyle says. God damn why didn't we bring a dog. Could've borrowed the Wheelers' bloodhound. Ugly as sin but it gets the job done. Know a man in Hastings with a litter of wolfhound pups now. Wouldn't that be interesting. Could hunt coyotes with those things.

Maybe we could get a pointer, Joshua says. They're good for birds.

Now where are we going to find a pointer?

Don't know. Maybe Nebraska City. Same place you found the greyhounds.

You won't need a pointer in New York. Unless you want to hunt city pigeons.

Didn't say it'd be for me. Nick'll still be here.

Well I wasn't asking what Nick wanted.

Okay, Dad, Joshua says.

There's something coming through the grass, Nick says.

Carlyle's head snaps sideways.

Where, he says.

Nick points. Just a little farther beyond that tree.

Closer and closer Carlyle creeps until his face is completely obscured by the shadow of an overhanging branch. Terrible deathbringer, enemy to men and beasts alike, his eyes now pinpoints of light amongst the shade. He seizes the brush and pulls it aside to reveal nothing more than a spooked warren of rabbits pouring out underfoot. Their nimble and endless bodies scattering in all directions.

For a moment Nick worries his father will be angry with him. But instead Carlyle turns back to them and says, Just rabbits. We'll have to look harder. His face cheerful and unfazed. Nick searches his father's expression for some lurking resentment and finds none. A few times he has seen Carlyle hide his anger and wait for a more opportune moment to strike. Yet here he perceives nothing, no artifice. The look of someone who could have been a good and honest father in another life.

Joshua says, Maybe we should head a little to the west. Isn't that where we found our buck last year?

That had been a good year. The hunt was easy. Joshua had sighted him from the ground early on. He was magnificent. In full velvet his antlers jutting from his head like an ornamental diadem. Monarch of the forest glorious in his exaltation.

They stalked him for several yards. Absorbed by the

sounds of the woods, the sound of their breathing. Waiting until the stag paused to drink from a puddle of clear and untouched rainwater. Then at Carlyle's hand signal Joshua unslung his rifle and shot him right through the skull.

xii.

NOW

In the arrivals lounge Nick paces. Half unwrapping his overpriced sandwich that he bought from a nearby kiosk, filled with ingredients he dislikes. The foolish and collective insistence that he ingest vegetables has hounded him his entire adult life. Today of all days he refuses to give in. He makes sure to remove the tomato slices and eats the rest with a nervous energy, far too quickly, like a dog unsure of his next meal. Then he crinkles the wrapper in his fist and tosses it in the trash. He mills about aimlessly for a little before deciding to read while he waits or at least give the appearance of reading.

Hunting in his briefcase for a suitable book, he props his legs on his roller suitcase like a makeshift ottoman. He settles on a slim volume of poems by Du Fu and makes sure to crease the spine multiple times to make it seem older. Wondering as he does this what Emilia reads; what Emilia likes to read. He likes to think he can tell the measure of a person by their bookshelf though often they are mere mirages, an intellectual image of what the person wishes to be. He doubts that Joshua reads and if he does it is hardly of consequence. Last he heard, his brother had ascended to a high position in a company with absolutely nothing to recommend him for such a prestigious thing. His brother, unlike himself, is a man easily admired—but admired from a distance, like all Morrow men.

The crowd goes by. He feels remarkably normal seeing these people and in this absurd normalcy there is a maudlin sensibility that disturbs him. His father would not have minced words remarking on their weaknesses, the despicable softness of their glances. A man and woman kiss ecstatically, betraying their long separation. Nick wonders if one of them has been unfaithful so fervent is their embrace. Like his father he enjoys spoiling good things.

In this parade of normal, unremarkable white people he searches for a tall woman with black hair. Just as Joshua says though the description is inadequate as speech itself has proven inadequate to describe the visage of another. Woman, outsider, wolf at the door. He could say Joshua is a white man who resembles himself with pale hair and pale eyes but that phrase is like an empty platitude without meaning. Without an understanding of their long and bloody history that stretches between them taut as fishing line. It also does not say what makes them white; having abjured all others their bloodline is impeccably pure. But none of this explains the deference they receive in public places, the oiled hinges of their social interactions. He is a *sir* to all strangers; his father is a *sir* even to his acquaintances.

So distracted is he by Du Fu's opening couplets he almost does not see Emilia walking toward him. Her large duffel bag rolling behind her with its wheels clacking obnoxiously on the tile floor. Emilia, Emilia Morrow, lovely and deathless Emilia! Her divine and regal look. The same as he remembers. As he can never forget.

Time has left her untouched, pristine. Her face like a burnished and reflective Oriental mirror. Raised before him he can see himself in it and perhaps this is what made Joshua fall in love with her instantly—the honesty of her gaze, nothing obscured in her features but bared entirely to the world. This kind of beauty cannot be created through artifice but is innate, translucent as glass.

What also remains is her unnerving magnetism, a slyness in her expression that cannot be wholly erased. If anything, she is more radiant than ever, to an almost unsettling degree. Even in her awaiting smile, beguiling as it is, there is something just out of place. Beyond the furthest reaches of his understanding, where it verges on the unknowable.

Nick? she says, almost hesitantly.

Of course. They have not seen each other in nearly twenty years. Nick is aware, painfully so, of how generic he appears. A man like any other man with brown hair and an unpleasant face. The classic mien of a Midwesterner, harmless and vaguely passive-aggressive. How could she recognize him without looking for Joshua in his features, though despite being brothers they are as alike as Earth and Jupiter.

Hello, he says. Let me take your bag.

No, she says. I've got it. Sorry I'm late—the flight was delayed.

Well, you made it.

I made it, she says.

I'll go get the rental car then.

Thanks for driving.

It's not a problem, Nick says.

He realizes on his way to the rental kiosk he could be role-playing the pedestrian suburban husband. Awaiting the return of his jet-setting wife. He takes no amusement in imagining this because everything about her marks her as his brother's one true love; though he and Joshua are separated by four years and a lifetime of resentment he understands immediately why she appeals to him so. Simultaneously delicate and not, his equal in beauty—Joshua would have never married a woman his lesser in attractiveness so he knew, of course he knew she would be arresting—liable to inspire jealousy in other men but forever loyal to him. Forever his own. Like a jewel in his garlanded crown.

She is silent as he negotiates with the attendant for the rental car keys. Standing a suitable distance away from him she busies herself examining the inside of her purse. The floor. The wall. As though if meeting his eyes for more than a moment would irrevocably shatter something between them. A subtle and ethereal peace.

What do you think? he says, gesturing toward the poster of available models on the wall.

Anything with airbags and seat belts is fine with me, she says, with a touch of humor.

In the windy parking lot he notices she is nervous. To see him? To be with him alone? He wants to say, There is nothing between us, no anger. But he cannot say this really because the anger of his father is his anger though he will deny it with such fervency he might even believe his own lies. A part of him will forever see her as an outsider, a pestilence upon their family. Had Joshua never transgressed they would not be this way; he would still be one among their happy flock. He could have married some vapid and acceptable woman who grew up only three towns over. Instead Joshua has led Emilia and no other woman through the threshold of his house, his bedroom. He has let the beast loose upon the sheep and for this crime Carlyle struck him from the family tree. Mangling the line of succession beyond repair.

What woman could be worth such misery? Yet here she is. Dooming them all to a bitter and ruinous fate. His brother's passion, the ardor of a madman, has torn through their family leaving disaster in its wake. Carlyle alone in his room shouting at nothing. At the ghosts of his boyhood. Nick crouching beneath the shadow of the Quonset ruminating on the arc of his predestined future which he can discern only faintly through the dark cloak of evening. The house in flames. Nick's face bloodied with gore. Wiping his hands of the little foxes that still haunt him in his dreams. Returning to Stag's Crossing, one day, as the herald of an even greater ruination.

He studies her in the hopes of understanding what drove his brother from his birthright; in all ways she appears to be the same as many beautiful women who are aware of their allure and delight in it. Her complexion bright and unblemished. Her mouth pert and rouged with deep coral. In every way she seems exactly the same to him as when he last saw her, the memory half-obscured. The day of her wedding. The days, the months, the years altering her appearance not at all.

Thanks for being my unpaid chauffeur, she says as he opens the trunk for their bags.

It's nothing really, he says. Thanks for coming. I don't know how you convinced Joshua to come back—

He didn't need any convincing. It was his idea.

He told me it was your idea.

She tilts her head slightly. Almost like a bird. Did he? That's so funny.

I'm honestly surprised you came.

I'm not sure what you mean, she says.

You were very specific about how you felt about my dad.

I know I offered my condolences.

But there was something else. About dying—

I think you're mistaken, she says, sliding into the passenger seat in one fluid and graceful movement. An easy smile gracing her lips. Her legs long and slender. Maybe you misheard.

I'm sure that's it, he says. Not wanting to fight about it. He puts the car into reverse and begins the agonizing crawl out of the lot. The afternoon light now turning slowly to the soft glow of evening.

It happens, she says.

It's going to be a bit of a drive. Do you want something to eat?

I'm good. We can stop on the way, maybe.

Works for me.

Were you reading Du Fu? she says.

I didn't know you knew him. I just picked him up recently.

I studied him a little in college. For my Chinese class.

Really, he says.

Yes, I find him a little boring. White people seem to find him deep though.

He does not know if she means this as a dig or an observation. He keeps his eyes on the road, his response measured.

Does that make me like other white people?

She seems surprised by the question. I don't really know. Does it?

Well, you're married to my brother, he says.

Sure. But that doesn't have anything to do with Du Fu.

If you can be married to a white man, but criticize white people—

Her face twists, briefly grotesque with disdain. That's a rather disingenuous interpretation of what I was talking about.

I'm just saying, he says. Unsure why he is even doing this, picking a fight so early on. Before they have even had the chance to really tear into each other. To learn about each other's weakest points and aim precisely for the center of the target. He was raised in an adversarial household, he supposes, and after many years all interactions take on the air of confrontation. Even if he does not want to, he feels bound to do so, like some unwritten law.

Do you get into these friendly debates with every Asian woman you spend time with?

Obviously not. Just you.

Lucky me, she says. She averts her eyes from his face as though she cannot bear witness to him. Trapped in such a small space they might suffocate each other.

It's not some abstract concept, you know, she adds. Race.

How is it not abstract? It's a social issue.

Your father doesn't seem to think it's particularly abstract.

My father isn't the same person as me.

I'm sure he isn't.

No, really.

I believe you. We're not our parents.

He doesn't know what to say to that. She states it so plainly and obviously—like it is something she has known her entire life. A mere commonplace. He wants to ask what her parents were like; if she is like them at all. He senses that she is not. No one else with quite the same walk, the same countenance.

She looks out the window. He looks carefully at the road. The rearview mirror which reflects nothing back except the vanishing remains of civilization. An hour or so more of this unpleasant landscape to go until they will reach the gates of Stag's Crossing where the past recurs; reinvents itself. Flowering like a fragrant and poisonous fruit in the shade of their willow trees.

At least twenty minutes pass like this, in complete silence.

I'm glad to see you, she says, finally.

You are?

Yes.

Why?

I wanted to ask if you liked those paintings I sent you. You've never said anything about them.

What paintings? he says, feigning ignorance. Even though he has one hidden in his suitcase, neatly folded and concealed between the pages of his notebook.

You didn't get them? she says.

I got them. I don't think it was a good idea to send them to me. Just like all those letters you wrote.

There's no law against writing your brother-in-law, Nick.

He finds it very difficult to articulate the irrationality of his brother's jealousy; the sheer paranoia of it, that manifests so similarly to Carlyle's hatred of anything born outside Stag's Crossing. How he cannot say, Your husband might kill me over less, though he still remembers Joshua's rage at the wedding that threatened to overflow into a brawl right there among the pews.

Instead he says, very cautiously, I don't think Joshua would see it that way.

Have it your way, she says. Is that why you left my wedding early?

I can't remember.

I think you do remember, but you don't want to tell me.

Weddings are hideously boring. Joshua and I got into an argument. I decided to leave. I'm sorry I couldn't attend. I'm sure it was lovely.

You know, before we got married Joshua told me a lot about you.

Oh? What'd he say?

Pretty much what you'd expect. But I wanted to know for myself, she says. What you were like. And now I know.

And what do you think I'm like?

I think you're incredibly arrogant and full of yourself, she says. She laughs a little at this like she can hardly believe that she has said it. A private joke.

At least I'm entertaining, he says.

Entertaining. That's an interesting way of putting it.

She is smiling with the left half of her mouth; more than that something deep within her radiates good humor and warmth. He could sit like this for hours within her aura, unmoving.

Do you want to listen to something on the radio?

No, she says. But I'm going to roll down the window and listen to the birds.

Trust me, I grew up here. They're overrated. Mostly sparrows.

I think they're lovely, she says. She rolls down the window a little and leans her head against it. Closes her eyes.

The wind going by plays with her hair which is long and dark just as Joshua said, as Nick has always remembered. Her hands show no sign of hard labor. Getting up at six in the morning to shovel cowpatty and pigshit palms blistering and peeling in the cold. Hers are the hands that would have once been rendered in exquisite oils, clasped together in her lap. The back of her left hand remains scarred, the skin healed unevenly. Her right is pristine. Her wedding ring, suitably ostentatious, glitters flirtatiously in the late afternoon light.

Xiii.

THEN

In the clearing they see a tree shorn of its bark. Torn away in jagged strips its white heart hangs open for all to see. Nick steps closer and kneels to examine the ground. Deer rub; deer tracks. The soft impressions of their fleet hooves. He imagines them cut down in their magnificence like young men felled by war.

Tracks going east, he says. His brother and father just coming up the hill.

What are you waiting for, Carlyle says. Let's go.

Now he has his particular hunting expression not so much the gaze of a born predator as it is the gaze of someone who is happy to lie in wait for hours until exploding with resentment; anger; a clean rifle shot to the brain. Nick's anger runs like electricity down the length of his fishing wire and into the vicious yank of the rod his brusque reeling until the fish lie gasping and dying on the riverbank.

Unlike his brethren there is no sublimated rage to Joshua's killing only the precise calculation of his violence; he never deceives or shrouds himself as an angler disguises his bait. When he hunts he is entirely himself present in his body the action of his arm lifting the gun and pulling the trigger a perfect and silent motion. Nick wants to be jealous of this but he knows he can never be like Joshua filled as he is with overwhelming wrath. Trapped in the radiance and sharp agony of youth he is barely cognizant that once he is civilized and domesticated these feelings will fade with time. As a man he will grow out of this sick fervor until he is reminded of it only rarely like an old and forgotten injury. What he will summon then will be only a shadow of the burning feeling of his hand against the metal siding of the Quonset his fantasies of putting rocks in his shoes and leaping headfirst into the Platte River that cuts through the landscape like a winding gash.

His brother's hair flashes in the sunlight as he passes. Nick marveling at him as he goes. In the wilderness they are like sprites of shadow and air flitting from grove to grove. Joshua nimble and silent as he navigates through the underbrush his face illuminated with unerring determination.

Eastward they go. The cold thrill of predestination creeping over Nick though he does not know what it means. What awaits them beyond the tree line has neither shape nor image; it comes in the guise of a doe but is not. Just over the hill through a gap in the pines they see it kneeling down to feed upon the emerald grass. Its underbelly a soft white color but there is no motherly gentleness in its eyes. No indication that it has ever mated nor birthed a fawn though the stags here are always vigorous in rutting season. Eating with uncommon zeal it feasts upon the grass as a starving man might gorge himself upon raw meat.

Joshua says, I've never shot a doe before.

Better meat, Carlyle says. Not as gamey.

They have stopped at the top of the hill hidden in the shadow of the trees. The angle is perfect. Clean shot if Joshua wants it. He begins to raise his gun but Carlyle stops him.

No, he says. Let Nick take the shot.

Joshua says, Dad—

I'm not going to tell you again. Nick will take the shot.

This must be a mistake. His father would never forsake his favored son in this way. Joshua now bewildered and resentful lowers his rifle and steps back. Letting Nick come forward to stand next to his father.

What are you waiting for? Carlyle asks.

Nick raises his rifle. Straight down the scope he sees the doe its silhouette clear and unmoving.

The doe raises its head to look straight at him.

He pulls the trigger.

He catches the doe just as it is leaping away but it is not a clean shot; he has wounded but not killed it. It falls on its side moaning and gurgling. Staining the ground beneath it a wondrous red.

God damn it, Carlyle says. He grabs Nick by the collar and pushes him toward the dying doe. Get down there and have a look.

Joshua goes as well. Something like triumph in his

gaze. Had Joshua taken the shot Nick knows it would have been decisive; a death blow. But Joshua did not shoot.

What did you do? Joshua says, kneeling down at the doe's side. Its legs still twitching and spasming in the grass. Gasping and wailing as it dies. Blood coming out of its neck where Nick must have missed the skull and gone through the spine, only paralyzing it. Already the air is filled with the coppery scent of blood which gushes onto the ground warm to the touch.

Carlyle comes up behind them leaning to look over their shoulders.

Fix this, he says. His voice bitter with displeasure. Don't waste another bullet.

Joshua and Nick stare at each other then the doe. The forest now silent as the nave of a cathedral Joshua gets the knife out of his knapsack and cuts its throat. The doe still gasping and weeping. Sounding almost like human speech.

Nick turns away before he can witness it dying. All the light going out of it. Its body immobile and the flesh already turning to rot. The grass sticky with blood will soon attract flies. In turning away he shows that he is weak but he is too tired to care.

It's done, Joshua says.

Then dress it, Carlyle says.

Nick pushes the doe onto its back and uses his knife to slit open the hide, cutting around the udder. Joshua helps peel the skin away from the muscle and Nick takes the knife again to cut through the layer of muscle around the organs. Slowly he goes from the pelvis to the breastbone

Joshua pulling up the muscle layer to keep him from cutting open the stomach.

Something's wrong, Nick says. He reaches his hand in to feel for the organs. He pulls out the liver, riddled with holes. Smelling like death, or worse than death. Before he can turn away from his father's unerring gaze he dry heaves into the grass.

Jesus Christ, Joshua says. He yanks on his side of the deer and the belly splits open. The innards sliding out of the animal and into the grass. Taking the stomach in his left hand he slices it in half; the interior is filled with writhing parasites.

Looks like liver fluke. The meat could be safe, but they're everywhere. Dad, what do you think? Joshua says.

They look back at their father who has studied this scene in silence. The deer slowly leaking its viscera into the grass.

Get up before that stains your shoes, he says.

Backing away from the carcass Joshua turns to wipe his hands on his pants. Nick looks closer, at the contents of its stomach that have tumbled out. In the four-chambered organ he can see the remnants of half-digested grass and sedge. Coiled tightly inside the rumen he pulls out a torn blue ribbon, wrapped almost into a ball. He has heard of deer eating plastic, rock candy, even parts of metal soup cans. Folding it over in his hands, the voice of Andrew Rasmussen enters his mind, unbidden: *Be good at school today, Daddy loves you.*

This is the same ribbon that Peggy showed him at the gates of Stag's Crossing, that fox carcass dangling in her hand. Something terrible has occurred here, something he cannot understand—the doe with her womanish gasping and dying, the dead dog-fox. A terrible retribution.

He knows he cannot tell his father or his brother any of this. The ribbon in his hand a mark of a greater crime, one that he cannot prove. Instead he lets it fall to the ground. Not wanting to be caught by his father and brother examining such a girlish thing. Not wanting his father to excoriate him for being just like his mother, tangled up in dark forces he cannot understand.

Carlyle says, What a waste of a good deer.

We can come back next week, Joshua says.

No. This is it for now. We won't get another chance to hunt until next year.

Joshua hides his disappointment well enough though he cannot hide from his own brother. Disappointment then resentment and confusion—why did his father ask Nick to take the shot? Where had he, the glorious marksman, gone wrong?

Perhaps later they will fight over this—settling the score with fists, howling, brambles in their hair. Nick's strikes small but calculating while Joshua pulls his arm back taut as an archer. His aim vicious and true. Nick fights even though he knows in the end he will submit. Lying in the dirt like a kicked dog. Something about him forever painful, forever wounded by this.

The trek back to the Ford feels endless. Nearing autumn the heat approaches the intolerable. Sweat glides down Joshua's forehead. He rubs it away with his hand the sleeve of his hunting jacket obscuring a glimpse of something beneath the truck. Vanishing upon a second look.

Here they have committed an unforgivable transgression. Leaving behind the half-butchered doe its viscera seeping into the ground. A prodigy, an ill omen.

A death deferred has come to Stag's Crossing, has lain down in the entryway of the grand house with the obeisance of a slavering hound. And there it will stay, waiting for the interregnum. The return from exile signaling the twilight of an empire.

Exhausted Nick throws his pack into the truck bed and flops down next to the tackle boxes. There will be no fishing on the way home so he has threaded his fanciful lures in vain. Joshua carefully sets down his rifle and closes the tailgate. He folds up his hunting jacket and lies down to ruminate in the strangling heat.

They ride home without so much as whispering. Cornfields passing so close Nick could stick out his arm and touch the stalks overhanging the fences. Joshua obsesses over the dying animal; Nick cleans his sleeve of lingering parasites.

Time will destroy all these memories. In their forties there will be nothing here except the easy and complacent amnesia of childhood. The silhouette of the forest vanishing behind them in the far distance. The sun glowing like a lit match. The summer air bruising their anxious faces with warmth and light.

Xiv.

NOW

He notices only later that Emilia has fallen asleep. Noticing only because he thinks of something pointless and amusing he wants to tell her but realizes she has long since stopped listening to his idle conversation. Her eyes closed and her breath moving evenly beneath her collarbone. She could be a statue of exquisite marble until a slight bump in the road makes her stir. Slowly she opens her eyes; yawns; stretches.

Nick turns on the radio—Rachmaninov and a hint of static creeps softly over them. Her face is beatific. Upon awakening she is languorous as a cat sunning itself in a windowsill. Her spine curves as she twists from side to side and then bends downward a bit to rub her neck.

We've got about a half hour before we get to my house, he says. *My house* as though he owns it though he does not. Who else could own Stag's Crossing except his father? The maimed king whose empire has gone halfway to ruin.

What does it look like? she says.

You've been here before, haven't you? he says. Careful not to mention his father's cruel outburst upon her disastrous arrival.

Not inside.

Like an apprentice at the master draftsman's table he conjures it in his mind; how even with only two stories it towers, casting its inimitable shadow over the land. The garden in full bloom then withered and dying in the winter. The Quonset near the house leering and metallic. The coop must be there too, the rotted swing. His small bedroom at the end of the hallway wherein lies the decayed corpse of his childhood.

It's immense, he says. My dad built it himself. Mixture of Southern plantation architecture and Gothic farmhouse, I guess.

Gothic farmhouse, she says. Fascinating. When I was a kid I just lived in a boring Pennsylvania suburb.

I'm sure it was nice, he says.

Not really, she says. My dad was an alcoholic.

I'm sorry to hear that.

Don't be sorry. He was an asshole.

That's a difficult situation.

Joshua told me, she says carefully, that your father used to beat the two of you.

You just got here, and you're bringing that up?

Why not? she says. We're family.

He does not have the heart to tell her that under no

circumstances would she be considered family by any Morrow. The best she can aspire to is a tolerated guest, one who is quickly ushered out with pleasantries and then relentlessly gossiped about afterward in the classic manner of Midwestern hospitality. Yet perhaps things have changed. Perhaps this time Carlyle will not throw her out upon first glance.

Yeah, a long time ago. Just when we were kids.

She is quiet for a moment.

So do you think that's okay?

What—hitting children?

Yes.

No, of course not.

But you're going home to see your father anyway. Even though what he did to you was wrong.

It's more complicated than you're making it out to be.

I didn't go to my father's funeral, she says. I don't know why you'd go to a funeral to celebrate the life of someone who used to harm you.

I'm sure Joshua made it sound like we were belted every day, Nick says. I had it worse than him and I turned out fine.

Is that what you tell yourself?

Listen, Nick says, I'm not here to debate the specifics of my childhood—I have no idea what my brother told you, but it wasn't that bad.

You're not here to debate your childhood but you're here to debate race.

Now you're just being unfair—

She looks at him as though she wants to say something

but does not. They are both silent Nick half looking at the road and half looking at her.

Touché, he says, at last. The Rachmaninov all at once seems profoundly loud and piercing. He turns off the radio. Utter silence greets him. The empty chasm between them wide as the space between galaxies.

He wonders if she is like this with his brother—high-strung, unintimidated. Prone to fits of pique, facile and cutting in her repartee. Or perhaps they are merely acting out their roles preordained by destiny. As he is set against his brother he is naturally set against her as well. Their rivalry immediate and obvious. He has the distinct sense that if he turns his back to her even for a moment she might cut him open with a knife.

Nick, she says. Look.

What?

To your left, she says.

Through the cloudy windshield Nick sees a group of palominos shy as young girls cantering through the long unmown yellow grass.

I've never seen horses up close before, she says. Always wanted one when I was a kid.

Well, come on, he says. Feeling a foolish impulse rising inside him—to please her, to hear her laugh in his presence. Pulling over he stops the car right off the road. There is no one else for miles. Nothing except Emilia and the horses and the sagging fence with barbed wire.

Are you sure? she says.

If the Rasmussens still live here they won't care, he says.

Who are they?

One of the families that has land neighboring ours. I used to be friends with their daughter, Peggy.

Are you still?

I haven't seen her in a long time. I think she ran off with a boyfriend or something. Maybe to California.

Oh. That's a shame.

She gets out of the car and follows him up to the fence.

Be careful, he says. There's barbed wire.

He nickers to the horses. The sight of them stirring in him memories of a long distant past—admiring the beautiful Arabian yearlings at the annual sale; racing his brother on borrowed Thoroughbreds.

One of the horses comes ever closer. Slowing to a light trot as it goes. Tossing its head from side to side its mane fluttering in the wind. Emilia reaches out her hand too close to the wire and he gently grasps her wrist and moves it higher just clear of the fence. He gestures softly to the horse who has come now right in front of them. Its mane pale blonde and its eyes filled with tenderness.

Hello, horse, she says.

They don't speak English.

How do you know? she says.

She says something to the horse again but he doesn't catch it. In Chinese maybe. Nearing dusk now the sky blushing a bright orange brings out the redness in her sable hair.

Is it what you expected? he asks.

Even better, she says.

Here, he says, just stroke its neck.

He lets go of her wrist and she pats the horse hesitantly. A strange, shadowed look comes over its eyes as she reaches for it. In its mahogany lens he can see only his dark silhouette and the empty stretch of road behind them. The horse flicks its tail up and shifts its gaze to something that Nick cannot see, behind Emilia—a passing horsefly, or the mistaken scent of a predator—before it spooks. Nick quickly pulls Emilia back as the horse lets out a frantic whinny. Rearing up on its hind legs like a charger, its hooves pummeling the air.

Easy, easy! Nick says.

With an almost impossible lightness, the horse jumps backward and turns away from them. Breaking into a breathless, heedless run as it returns to the safety of its herd that watches from a distance. Shaking its head back and forth and tossing its mane in the billowing wind.

Emilia stands in the road, looking neither pleased nor disappointed.

Sorry about that, he says, sheepish. Must've been one of the ones they're still training. Some wild horses aren't used to people yet. They get nervous.

It's okay, she says. I'm glad you weren't hurt.

Well, thank you kindly.

When it reared up—it reminded me of one of those equestrian statues. I saw a few in Vienna.

You've been to Vienna?

It's beautiful in the winter.

He says, not at all jealous, Did Joshua take you there?

Oh—no, she says. It was a long time ago. Before we met.

That sounds very nice.

Imagining the crystals of frost in her black hair. Allowing himself to imagine it. The act of fantasy itself like a long-ago transgression.

We should probably go. Your dad must be waiting for us.

Right, he says.

In the car she leans her head against the cracked-open window once more.

Thank you, she says. So softly he almost doesn't hear. So softly he does not turn to look at her even. Her body perfect and still. Casting no reflection at all.

XV.

THEN

His father wakes him, axe in hand.

Come on. Your brother's already up, Carlyle says. Through the open door Nick can see the blurry outline of Joshua's shadow as he struggles to get his coat on. Dawn has only just arrived at Stag's Crossing, a purple bruise blooming in the sky.

Nick rubs his eyes. S'early.

Firewood needs cutting. Trees need felling. Get moving.

He gets up and puts his clothes on. Downstairs he finds Joshua spreading butter on a slice of toast. He takes a piece for himself and eats it with one hand. Getting into his boots with the other. By the time he has swallowed the last crumb his father has already come up behind him and unlocked the screen door at the back of the house. Nick retrieves his coat, his small axe, his gloves.

With Carlyle leading they pass the henhouse, the rooster not yet risen for its morning cacophony. One of the dogs lounges beneath the house's long shadow, dozing with one eye open. Broad-chested and stout it is a strange cross between a greyhound and a neighbor's bear-baiting terrier that infiltrated the bloodline years back. It retains the slender legs of a greyhound, the wild teeth of a killer. Watching as they wind round the henhouse and head toward the creek and the woods that abut the southern part of Stag's Crossing.

The summer has been good to them. The cornstalks high as ever. The creek has flooded twice already, its soil soft and wet with the memory of rainfall. Imprinted in the ground are pawprints, spaced close together. A sluggish and uneven pace. Strange for the fleet-footed hounds that roam Stag's Crossing, who are so light upon the earth they are likely to leave hardly any trace at all.

At the edge of the woods Carlyle stops and points to a tree that has sprouted branches too long for his liking. When he first came to Stag's Crossing and saw the woods south of the old farmhouse growing, ever growing gnarled and covered in thorns he knew it would be impossible to cut down all of it. Once his thousand acres were nearly all forest. Now all that remains is a pathetic remnant of its ancient self, the canopy cover so thin that light pours through and dries the unshaded soil in the blistering summer. Every summer he finds yet another tree reaching its envious branches toward the house, hoping one day to reclaim all that is man-made at Stag's Crossing, perhaps even Stag's Crossing itself, all that Carlyle has hacked and cut into the earth and made his own.

This is the one, he says.

Joshua is ready with the axe. He is always ready.

I've got this, Dad.

Go ahead then, Carlyle says.

Nick turns away from this scene as Carlyle instructs Joshua on the height and placement of the first cut. His mind wandering to the tracks in the creek, the soft imprints in the grass that lead deeper into the woods. With his father's back to him and Joshua engrossed in the minutiae of tree-felling, Nick simply walks past them and deeper into the woods. They might notice his absence in a few minutes or a few hours, however long it takes for Carlyle to recall Nick's existence and yell for him to come back to the house immediately or there'll be hell to pay, Nicholas Edward Morrow—

Nick hears Joshua shouting, Timber! The tree falls, a small crash in the distance. They will come looking for him soon; he hurries. Passing a cairn of rocks, then another. The graves of the dogs that Carlyle was particularly fond of, memorialized with a strange tenderness that is slightly morbid. His father always buries them out in the woods so he does not have to see their graves from the house. Just like the graves of his wife and son. Buried past the creek, so far from the house Carlyle is reminded of them very little—exactly how he likes it. Yet from time to time he will see her delicate features lingering on the face of his second son. Forcing him to remember what he has long since deliberately forgotten. With such brutality he recalls her in the particular coloration of Nick's hair, the placement of his nose. Perhaps the only creature besides the dogs for which he has ever felt true affection.

Beyond the cairns Nick sees blood mingling in the grass. Having dried several hours ago it is like rust on the ground. Beneath one of the grand trees lies the pregnant bitch his father had so prized. Its sleek coat darkened with gore. From its slit belly spills its intestines and the remnants of its unborn litter. A deep slash has opened its neck and flung the head several feet away. Its dead eyes looking toward Nick without emotion.

He turns around. If he looks for another moment he will faint or vomit and he cannot let his father see that. Carlyle catches up to him easily with his long, unhurried strides. Joshua following obediently behind.

Joshua says, Look, the dog—

I know.

Carlyle approaches. Examining the scene with an air of detachment.

What do you think it was?

A mountain lion, says Nick weakly. His hands are balled into fists; he looks at the ground. He knows a mountain lion could not have done this.

Haven't been mountain lions in Nebraska for over a century, Carlyle says, advancing on him. There are things beyond our understanding in these woods and elsewhere. You'd know this if you weren't a lazy fool. But you are, aren't you?

He grabs Nick by the collar and pulls him closer to where the dog lies. Forcing Nick to look at this tableau that disgusts him so, to inhale the vicious aroma of the animal's dying, its desperation as it fought to survive and could not. Some creature of unknown provenance, some beast from elsewhere had done this. Not one that any Morrow could name.

This wouldn't have happened if you were looking after the dogs properly. Wouldn't have happened if you kept them out of the woods. A family like ours has enemies, we can't afford to be careless.

Nick says, Dad, let go, please—

He feels Carlyle throwing him to the ground; he rolls over onto his side and covers his head without even thinking of doing it. Accepting his fate as his father uses the wooden handle of the axe on him and his thoughts drift effortlessly elsewhere. To the wonderful life he will have once he is free of this place, this family. To the half-remembered face of his mother, a small comfort.

Lying there in the dirt he sees out of the corner of his half-shut eyes the faint imprints of tracks on the bloodied ground, not one of the dogs but coyote or wolf or even fox—but what fox could possibly kill one of his father's glorious hounds?—but it must be, he knows it by sight alone, the tracks of a creature more cunning than any of them—no fence around the coop or locked door could keep it out, it will come back until it has eaten them alive with the hens and picked its teeth with their bones—the very thought driven from his mind by another blow from the handle of his father's axe against his ribs, so painful it rips a shriek from his clenched mouth. He is sick with it, this agony that enters him like a calf at his first branding. Scratching hopelessly at his face with his hands he wills himself to die.

Dad, stop!

Carlyle pauses, his arm halted in midair. Nick watches as Joshua throws himself between them, his arms outstretched in supplication. At seventeen he is just as tall as their father, just as strong. Not yet grown into the fullness of the glory he will possess as a man though the flash of his golden hair augurs it. Anticipating his handsomeness, his blazing defiance.

Without a word Carlyle strikes Joshua with the axe handle, so hard he is violently thrown to the ground where he lies in the dirt as pathetic as a stillborn calf. Blood seeping through his sleeve where he caught the blow.

They are silent after this. Watching their father turn and walk back to the house. Refusing to acknowledge Joshua's sniffles of agony, Nick's accusing stare. Unaffected by what he has done, as though some other man has come in and beat Nick within an inch of his life, another father in another family who wields an axe handle with the grace and fervor of a duelist.

Eventually Joshua rises and helps Nick to his feet. They do not speak of what has transpired. Instead they take their axes and return to the tree line where Joshua shows Nick how to chop the firewood exactly the way their father likes it.

Joshua says, Here, take these. Placing a few perfectly cut logs into Nick's outstretched arms. I can't carry any more, my arm hurts.

It's okay, Nick says. I've got it.

You'll have to take care of this stuff once I'm gone for college, Joshua says. Dad needs help. You can't leave him alone.

They carry the firewood back to the house. Carlyle

has already retired to his study, where he is not to be disturbed. Joshua busies himself with schoolwork. Nick goes up to his little bedroom and lies on the bed with his hands balled into fists. Tears pricking his eyelids, arriving unbidden.

He knows better than to ask his father to apologize for his myriad injuries, of the flesh and not, for Carlyle has done nothing except what is expected of him. Disciplining his boys, unruly as they are. Molding them into exactly the kind of men they are supposed to be. So that in ten years, or twenty, or however long it takes for Joshua to find a wife, he might strike his son in turn and think nothing of it. And Nick, whether fourteen or forty-three, will still awaken to the nightmarish thud of the axe handle against his ribs. Delirious, shivering in anticipation of the next blow. Even when it never comes.

XVI.

NOW

Nearly twenty years since he has last set foot in the house of his father and already he cannot speak truthfully of it as though Stag's Crossing is merely a place he had invented as a child, a sepulcher of the imagination. Yet after a leisurely evening drive he sees the weathered buck's head with its unblinking glass eyes. The rusted and curlicued iron gates. Straight ahead no more than a hundred feet away. Hanging open; waiting. As he remembered as he has dreamed. Turn back, he tells himself. Yet like a man having a vision of his death he is transfixed and cannot retreat.

A hysterical spasm propels him forward. Forcing him to drive at a measured and deliberate pace up the gravel path now overgrown with weeds. A greyhound with white hairs dotting its muzzle dashes in front of him and he nearly swerves to avoid hitting it. Light as a ballet dancer it dodges and leaps away.

Beyond the tangled and thorny driveway lies the house, its handsomeness without equal. Brought forth from the dirt by a virtuoso with the saw, the carpenter's blade. The first floor awash with light. Cascading from the windows, the open double doors. Beckoning to him now at forty-three a remnant of himself; no longer as he was when he last came here with no intention of returning.

Emilia says, Your home is beautiful. Her voice filled with feigned astonishment like she has never been here before though she has, she must remember that place where at last Carlyle showed himself to her the person he has always been—a delusional old man, cataleptic with rage.

Well. Here we are, he says. Parking the car out front. In the humid summer air he can hear the crackling hum of the television, the dry melodic music of the brown field crickets. He gets out of the car and softly closes the door behind him so as not to startle the dogs, the grasshoppers. Having rained only a few days before the ground beneath him is warm and wet. Emilia comes to stand next to him slowly almost warily. No one left in the yard save them and three long-limbed greyhounds lounging in the grass. Unloading the luggage from the car Nick hears nothing other than the creaking of the trunk lid, Emilia fiddling with the handle of her suitcase.

Three greyhounds approach them. Even the oldest with the white hairs on its snout must have been born long after Nick last came to Stag's Crossing; they live fifteen years at the most. Less, if they are impaled on a tractor spike. The one leading is particularly hostile. Pulling its lips back into a snarl.

Easy there, Nick says.

Odd choice for a guard dog.

They're meant for hunting, Nick says. My dad likes the look of them. You ever seen one chase a hare? Small animals don't stand a chance.

They don't seem to like you very much, Emilia says, stepping forward. This seems to agitate the dogs even more. One turns on its heel and takes off immediately; the other two slowly retreat, hackles raised. Staring her down with a wild fervidness in their eyes before she waves them off. Finally they too turn and depart, disappearing into the shadows of the night.

They don't seem to like you, either.

Fine by me, she says.

As he steps onto the patio he sees no sign of welcome—no one to greet him as his mother might have, had she lived longer. For years there were rumors that his father would remarry; yet in all the years Nick lived at Stag's Crossing hiding himself among his father's books like a fugitive he never saw his father so much as look at another woman. So much as spend more than an afternoon playing cards with other men for whom he put on a show of congeniality but later would brutally dissect—Max Young uglier than a donkey's backside; Teddy Miller whose wife steps out on him every night like a streetwalker. The tragedy of human relations; the fatal weakness of sentiment. Having driven this philosophy into his sons with the sharp awl of his conviction he has rendered them distant and cold. Joshua prone to an icy glory. Nick forever and correctly accused of apathy. Filled with a serpentine haughtiness he no longer cares to disguise.

In Emilia's presence utter confusion overtakes him—remembering the way his brother spoke of women once, dismissed them with a wave of his hand—here she stands having lured Joshua from his ancestral sanctuary. Captivating him somehow into a grand intimacy, a ceaseless and riveting attraction. Nick is long past the age where such an indulgence would register with him. Finding fleeting pleasure in a tangling of bodies afterward he is warmly satisfied; he might open the window or pull the blankets above his head. Lingering in the moment. But that was him in a younger and more virile lifetime. In his forties at last he has solved the puzzle of sex, the problem thereof, wanting it now only for the vague and abstract pursuit of pleasure.

He follows her to the front of the house wondering if Joshua had followed her similarly twenty years before. Watching her delicate glances; how she brushes her hair behind her ears with a kind of sweetness. The closer they come to the house the more overpowering the light and static appear to him. Their approach doomed and inexorable. A part of him is both inside and outside his body. Going to the doorway he is beguiled by the brightness—all the lights in the house switched on brilliant as fireflies held close to the naked eye.

In the living room sits the man he calls Father, Dad, master and maker. Leaning forward in his leather recliner he is thinner than Nick recalls. His hands gripping his knees as he looks deep into the flickering kaleidoscope of the television. The signal grainy distorting the image with static. Emilia's low-heeled shoes hit the polished hardwood floor and Carlyle snaps his head around to look at them standing as he does. Almost leaping from the chair like a dead man reanimated. His skin has taken on the hue of rotting balsa. He is resplendent in the ascetic harshness that inhabits every fissure of his face, every line around his eyes and mouth that now twists upward into a smile. A grotesquerie. No part of him could be called fatherly or kind. No fat cradling his bones the veins of his hand visible, bluish with sickness.

Turning off the television he gestures to Nick. Come here—let me see you. My eyes are bad.

Emilia stands back, to the side. Her long dark hair shrouding her expression with shadow. Nick walks closer. Willing his feet to drag him there. The doors hanging open behind him the house weeping incandescent light all over the lawn.

You look exactly how I imagined, Carlyle says. Like your mother.

Thanks, Nick says. Knowing it is not a compliment to be unlike his father. To be a Morrow unlike Carlyle is to be a Morrow who hardly exists.

Where's Joshua?

Business meeting. He's coming tomorrow.

And this must be Emilia.

Hello, she says.

It's nice to meet you.

It's nice to meet you too, Carlyle, she says. You have a lovely home.

Why thank you. I built it myself. Even laid the foundation by hand, he says. But you must be hungry—do you want some food? I don't have much, but there's some meat loaf I could heat up.

We're really tired, Dad, Nick says. I think we should all get some sleep.

Of course, of course. Must've been quite the drive. Traffic from the airport gets worse every year.

I'll take my old bedroom, Nick says.

Oh, no. I couldn't. You're a guest, Carlyle says. I'll take your little bedroom—I'm an old man, I don't need much room anymore with my old bones—you'll have Joshua's, and Joshua and Emilia can take the master.

You're too kind, Emilia says.

Not at all. It's my pleasure.

Let me help with the lights, Nick says.

No, no, I'll do it. Get some rest. Already Carlyle is walking through the kitchen flicking switches as he goes. Extinguishing the house of all life.

Emilia goes up to the stairs dragging her slim suitcase with her. At the top floor she looks around—unable to choose between the three identical doors carved from heavy pine. Nick points her to the largest bedroom overlooking Carlyle's study.

The master is that one. With the gold doorknob.

How fancy.

I've never really been in there.

Never?

No, but I know the bed is big enough for two at least. You also have your own bathroom.

I guess it'll be an adventure, she says. Like sleeping in a grand hotel somewhere exotic.

It's Nebraska, not Paris.

Are you always so pessimistic?

I lived here for half my life. I'm just being honest.

I like that about you.

Thanks. Most people don't.

She smiles at this.

Anyway, he says, I'll be next door. Let me know if you need anything.

Thank you, she says.

His brother's old bedroom is larger than he remembers. The feather mattress soft and comfortable; the freshly washed quilt smelling pleasantly of detergent. Carlyle must have washed the sheets like Nick always used to, carrying them down to the little laundry corner on the first floor with the boxy Maytag washer. How strange to think of his father doing housework like a woman.

He takes off his shoes and socks. Unzipping his luggage he takes out the little painting, folded over until it is no bigger than his palm. He unfolds it and places it on Joshua's old desk, engraved with his initials. The unnamed woman in the painting looking back at him coyly from behind a curtain of black hair. Fishing for a pair of boxers and an old nightshirt he changes quickly and crawls under the duvet. Through the wall he can hear the shower running. He is warm all over; he pulls the sheets over his head. Imagining Emilia showering though he does not want to think of her like that: nude and pale as a newborn lamb. Yet she is so close he can see her without even looking. Her hair long and dark and wet with desire.

Xvii.

THEN

The fox returns the next year. Nick does not see it—only the cleverness of its work. January is brisk and cloudless but the fresh snowfall each morning hides nothing. The decapitated hens, the roosters with missing legs. One weekend he is shoveling snow near the coop and sees broken eggs scattered all along the outer fence. Cracked open, the yolks spilled out on the ground. Discarded with the refined and mocking air of an epicure.

The difference between wolves and foxes his father says is that wolves love to hunt and foxes love to play. A tantalizing trail of blood in the half-melted snow. Wolves only have enough foresight to kill and upon their killing they will feed ravenously and strip the bones. But foxes; they are quick-witted and brutal. When they hunt they do so with finesse stalking and pouncing then snapping the spine in their slender jaws.

At school Nick's class studies the various predators of the Sandhills though no wolves have stalked the plains for more than fifty years. Passing around the skeleton of a raccoon the skull of a *Canis familiaris.* Taught to recognize the signs of rabies and help with the birthing of calves they are strangers to many things. The seduction of literature; the perfect and refined beauty of mathematics. Nick does not even know if he will go to college as it seems like such a useless and far-off concept. He rarely reads books of substance and when he reads he does not pay attention at all. He reads only to be away from himself, to see himself at a distance, but when he closes the book its contents appear unfamiliar to him and he cannot remember anything from it.

Considering all possibilities in his mind—suicide, exodus, escape—he dreams of fleeing to some unknown and untouched paradise. Yet he knows this is a pathetic fantasy for no place on earth remains unmarked by his father's righteous hand. Carlyle had not gone to college instead he had gone west to seek his fortune like many young men of his generation. Settling in Iowa, the Dakotas, Nevada where they gouged open the land with plows and fed upon its offspring. Killed the young and sucked the marrow from their bones.

At first he hopes his father simply does not notice. Carlyle rarely goes out to the coop spending most of his afternoons surveying their fields instead. But in the winter sometimes he checks on the chickens and after several unlucky passes he sees the fox's leftovers rotting in the iced-over dirt. Pushing the remains aside with his shoe he sees they are fresh.

He walks back to the house where Nick is sitting on the front porch feeding the dogs. Shivering a bit in his grand winter coat though the dogs need to be fed and he will be the one to do it without his brother there.

Fox in the henhouse, he says.

I saw, Nick says.

Seems like you've known about this for a while, Carlyle says.

Just a week, Nick lies. I've been busy with school.

Don't look that busy to me.

Nick puts down the dog dish. The greyhounds crowd around him licking at his face.

And what are you going to do about it? Are you just going to let this happen? Carlyle says.

No.

Then stop being incompetent. Joshua's not here to help so figure it out yourself.

Okay, Dad, he says.

One of the greyhounds gently knocks against him with its lean and tawny shoulder. Nick pours more dog food into the metal bowl and walks into the house taking off his shoes and coat so as not to track in snow. Goes through the kitchen to the study where his father's rotary phone lies on the grand mahogany desk. When he was a young boy he could barely see over the top where sat his father's beautiful books; his collection of letters. There he has displayed photos of his infant sons, his wife. Nick's mother whose image he knows though he can barely remember her, only the imprint thereof. The way his father will sometimes say, Your hair is just like your mother's. Thick as a bay roan.

He dials Kenny who sits in front of him in math class and lives fifteen minutes away if you drive recklessly enough on the gravel road. Kenny the neighbor boy in Carlyle's parlance. Scrappy little thing he has been held back once already. Kenny's father is the type of the perpetual laissez-faire drunkard who lets him borrow the truck whenever he likes. Five years from now Kenny will be dead having been engulfed by a hail of corn in his father's grain bin. Nick foresees tragedy for him but knows not its final form; he says nothing of it.

Hi Kenny, Nick says. It's Nick. Need to run an errand this afternoon. Can you borrow your dad's pickup?

Was planning on heading to town anyway, Kenny says. Give me twenty minutes and I'll be over.

He puts his coat and shoes back on. He is so tired he could fall asleep right there as he sits on the front porch throwing old tennis balls at the dogs who were not made for fetching but killing rabbits. Coming back to the house clutching the progeny of hares in their jaws their mouths mottled with gore. Something haughty about them; sinister and nimble in their walk. Sometimes they chase the barn cats across the wide and fallow fields for the pleasure of it. Nick watches them and marvels at how they are like an extension of his father, swift and unerring in their bloodshed.

Smooth and radiant as a racing stallion comes Kenny's Studebaker to the gates of Stag's Crossing. Gleaming bright and cherry-red in the pleasant afternoon light Nick is transfixed by its halcyon glory.

Kenny rolls down the window. Nick, come on! he says.

Nick runs to meet him. Down the narrow driveway and then past the gate he dutifully latches behind him. Swinging open the passenger-side door he is nearly beaten back by the rank scent of chewing tobacco. At fifteen Kenny has already picked up one of his father's many vices. Gnawing on his Skoal with the comportment of a philosopher.

He brushes his coppery hair from his eyes and says, You're taller.

I grew a lot in November, Nick says. In the doorway of his room his father has been marking his height with a pencil. Almost as tall as Joshua now. Thinner and with a nervous disposition.

Gonna try out for the football team?

I'm turning traitor and joining Alabama, actually.

After what happened at the Orange Bowl I don't blame you.

Sounds like it was a bad time.

My dad nearly threw the TV out the window. Even started calling Devaney names. He's always hollering at the players too like they can hear him.

Does he do that in the stadium?

Yeah, he does. If you had come to the Colorado game with me you would've seen him.

It's okay. My dad needed me here.

To do what?

Dunno. He doesn't watch football. Thinks it rots your brain.

I mean, he's right. But you still should've come to the game.

Next time, Nick says.

Promise?

Promise.

Kenny turns up the heater inside the Studebaker.

Goddamn, it's cold out. Why're you going to town in this weather?

Why're *you* going? Nick shoots back.

My dad ran out of beer, Kenny says.

You can get that in Fremont.

Not the kind my dad likes.

Can't he go get it himself?

He's sleeping.

At two in the afternoon?

Kenny shrugs.

Nick says, Well, my dad's pissed too. We've got a fox up in the coop. I would've shot it by now but I haven't hardly seen it.

Sure it's not a coyote?

It's not a coyote.

That makes two foxes in a year. You're gonna turn into Ben Wilkerson. Found a whole family of em on his land.

I think it's the same one as before.

Then if you're not quick about it you won't have any chickens left by spring.

I know. Got no choice but to kill it.

That why you're going all that way?

Yeah. Traps and bait.

You know all that stuff looks the same to me right.

Well that's because you're an idiot, Kenny.

Ha-ha, Kenny says. Unusually pensive he thinks to himself for a moment. If it was your brother he would've just gone out and killed it. None of this fancy stuff.

Good thing I'm not Joshua, Nick says.

No, Kenny says. You're not at all.

For once Nick is not tormented by this difference. Outside the tyrannical presence of Stag's Crossing he is free to be as he is, however God might have made him. No longer overlooked by Joshua's lingering shadow. The image of his mother flitting briefly into his head, whom he is often told he resembles like it is a bad thing. Were he not in the presence of another boy he might weep to think of her, dead now almost nine years. One year Nick came downstairs having picked dandelions and dried them between the pages of his Bible just for the occasion and asked Carlyle if he would like to lay flowers on the grave and his father had said, Not today. I'm taking Joshua to town with me.

Still now he thinks of it. How falls the lightning, the rain upon those two engraved slabs. *Beloved Wife & Mother. Beloved Son.*

Xviii.

NOW

Late afternoon conversation fills the house. His brother's wife—his father. From the second floor Nick can hear their voices. Not their words but the timbre of them. Having grown up listening to his father's daily sermons there is no mistaking the earthy darkness of his speech. The distinct Southern inflection in his cadence. His vowels rich as brandy, meant to be savored.

Getting up to open the blinds Nick is stiff and ungainly as an old man. He is already an old man by his childhood reckoning though he does not like to think of himself that way. In his forties his intellect is still piercing, still capable of wounding beyond repair. And what is violence if not a young man's game? His viciousness merely another stratagem, a diagonal move across the chessboard of human relations.

He goes to the bathroom to wash up and put on something more respectable than boxer briefs and an ugly bathrobe. Absurdly he wonders if he should put on a tie or else apologize for rising at such a late hour. Were he the Nick of his childhood Carlyle would have already barged into his room at six in the morning yelling for him to get up, God damn it. But today he has been left alone to sleep late and do as he pleases. As his brother was once permitted.

Settling on a white dress shirt and neatly pressed jeans he combs his hair and prepares himself for the scene that awaits him downstairs. What might his father make of him now—writer, hierophant, teller of tales? Or else the critic of the hour, the playful vivisector, taking exquisite pleasure in his acrimony? Last night they had seen each other only for a few moments and Carlyle had said nothing. Raked over him with his eyes and then said that Nick looked like his mother which is to say that Nick bore no resemblance to him at all. Yet he is a Morrow in face and body and hatred; the marks of his father have made him son enough.

Treading silently down the steps he hears bits and pieces of conversation floating through the air delicate as dandelion seeds.

—and that's when I bought my first greyhound, Carlyle says. I must have been about fifteen. Always loved the look of em. When I finally got one of my own I was absolutely amazed.

And you've bred them since?

Yes.

What an incredible story.

It's nothing, really. My boys gave me a lot of help. Didn't you, Nick?

Nick freezes. His hand resting lightly on the banister.

Knew someone was coming down the stairs. My hearing is still pretty good, Carlyle calls out.

Sure is, Nick says.

You're up late. Why don't you come grab what's left of lunch.

Nick walks through the kitchen and into the dining room. Passing through the narrow doorway separating the two he sees Emilia sitting nearest to the window, looking out. Carlyle has taken his rightful seat at the head of the too-large table. Proud and unbowed even in his infirmity. He gestures toward the centerpiece—calla lilies in a violet vase, a tray of half sandwiches. Nick pulls out a chair and sits, awkwardly, the latecomer. Unwrapping a cucumber sandwich with both hands he eats hesitantly like a child.

How is it?

Great.

In the past he did not eat if his father had not already begun his meal. He was never invited to gorge himself. Eating only what was given to him and like any mongrel born at Stag's Crossing he was happy to starve.

He licks a stray crumb from the curve of his palm. Emilia, still looking out the window, plays idly with a strand of her hair.

While you were asleep I drove your rental back to Fremont, Carlyle says.

Oh. Thanks. Did you get a ride back from one of the Rasmussens?

Emilia followed me in my truck, Carlyle says. Then I drove us both back.

I'm surprised you let him drive, Nick says.

Emilia says, I don't know what you're talking about. Carlyle's a great driver.

I only hit a few curbs on the way, Carlyle says, winking.

There is a phantasm of uncomfortable mirth in the air—a wry joke told to a roomful of strangers. Nick has never considered his father to be a good-humored man. Choleric and unstable, perhaps. Now Carlyle sits beatifically at the head of the table trading jokes with pariahs. His son, made furious and bitter by history. His daughter-in-law, who has descended upon them like an unexpected pestilence.

For a single delicious moment Nick allows himself to glimpse a brief and hallucinatory American fantasia, one in which beauty and true love might free the country from the strange malaise that makes itself known in Carlyle's unadorned speech: Oriental, chink, *you brought that bitch into this house.* A stranger at Stag's Crossing! His civility now is only spectacle—the practiced manners of a leashed and muzzled hound. Nick of all people knows what his father has said about her when she was not around—that she was *that woman* who had turned Joshua cunt-struck, doing the work of the Devil or someone even worse—she had spirited Joshua away, bewitched him, changed him forever into something he was not. Yet perhaps as she ascends the ancestral threshold his father will finally see her and welcome her as a member of the family. For her flesh is now commingled with Joshua's—she will die with him and be buried in that same ashen sepulcher. Her lovely head haloed with dead flowers.

He might even become used to her presence seeing her glide through the kitchen every day on the way to breakfast every morning. They will never be close but they can be cordial. Out of politeness she will show Carlyle pictures of her dead family and he will see then that she is perfectly ordinary. Even less than that: her heritage unremarkable and pedestrian, heir to nothing. Unlike them she has neither money nor history. And Carlyle will marvel at the end of this long and delirious season how he could have ever thought poorly of her, this nice girl from Pennsylvania who could have been good in another life had she another name and another face. Standing at his deathbed barely holding back tears she will weep with gratitude when Carlyle forgives; makes amends; calls his lawyer to restore Joshua's thousand-acre birthright. Blood returning to blood. A final act of generosity.

No. His father will never tread the path of redemption. Even after such a long absence the pleasure of homecoming has soured—there is no sunlit blur of nostalgia to elide Nick's years of exile, disillusionment. He knows better than this—knew as soon as he saw Carlyle sitting motionless in front of the television that the time for repentance is long past. Carlyle may say he wishes to reconcile but there is nothing to reconcile. His father will always be his father. And he will always be his father's second son.

Gravel scatters in the grass. He hears a car pulling into the driveway.

Must be Eli, Carlyle says.

He's visiting? Nick says.

Picked Joshua up from the airport.

I wasn't aware Joshua couldn't drive himself.

I'd never ask him to do that. Have you seen the roads lately?

Yes, I was just on them last night.

Carlyle's mouth pricks with displeasure. That's not what I meant—

Come on, let's go say hi, Emilia interrupts. She gets up from the table and goes to the door. The skirt of her linen sundress swinging as she walks. Nick follows her into the foyer where the light is rich and seductive. Where he often dreamed as a boy of lying down and sunning himself like an animal stretched out along the strip of light coming through the window, dashing itself across the floor. The sun catches the dust motes, the obsidian glint of her hair. He is standing so close to her he could almost touch it if he wanted to. If he let himself.

Someone bangs on the door. Loud stentorian knocks like a jackhammer.

Coming! Emilia shouts. She turns the lock and pushes open the double doors that swing outward with a great heave of air. On the porch stand Joshua and Eli. As grown men they could not be more different. Eli tugs at the sagging strap of his overalls, his boots muddied with dirt. Joshua is still wearing his work suit, stiff and lawyerly, running a hand self-consciously over the wrinkles in his sleeve. His fancy luggage in a pile on the stoop. At forty-seven he has changed, certainly—no longer possessing the charm of young men who are beautiful and believe they will remain so forever he has instead been gifted with a sharp and refined handsomeness in middle age. His hair formerly a light blond now a deeper, burnished gold. Elegant and patrician as ever only the slight hint of a flat Midwestern accent betrays him—he remains a child of the same God as Eli. God of the Sandhills, of his father and brother alike.

Nice to see you, Eli, Nick says. Been a while.

You too, Eli says.

Would you like to stay for a little? Emilia says. You could have a beer and catch up.

Nick looks at his father, whose face betrays no anxiety, no anger. When he was a child he knew that to invite anyone other than family into Stag's Crossing was forbidden. Yet here Emilia is, a stranger herself, playing at hostess.

Sorry, can't. I've gotta get back to the farm, Eli says.

Thanks for the ride, Joshua says.

Anytime.

Eli waves goodbye to the family gathered before him and begins walking back to his truck. His figure receding into the distance.

Joshua, Nick says.

Nick.

Hey, Emilia says. You made it. She rushes forward to embrace him.

I made it, Joshua says. Wrapping his arms around her he smooths back a flyaway strand of her hair. Such vulnerability in his gesture, his gaze it is almost painful to witness.

Nick coughs and says, Let me help you with your bags.

Thanks, Joshua says. Disentangling himself from Emilia he reaches for his roller suitcase and goes inside. Nick following behind with one of Joshua's duffel bags in hand. Emilia carefully shuts the doors behind them.

Carlyle waits for them in the hallway as he has waited for decades. His shadow growing lean and menacing as it crawls across the floor. Gaunt and haggard he may be but his presence is still commanding, magisterial.

Hello, Dad, Joshua says.

Welcome home, Joshua.

Thank you.

Why don't you get set up in my old bedroom. We can start making supper when you're ready.

What's for supper?

What about a nice rib eye? I know that's your favorite.

A hesitant smile flickers across Joshua's face, decisive as a lightning strike. Heir apparent triumphant; in a single sentence his father has shown which of his sons will hold Stag's Crossing after his passing. Which of the two will reign here in all his glory, will lay his claim over the territory, the conqueror unconquered.

Carlyle says to Nick, I can take that bag. Just stay down here until we're back. Emilia, why don't you get out some of the steaks from the freezer and start preparing them.

Dad—not with your back—

Stop worrying about me, he says sharply, pulling it from Nick's shoulder and carrying it upstairs. His steps heavy with age. They watch him climb up to the second floor and disappear into the master bedroom with Joshua. Closing the door behind him.

Sorry about my dad, Nick says. I can help you with the steaks.

It's fine, Emilia says.

No, really.

I said it's fine.

Okay, Nick says. If it makes you feel any better, you're married to his favorite son.

Her laugh is tinged with acid. Which seems to have gone over well, seeing as he got disowned over it.

Nick shrugs.

What I don't understand is the sudden change of heart, she says.

He's dying.

So he regrets it?

My dad doesn't really do regrets, Nick says. I think he wants to make a big show of reconciliation right before he dies. It's the lingering Christian in him.

How kind of him, to forgive Samson for running off with Delilah.

Nice Biblical reference. Very apt.

I converted to Lutheranism for the wedding, she says. It didn't take, but it's the thought that counts.

I didn't know that about you.

I'd say you don't know much about me at all, she says.

Give it time. I'm sure I'll find out all your secrets.

Will you now, she says. Her tone arch, dry as brut champagne. Yet her face betrays her: a slight redness creeps over the bridge of her nose like a moody sunrise. Quickly extinguished as Joshua and Carlyle come back down the stairs.

Why don't you two start getting everything ready while Joshua and I take a look at the fields, he says.

We both grew up here, Dad, Nick says. I don't think Joshua's forgotten what the place looks like.

We'll be back in an hour, Carlyle says. Already putting on his boots and coat. Shortly after Joshua follows, quickly kissing Emilia on the cheek.

See you in a bit, Joshua says. Love you.

Love you too, Emilia says. She watches Joshua dutifully trail his father out the south exit, the screen door slamming closed behind them.

Guess we should work on dinner, Nick says.

Emilia says, I hope you burn his steak.

My dad's or Joshua's?

Chef's choice, she says.

He glances sideways at her. Considering if she is attempting to goad him into something. Dangerous, unknown territory like the cavernous and mountainous lands beyond the border of Nebraska, the distant province of the coasts. He thinks, briefly, of flirting with her—a risky avocation, should he choose to pursue it. The urge to flirt with women long buried within him, an impulse that has lain dormant for years.

Nothing good could come of this, he decides. To have what his brother has laid claim to long ago, to revive an ancient resentment over what Joshua possesses by birth that he cannot.

In her expression there is no sign of the brief blush from before though he can sense its presence lingering against her skin. He wonders rather like a voyeur if she blushed the same way standing at the altar, Joshua lifting the white veil to reveal her lunar face beneath. Or if she might flush similarly in the morning, lying bare-skinned amongst a tangle of bedsheets. Smug with the forbidden knowledge she has extracted from him while committing this transgression that brings him a near-Levitical pleasure to envision; searching her gaze he might find at last what he has been seeking his entire life, what men often believe they will find in women, held inside her like a precious pearl within an oyster. Salvation—liberation—absolution. Or better yet a clever imitation thereof, wrought from gleaming pyrite. Almost like the real thing.

Xix.

THEN

As Kenny pulls the Studebaker into town Nick sees the snow has already begun to fall fine and gentle as powdered sugar. Dusting the roofs shimmering and delicate. Empty are the streets on a Saturday afternoon so cold it is nearly wounding. Shearing the skin from his nose and his eyelids. The wind has torn the black wet bark from the trees leaving them naked and defenseless. They pass the diner with its window iced over and through it he can barely see the silhouettes of transients gathered for their hash browns and coffee. A single man standing outside smoking beneath the lamppost.

Past the diner Nick sees the dressmaker's shop with the beautiful gowns in the window. Pink and blue festooned with ribbons so delicate Nick can hardly imagine holding them in his cracked and callused hands. In a girlie magazine Kenny had stolen from his father they had seen as voyeurs the image of a woman tangled in silk ribbons like a gift to be unwrapped. His face was red like the shell of a lobster and he had to turn away Kenny laughing as he did.

Let's go to Wine and Spirits first, Kenny says.

Fine with me, Nick says. In his back pocket he carries the money he earned last summer detasseling corn and working at Stag's Crossing. His body sore from bending over to chop and carry the firewood. His hands bloody with corn rash. His father tossing him each dollar casually as he tosses raw meat to the dogs. Yet amongst Nick's meager possessions his fifteen dollars are akin to polished gemstone. Held tightly in his fist he still feels its brilliance its sparkling in his palm. Were he to open his hand he would see the worn and crumpled paper but it matters to him not at all.

Kenny the profligate finds this silly. His father might give him fifteen dollars on a regular Wednesday afternoon and Kenny will think nothing of it. Kenny's father shedding his largesse without subtlety. Bestowing it upon his son with the desperation of a man seeking forgiveness for his crimes.

Kenny parks the Studebaker right outside the liquor store. A drunk in tattered clothing bangs on the window. They pass him without speaking. Inside Michael Miller has set up a gas heater behind the counter his cheeks glowing pinkish from the warmth. He and Kenny exchange the hellos of old and well-acquainted friends as Nick loiters in the front near the neat shelves of vodka.

Help me with this, Kenny says. On the counter are four

packs of Carling Black Label. Nick helps him carry them back to the car the glass bottles rattling against each other as he goes. Kenny wheezes as he opens the tailgate and lifts the packs into the truck bed. Nick carefully places his bottles alongside Kenny's.

At last, Kenny says. Victory.

You should stop smoking, Nick says as he hops back into the truck. The cab smells of tobacco and only tobacco. It's probably not good for you.

You're no fun, Kenny says.

Nick looks at him as though he might be offended but his face is unemotional. Too much time with his father has given him the ability to tune his mind to dead air. Feeling only the sensation of being alive—but at a far remove, as though nothing is really happening to him at all.

Kenny drops him off at McFarlane's Hunting and Fishing. Family-owned since 1917 it is mostly run by two kids at their high school—Linda McFarlane and her younger brother Henry. Linda is seventeen and engaged already. No one knows anything about Henry and no one asks. Occasionally Nick sees him walking down the hallway carrying a worn-out issue of *Field & Stream*. He has the build of a prizewinning steer, a blacksmith. A tall and haughty bull leading the herd. His shoulders strong and muscled; his voice low and serious. Sixteen and he could be mistaken for a man, fully grown.

I'll be back in a bit, Kenny says. However long it takes me to drink a beer so I don't die of frostbite.

It won't actually warm you up. Your body temperature will drop which is why you feel warm.

Who are you, my mother?

I'm just saying.

You're ridiculous, Kenny says.

Nick goes inside. The door tinkles; a light and pleasing sound.

Linda hears the bell and comes out front. Even indoors she wears a winter coat and hat. Slim and pretty her hair is a light brunette.

Hi, she says.

Just you today? he asks.

Yeah, she says. Saturdays my dad goes to Kearney to sell seed. So it's just me and Henry.

Where's your brother?

Henry? He's just out back unloading some junk.

I've got some questions for him, Nick says.

If it's about seed you should wait for my dad to get back today, Linda says.

It's not about seed. It's about foxes.

All right. I'll go get him. Give me a second.

Linda comes back with Henry who is carrying a cardboard box filled with metal tools. He puts it on the ground and leans against the counter sweating a bit. Wiping the sweat off his face with his elbow. His arms are thick and already growing patches of wiry black hair.

I need some help, Nick says. Got a fox on our land and I don't know the first thing about trapping it.

You sure it's not a coyote? Henry says. Need a different lure if it's a coyote.

No, we heard the barking. Definitely a fox.

I'd recommend a dirt hole set paired with a fox-specific bait and lure, Henry says. It's not hard to set up. I'll have to order the materials for you though. We just ran out of traps a few weeks ago.

That's fine, Nick says.

It'll be four dollars, Henry says. To cover shipping.

Nick digs around in his pocket for the money and hands Henry the four dollars. Henry counts them out on the countertop and puts them in the till.

Write down your number for me, Henry says handing Nick a piece of paper and a pencil.

Can you show me how to set it up?

Sure, if you want me to.

That'd be swell, Nick says.

Linda goes into the back to clean. They can hear her shuffling and scraping the broom against the floor. Leaving them alone.

Henry extends his hand to shake. His grip is callused and slightly warm. His thumb comes up over Nick's knuckle and something passes between them strange and inexpressible. Sinuous as the bending of the tide beneath the moon. Mesmerizing, obscene.

Nick slowly pulls his hand away and puts it behind his back. A tremor, a fluttering growing beneath his wrist.

Henry says, I'll call you. He does not seem to have noticed anything. Already he is turning away to fix the shelving beneath the counter.

Thanks, Nick says. Please do.

He hears the Studebaker before he sees it. For lack of a trumpet Kenny announces his arrival with a fanfare of obnoxious honking.

Your chariot awaits, Henry says.

Very funny, Nick says. He walks to the door and closes it gently behind him. Escaping as he does the prison of his imagination for had he stayed for a moment longer he does not know what he might think of. What he could imagine standing there just the two of them together. Waiting, alone.

Come on, Kenny says. You walk like an old man.

I'm cold and stiff, Nick says. His gait that of a broken-down dog with a broken-down body. As he gets in the car he looks back at the store just once and sees Henry give him a short wave. He waves back and later he will know as a man and not as a boy that he had ruined himself then and there sitting in Kenny's car with the winter ice on the road shining, serene.

His brother had once shown him a giant tan silk moth, larger than a man's fist, monstrously beautiful. Carefully Joshua had placed it on a tree branch and Nick saw the patterning of its wings like eyes. Like Henry's eyes a rich auburn sublime and enticing.

Nick is torn violently from his old form which he has shed like a chrysalis. His body unraveling as he goes. The moth's body—his body—is an oculus. A wound, an opening into the future. In the windshield he sees the reflection of his open mouth; his tongue lying heavy and dead against his teeth. His mouth open slightly as Henry puts two fingers into it and Nick can do nothing other than swallow them down.

Xx.

NOW

History has spared none of them. Even after twenty years or more away from Stag's Crossing they return so easily to the old way of life. Joshua is inseparable from his father. Following him around the house as persistently as any of the dogs that scramble underfoot, having been dethroned by the reappearance of Carlyle's errant sons. Nick observes his father and brother standing on the patio, speaking to each other with an enviable casualness. Their secret language known only to them, undecipherable by outsiders.

In the living room, he comes upon Emilia sitting on the sofa. Thumbing through a book. Her face furrowed in study. Today she has worn a pale turquoise dress and tied her hair up into a loose bun. He takes notice of her slender fingers, turning over each page with a deft gentleness.

He sits down next to her and leans over with interest. What're you reading?

The glossy pages reveal image after image—vibrant Japanese woodcuts, intricately carved. Samurai, gods, spirits, beautiful women.

Ah, an art book.

Well, I am a painter, she says, snapping the book shut. He glimpses the title beneath her slender fingers. *Ukiyo-e: An Introduction*. Is there something you need, Nick?

So how long do you think you'll be stuck here? he says.

As long as Joshua wants, Emilia says. Your father doesn't have very long, so I doubt it'll be an extended stay.

You seem pretty confident about that estimate.

In my limited experience, men with your father's level of assholery tend to live miserable, often short lives.

And yet you had a nice exchange with him the other day.

He's tolerable, in small doses. Hopefully we'll be able to keep it up until the funeral.

You really don't like him.

He disowned Joshua after marrying me. Is that something I'm supposed to be thankful for?

Well, I think there's some regret there, Nick says, feeling distinctly like he has waded into yet another disagreement without intending. The conversation taking a sharp turn into a direction he does not like. Torn between being overly friendly to Emilia, perhaps out of some misguided remorse, and defending the only family he has ever known.

Did you expect me to be excited to come here? she says.

To be stuck here with a man who despises me, and get into pointless arguments with my brother-in-law? He's a real asshole, Nick. I hope you can realize that one day, the things he did to you and your brother—

Come on, Emilia—

She sighs and puts the book on the coffee table in front of her. Smoothing down the front of her dress with anxious hands. The fabric still and cool as the surface of a pond in the wintertime.

Her face is radiant in the afternoon light. She forces a polite smile and says, Look—let's not fight.

Okay, he says. Putting his hands up in mock surrender. No discussions of Du Fu.

The past is behind us, she says, and gives a short nod.

Right, he says. Have you seen the creek?

She shakes her head.

It's a real historical landmark, he says. For Nebraska.

I'm sure.

And, uh, he begins, I guess my mom's buried nearby. So that's—that's kind of its own thing.

Is she.

Yeah. With the baby. He rises from the sofa, uncomfortable. I was going to go see her. It's been a long time.

And you want me to come with you, Emilia says. Why?

I mean, you don't have to. Maybe you should wait until Joshua gets back.

No, I'd like to see it. I was just wondering why. If you don't want to tell me, that's fine.

She stands up and for a few moments they are standing uncomfortably close together, like two celestial bodies with briefly intersecting trajectories. Emilia tall enough to be almost eye level with him; he glances down at her before she ducks her head and moves away.

Uh, he says, let's go out the back. Faster that way.

Outside the greyhounds have begun to crowd at the screen door, yelping excitedly. A few of them even jumping up and scratching at the door with their front paws. Git, he says, shooing them away; they disperse, dejected, their tails whipping back and forth in the yellow grass.

He leads Emilia south of the house, past the ancient relics of his childhood: the coop now a pile of rotting wood. The dogs having chewed up near everything they could get their teeth on, these remnants are a shattered wreck of what once was. Past the coop and down a slight incline a rowdy group of three greyhounds tussle in the dirt, only stopping to look at Emilia as she passes.

Emilia points at the crops growing high in the distance. Your dad still has time to farm?

No, he rents the land to other people. It's hard to make a profit now with a family-owned farm. Most of them have been bought up now.

Joshua said your mother's family owned oil wells too.

I think those dried up years ago, Nick says. Was nice while it lasted. The money, I mean. But we have more than enough of it.

Very magnanimous of you, she says.

There were lean years too, he says. Had to sell off some of the land. We're only a thousand acres if you round up now.

On the western side of Stag's Crossing Nick points at the tree line in the distance. Those're the woods, he says.

Are they haunted?

Nah, Nick says. The dogs go in there to hunt sometimes.

Hunting?

You ever seen a pack of greyhounds hunting? It's quite a sight.

No, Emilia says. I haven't.

They come to the ribbonlike creek that slashes through part of the woods and the western half of Stag's Crossing. The water is clear and ripples gently through his reflection as he stands along the bank. Looking down at himself, so much older than the last time he came to this place. Now he must witness his father's thousand acres in decline. The land in its agonistic death throes. Carlyle Morrow's dream of utter mastery dying with it—neither he nor his sons will ever rule over a tamed Stag's Crossing, for who can lay claim to the wild prairie, the locusts that swarm the fields, the history that has shaped their family since Carlyle drove the first nail into the foundation of the house?

At the water's edge they walk in silence. Finally coming to the place where the ground was evened out by his father some thirty years before. Out of sight from the house, a small and quiet plot of land that was meant to be forgotten.

Nick leans over and moves away the weeds that cover the twin footstones. With his bare hands he brushes away the dirt and dust that have settled atop the engraved letters. No one has come here in many years.

Emilia says, Here, let me help. She touches his mother's footstone with tender reverence; sweeping her hand across the surface, she uncovers the lettering beneath the name:

Beloved Wife & Mother. Carlyle's only sobriquet for this woman who bore him two sons and could not bear, could not endure a third.

Should've brought flowers, he says to no one in particular.

Emilia says, What was she like? Joshua never talks about her.

I don't really know. I was so little when she died. But don't ask my dad, it's not something he talks about.

But you must remember her a little.

I guess. It's a little painful for me.

Tell me, Emilia says.

With the sun at her back, he can hardly look into her eyes.

What?

She gestures to him with one hand. The left one, scarred, the fingers at strange angles. Beckoning. *Tell me.*

There is a metallic taste congealing right behind his teeth; his tongue moves, an alien intrusion in his mouth. His jaw opening and closing like a ventriloquist's dummy. Completely mesmerized.

He says, Once, she told me I had a gift. For reading people and their memories. That I had gotten it from her, that I was like her in many ways. I think she's the only person in my life who ever loved me.

That's very interesting, Nick, she says. Thank you for sharing it with me. The corners of her mouth turn upward into a smile. Exactly as she did at the wedding, exactly as she now does with an intensity that evaporates all conscious thought. Her expression innocent, as though nothing at all peculiar has happened between them. Yet beneath this he senses a growing attraction—a spreading madness like rot in an orchard. Ill-fated, completely irresistible.

Emilia, Joshua says. He has walked all this way from the house. Down to the southwestern edge of Stag's Crossing before it is swallowed by the woods and what lies beyond the trees that sway listlessly in the wind.

I've been looking everywhere for you. What are you even doing here?

Nick wanted to show me this place.

And you just went with him?

Why not?

My God, you two are like children, Joshua says, rolling his eyes. He reaches for Emilia, who takes his hand. The gesture completely natural, filled with warmth and affection. Nick watches this, not comprehending it at all.

Come on, let's go back. It's almost dinnertime, Joshua says, tugging on her wrist. As Joshua pulls her away, Nick notices she turns back to look at him, just briefly. The force of her gaze intense and enigmatic, almost daring him to look away. Then she turns back to Joshua and it is like nothing at all has happened; she wears the same politely neutral expression that betrays little beneath it.

He tries to recall his mother's voice, so often a comfort to him in the nadir of his misery. But he finds that he cannot retrieve this memory any longer; like so many things at Stag's Crossing, it has been forever lost. If he were to kneel at her grave and press his ear to the stone he would hear his mother's voice once again, clear and crystalline. He is too old for such childish superstitions, too old to listen to the warnings of his mother dead now for decades and useless to him except as a revenant from his derelict past.

Yet even now there is an echo of her in the air, as he stands atop her bones. A frisson of unease. *You brought that bitch into this house.*

When Joshua and Emilia have finally gone, Nick begins the trek back to the house. A lone greyhound comes up to him, sniffing at his hands and his pockets.

I don't have anything on me, he says.

A few other greyhounds come by, following the first. Trailing him as he walks, making pathetic whining noises. He remembers a similar tableau when his father had once thrown him out of the Ford. Sending him tumbling into a ditch by the side of the road. The greyhounds leaping from the bed of the truck and crowding around him. Licking at his bloody face, his bloody hands.

Xxi.

THEN

Even in the dead of winter Nick's room is full of flowers. Aster, primrose, spiderwort, poppy mallow for his mother. Some are preserved between the pages of his books with newspaper and butcher paper he has fetched from the trash, whatever of his father's discarded effluvia he can scavenge. Others he hangs from the rafter in his closet and dries them there, in the dark corner where Carlyle might not see them and mock him for his sincerity. He cannot apply himself similarly to his unartistic labor at Stag's Crossing; he lingers in the fastidiousness of petals and leaves, taking care to braid the stems before they dry. He knows that his father judges him too girlish, too maudlin for the unremarkable acts of daily life: cutting wood, feeding the dogs, latching the gate around the coop.

Nick senses he is destined for a life beyond Stag's

Crossing, a future that appears so far away he can hardly comprehend it. Yet he knows that no matter the distance between himself and Stag's Crossing, a thousand miles to match the thousand acres, some part of him will remain trapped here. Looking up at his father from where he kneels at his feet, brought to heel at last.

With Joshua long gone it is up to him now to tend to that place the dogs will not go, the twin graves for which Carlyle could only bother to assemble two flat footstones. Names, dates, a meaningless platitude inscribed in stone.

His father has not been in the house all day. Out hunting in the snow for prairie grouse. Striding the length of the fields as though by looking upon them the frozen ground might learn to fear him as much as his sons.

Having fed the dogs and done his math homework already Nick judges that he can make good time to the grave if he walks fast. Carefully he takes the flowers in hand, tying them together with twine. A real bouquet, like something in a wedding magazine. Putting his coat and boots on downstairs he carries it in his left hand, his fingers wrapped tightly around the stems. As he walks outside, one of the dogs trailing him, he allows himself to feel a small amount of joy. It has taken him months to assemble such a collection—plucking phlox from the roadside as the men driving by looked on in curiosity, wandering deep within the woods for those open places where sunflowers still sprout.

He follows the frozen creek until he can no longer see the house in the distance if he twists his neck round to look. In the lancing daylight there is no specter of death to follow in his footsteps; only the plainness of his grief. The fact that he had begun the day so well, thinking politely and distantly of his mother so as to not forget her, and even giving a few prayers for little Christopher; yet halfway to the grave he can feel his cold eyelashes pricked with tears. His grand repertoire of feelings is his terrible weakness—more than Joshua or Carlyle, he cannot sublimate his desperate longing. The memory of holding her limp hand as she died.

Carlyle was quick to bury his wife and third son and even quicker to forget about them. Instead Nick and Joshua have taken turns visiting, cleaning, speaking about nothing to the graves that do not answer back. On warm nights Nick will lie down with his ear pressed to his mother's grave and hear her again, as he might through a telephone line full of static, distorted and uncanny. Here there is a real haunting, a tremolo in the wind that suggests an ever-beating heart. Yet the house at Stag's Crossing is empty of her presence; Carlyle has made sure to remove almost everything that was once hers—her brushes and combs, her cosmetics, her beautiful dresses. The crib for the nursery thrown out with the refuse. The name Christopher never uttered again on these thousand acres.

Nick lays the flowers down upon the footstone, obscuring his mother's name from view. He places a flower for Christopher also. Satisfied with his handiwork he turns back to the house, the snow just beginning to fall. He catches a flake on his dark sleeve and marvels at the geometry of it as it melts before his eyes.

Been looking for you everywhere, Carlyle says. What're you up to here? He carries his rifle casually in his arms.

In the winter he wears only a light jacket, impervious to the unflinching cold. None of the dogs accompany him though it is as good of a grouse season as any. The last hound that did came too close to the graves and lost its way; it fell into the creek and drowned.

Visiting, Nick says.

This old place? What for?

Joshua and I used to do it. Together.

Well, Joshua's not around anymore. So why're you still wasting your time here?

I thought—I thought maybe they were lonely.

Lonely? They're dead, you little fool.

Nick feels hot tears coming into his eyes, unbidden. He looks away. It's Mom—

Don't, Carlyle says. Don't start with that. You don't know the half of it. Acting like you knew her. I was the one who married her.

Dad, come on.

Carlyle goes to the graves, sees the flowers on the footstones. He takes a fistful of them and scatters them in the frozen grass.

How long did it take you to make these? Months? When you could've been helping out around here, helping with the planting. You've grown up soft because we've always done well, but when I don't have the money to spoil you, you're nowhere to be found. Why is that?

When his father is like this Nick knows better than to answer. He stays silent, looking at the torn petals on the ground. All that he has wrought for his family, in pieces.

Too much like your mother. Too much of that woman in you. Soft. A real bleeding heart. A woman like that, she ruined me for all the others. One day you'll love a woman as much as I did and you'll understand.

Even at fourteen Nick knows he is incapable of such a thing. Inside he is a shattered wreck of a boy. So flawed in his creation God should have tossed him away.

Don't cry or I'll give you something to cry about.

Nick wipes his eyes.

I'm not— His face turning red, he closes his mouth before he says something unwise.

Listen to me. When your mother died I never let another stranger set foot on our land again. And this place flourished. You fail to understand that there are people out there, forces outside Stag's Crossing, that conspire against us. That would do anything to have what we have and can take it away if we're not careful.

In Nick's young mind the pronouncements of his father bring to mind only scattered images: the doe with Peggy Rasmussen's ribbon in its stomach, the footprint in the woods. The creeping dread of living alone on a thousand acres, beset by enemies on all sides. With the land so flat and the days so long and unending there is a bit of the mysterious in every interaction with the creatures that roam these parts—a strangeness unknowable and omnipresent, a hook embedded deep in the gut.

Having let forth his torrent of rage, Carlyle falls silent.

At last, Nick says, Are you finished, Dad?

His father has already turned his back to him. Muttering aloud to the carved rocks, the vast stretches of snow—that woman—not enough rain for the rye—an awful summer—oil wells running dry—my two boys—worse than useless—

Nick walks back to the house alone. Passing the coop insulated and filled with pine shavings for the winter a greyhound comes round and joins him. He sees his father has wrapped one of his old jackets around the dog to keep it warm. Tenderly tying the sleeves around its belly where the ribs always show, the mark of a well-bred specimen.

In the morning it will be as it was before. Waking early to feed the dogs. Walking to school or if his father is feeling generous he will drive him part of the way. Wandering the hallways with his book bag full of things he does not care to read, any thought of the savage exchange with his father obliterated from his mind by the sight of Henry waving to him in the hallway, a passing glance as swift and momentous as a fish striking the line before it is caught on the hook and reeled ashore.

Xxii.

NOW

Much to Nick's slight disappointment, the evening—and several evenings not unlike it—passes without so much as a single dramatic outburst. His father and Joshua return from their dinnertime walk; Emilia sets the table; they eat. There is talk of everything and nothing. The weather (poor, as usual), the crops (good, as usual), Joshua's job at a bank where he moves money back and forth in an aimless dance of wealth. Occasionally Carlyle opens a window and smokes a cigar, the smell of it causing the kitchen to reek of damp tobacco. He remains in a remarkably pleasant mood. Always good to have my sons back home, he says. As though neither of them had ever left.

They do not discuss his imminent, approaching death; nor the uneasiness that permeates Stag's Crossing, that has seeped into the floorboards underfoot. How quickly they both set out to defy their father—never to return to Stag's Crossing, never to look upon the face of the man who had made such a grievance of their childhoods. And now Joshua has come back as faithfully as any of the greyhounds that still roam the premises. Nick moments ahead of him, already lying pathetically at his father's feet.

Shut away in what was once Joshua's old room, Nick has kept himself busy. Writing feverishly and pausing only to look out the window down at the gravel road leading up to the front of the house. The menacing slope of the driveway. Over the years he has gotten into his head the strange idea of one day writing about Stag's Crossing, though he wonders if he might even possess the words to give it shape and form.

When he emerges later that day having written nothing and read even less, he carefully goes downstairs and finds himself in the midst of preparations for a minor feast: Emilia has peeled and mashed potatoes and impeccably seared four rib eye steaks, leaving Nick to steam the beans and fetch the tablecloth where it was hidden in a dusty cabinet near the fridge. Running his hands over the worn cotton he feels the frayed edges, the slow separation of warp and woof. Taking it to the table to spread it out in an ocean of blue fabric he realizes it is the same tablecloth his father has used since he was a child. Standing barely taller than the table itself he was fascinated by the fabric, the feeling of each individual fiber beneath his fingers like the wild rills of an unknown tide.

Smoothing down the tablecloth he sees Carlyle and Joshua coming through the backyard. One of Carlyle's elegant hounds trailing him, lunging forward to lick his hands as he walks. What a pair they make—father and son, Joshua in full glory, Carlyle almost uncountably aged.

Emilia comes up behind him and taps his shoulder. Wordlessly she passes him the plates of food, the silverware, a pitcher of water, a vase of freshly cut daffodils.

Where'd you get the daffodils? They don't grow around here.

I thought you said you were going to find out all my secrets, she says. I can't just give them away.

Just this one, then.

No, she says. Not yet.

Carlyle comes through the back door just as Nick sets down the last plate. He pretends that his hand does not shake upon hearing his father's calamitous voice echo through the still house.

I'm back! Carlyle says.

We're back, Joshua chimes in.

In the manner of a pathetic and voiceless factotum Nick waits for his father's approval of the meal though it was Emilia who had done most of the cooking. Her delicate wrist moving back and forth in a hypnotic repetition as she deftly peeled each potato. Mincing the garlic with subtle and sure strokes of the knife.

Smells good, Carlyle says. He drapes his coat over the back of his chair and takes a seat.

Thanks for doing this, Joshua says. He pecks Emilia on the mouth and moves to seat himself at the right hand of his father. Most men in their forties possess only the wilted shadow of their youth but Joshua with his face bright with expectation remains glorious as the day he married Emilia. As she pulls out her chair next to him he whispers something slyly in her ear that makes her laugh, high and charming as the ringing of a bell.

Like insects frozen in peerless amber his family has remained unchanged for thirty years. Carlyle the unquestioned authority; Joshua the splendid right hand of God. Nick filled with a resentment so magnificent and overpowering that parts of him have atrophied in its wake. Emilia remains an object of fascination and loathing—having married into the family she remains one of them and yet not, a stranger in the bed of another, a guest in the house of her husband.

Emilia, why don't you say grace? Carlyle says.

She extends a delicate hand to Nick across the table, which he takes. Her voice low and halting she begins, Come, lord Jesus, be our guest—

—and let these gifts to us be blessed, Carlyle says impatiently. With a grand sigh of distaste he releases their hands and reaches for his steak knife. Shearing past the outer layer of translucent fat he exposes a perfectly red center. He spears a piece on his fork and chews thoughtfully before nodding. Excellent, he says. Thank you, Nick.

Emilia did most of the work, actually. You should be thanking her.

Well then, thank you, Emilia.

You're welcome, she says. Let's eat. Without hesitation she slices apart her meat with startling efficiency and Nick realizes as she lifts each piece to her mouth that she has barely cooked her steak at all and is eating it almost raw. The fork scraping against her teeth and lips leaving small traces of liquid that she licks away with a swipe of her tongue. Something about this movement registers as both erotic and repulsive to him. Finding himself unable to eat he moves around the pieces of food on his plate aimlessly and allows empty conversation to fill the dead air.

How was the walk? Emilia asks.

It was nice. This time we went to the western end. Lots of changes around here though, Joshua says. Little farms being bought up by corporations, things like that.

But we're still here, Carlyle says.

We're still here, Joshua agrees. Raising his glass of water in a mock toast.

There is no intimacy in this talking amongst each other. Like they are speaking of people not themselves it is a hollow gesture. Joshua and Carlyle mention the weather, the crop cycles. The harmless quips of dilettantes. Were they to reveal themselves fully to each other there would be no need for them to wear the masks of men—they could bristle and howl and bare their teeth as they pleased. Yet the years have civilized them; instead they must content themselves with the slim knife held just beneath the table, the backhanded compliment aimed so precisely it strikes with the violence of a force majeure.

Carlyle says, Emilia, the mashed potatoes are perfect. I'm surprised you're so good at cooking our sort of food.

Emilia flashes him a smile that could incinerate the entire house and the fields surrounding it. A thousand acres set aflame in an instant. Thank you, Carlyle, she says. How kind of you to say. Then she pierces a green bean with her fork and chews it, slowly. Still smiling.

Carlyle says, I've been meaning to make a family announcement about this, but now that Joshua's back it's a good time as any. As you all know, I'm not in good health.

Dad, we don't have to talk about this right now, Joshua says.

I didn't ask for you to interrupt me, Joshua.

Nick sips his ice-cold water and waits. Joshua opens and closes his mouth, fishlike, before deciding not to further tempt his father's rage.

Having you both back has given me a lot to think about. About how important family is. I know we've had our differences over the years, Joshua, but I've decided to put you back in the will.

It makes perfect sense: with Carlyle dying, Joshua must be restored as the anointed successor. Stag's Crossing no longer passing to the weakest of the litter but the rightful heir ascendant. Nick must have known when his father called and sent him to fetch his brother that this would be the true purpose of his quest. Nothing more than his father's errand boy.

You'll have all of Stag's Crossing and half of whatever money's left. The other half goes to your brother but I know he doesn't want this place. It's yours.

Joshua looks at his father, then at his wife. He grips the edge of the table with trembling hands and does not answer.

Emilia cuts in smoothly. What a generous gift. Except we don't need your money.

I know you don't need my money. You don't need anything from me at all. I'm giving it to you. Freely. It's called a gift, Emilia.

Oh, we couldn't, she says. That same smile from before, unwavering.

Emilia's right, Joshua says, composing himself at last.

Color returning to his face little by little. We have our home in California. We wouldn't be able to take care of this place—we can't move back—

I knew you were here to bury me, Carlyle says. I just didn't know it would be like this.

Nick half expects his father to strike Joshua, as he might have years ago during one of his volcanic tirades. Instead Carlyle slams down his fork and knife, getting up from his chair to lumber toward the staircase that rises like a curved spinal column high into the unbreathing rib cage of the house.

Dad, Joshua says. He tries to stand up.

Leave him, Emilia says. Her hand on Joshua's elbow. She leans over to whisper reassurances in his ear and through the wide window behind her Nick sees a vision of Stag's Crossing if it does not pass to Joshua. Burning endlessly in the distance until it is consumed by its own recurring, fugue-like ruination.

Xxiii.

THEN

A feverish anticipation wakes him early, shivering. In his sleep he has kicked all his blankets to the floor. He gets out of bed to scoop them up and fold them neatly atop his fitted sheet. Halfway into his long-sleeved shirt and blue jeans he walks to the bathroom where only last summer he might have found Joshua already there before him, the early riser. Shaving blond flecks from his chin with his father's hand-me-down razor. They would fight over who would use the toilet first. Inevitably Joshua would win and Nick would wait outside for him to finish his morning piss before shoving past Joshua to brush his teeth. Spitting the frothy residue inelegantly in the sink then going downstairs to make breakfast for himself.

With his brother gone he is left alone in the house; his father goes every morning at five-thirty to walk through the fields and survey Stag's Crossing as God might study his own creations. Leaving Nick to make his own bed, cook his own breakfast. As Carlyle has done since Nick was a child and could stand at the stove without burning himself. A strange tenderness to his way of teaching Nick how to flip the eggs, slice and toast the bread.

Careful not to slip and fall in his soft white socks Nick creeps down the spiral staircase to the first floor. Seven on a winter morning and it is still dark outside. He turns the lights on in the kitchen and watches the gentle lamplight illuminate the quaint interior décor. A charming painting of wildflowers hangs over the sink. On the countertop his father has left a folded-over page torn from a bird-watching magazine. Field sparrow in flight.

Inside the fridge he finds a half-empty pack of beer, a slab of deli meat, various cheeses of indiscernible origins. Lettuce, cabbage, spinach, carrots. Rummaging around he finally finds a large ceramic bowl filled with fresh eggs. The bloom still intact covering the shell with a light sheen. He grabs three of them then a frying pan, salt, pepper, sour cream. Butter and sweet milk from a glass bottle. Breaking open each egg with a gleeful and boyish brio he grabs a spoon and stirs them together with the milk and the salt until creamy. Melting butter in the thin frying pan he gently heats the mixture until the golden liquid thickens to an edible sludge. Hastily he dumps the scrambled eggs onto a ceramic plate, fetches a knife and fork, and falls upon his breakfast like a ravenous animal. Too impatient by far for waffles or English muffins he shovels the eggs into his mouth before wiping his face with the lively demeanor of a bon vivant.

He washes the dishes and cutlery in the large porcelain sink wincing at the scraping of the knife against the plate. A greyhound coming through the kitchen begs for left-over bacon. The smell of yesterday's grease lingering near the stove.

At seven-thirty his father returns wearing his heavy dark snow boots.

Get your bag, Carlyle says.

Nick leaves the dishes in the sink and grabs his back-pack, his coat, his knit winter hat with earflaps. Bracing himself against the cold he follows his father into the front yard. The wind slaps at him. Carlyle has pulled the white Ford up to the house, the engine still idling with a metallic sputter. The leather seat is warm and Nick resists the urge to sit on his hands. His father never one for pleasantries does not speak as he descends from the driveway to the road leading from the wilderness of Stag's Crossing to the edge of civilization.

His father takes an unusual turn; left when it should be right.

School's that way.

I'm not driving you there.

Then where are we going?

Omaha.

That's an hour away.

Need to go look at some steers.

I didn't know we were going to get cattle.

I didn't say we were going to buy them. I said we were going to look at them. Don't have the money for that, anyways. Maybe next year.

Knowing better than to argue Nick instead closely examines the grooves of his open palm. His mind wandering like a stray lamb far from the flock. Were Stag's Crossing to expand it would not be through the act of men laying down fences but like the festering of an open wound. A thousand acres of weeping flesh left to rot in eastern Nebraska and now his father wants to buy cows to graze it. Smug potbellied pigs to slaughter just before Christmas.

Most men would be pleased with one thousand acres but Carlyle Morrow has never been like most men. Already he dreams of expansion, domination, granaries bedecked with seed. His sons grown limber and strong presiding over an empire forged with the keen and ravening edge of his ambition. Yet in only ten years his children will betray him in their own inimitable ways—Joshua marrying out, Nick exiling himself to a foreign land. And in their absence Stag's Crossing will lie silent and fallow as the fields surrounding it. This place: no place for young men.

Nick in his boyhood fervor has turned his mind to fantasies of a more animal nature—not specifically of Henry, though of other young men like him, and young women besides. Languorous summer evenings that stretch almost endlessly into the future, perfectly humid, pearling his body with sweat. His skin flushed to a light peach. With meticulous pleasure he catalogues these images and hides them away beneath the floorboards of his mind. Knowing he cannot reveal them to anyone else lest he be exposed as a fabulist, an abject fraud.

Carlyle says, Your friend Kenny, he ever taken you to the Stockyards?

No. We just drive around town together usually. Sometimes we go to Lincoln.

That's not a bad thing. I wish I had spent more time with my friends when I was a kid.

Nick cannot imagine his father as a child. Cannot imagine his father as anything other than Carlyle Morrow, tall and unbowed. In his forties his eyes have sunken in slightly giving a strange thoughtfulness to his expressions. A cunning in his gaze that seeks out all manner of weakness and waits to pounce as a jackal waits for the exposed flank of a leaping gazelle.

Your brother called the other day while you were outside feeding the chickens, he says. Asked how you were doing.

And what'd you say?

I said you were doing good. We're both doing good.

Did he have any exciting news?

Not really. Says life in the big city is keeping him busy.

What's he studying?

No idea yet. I told him to go for something practical—biology, maybe.

Joshua once told me he liked history class the best.

Carlyle says, Joshua doesn't need any of that. He'll just get to thinking he's better than the rest of us.

Nick looks out the window. Sensing another one of his father's tirades forceful and turbulent as whitewater. Washing over him like the eddies of the river, so fresh and clear he can see through its translucent surface the sleek bodies of leaping salmon, minnows by the fistful.

Carlyle continues, When I was a kid I didn't need any of that stuff. School, books, nothing. Just me and my dad working the land together. That's why I raised you both the way I did. It's important to know how to build things with your hands. How to hunt and fish properly. How to take care of yourself. Take care of your family.

Carlyle turns on the windshield wipers and Nick listens to them drag the flecks of ice across the glass. His father's voice blending with the rhythmic scraping as Carlyle drones incessantly, contemptuously, luxuriating in his venom. There is a bitter pleasure to his condescension, alluring as nectar, and Nick has learned to drink from the same source until he is choking with it. Until it has corroded and burned everything inside him.

Nick? Are you listening?

Yes, Nick says, without enthusiasm. His body feels far away from him and light as papier-mâché. His father looks at him skeptically but does not reprimand him for his lack of concentration.

Do you think Joshua will come back? Nick asks. When he speaks his voice sounds like another person.

Of course he'll come back. Where is he going to go.

I don't know. He could stay in New York, I guess.

Well, if he does it'll be his loss, Carlyle says. Anyway, you'll go to the University of Nebraska and come back here to help your old man, right?

Yeah.

Because if you leave you can never come back. You know that.

Nick takes a long look out the window. Endless strips of plowed land on either side. Ice on the road, snow drifting through the air.

He says, I know, Dad.

Should he stay at Stag's Crossing he knows it will be the death of him. The thought of another decade here fills him with the conviction that his destiny lies elsewhere. Otherwise his father might one day find him in the Quonset hanging by his knotted belt. Good leather wasted on a pointless suicide. Sometimes he imagines it when he is alone and the darkness of his room creeps up on him, unexpectedly, forcing him to relive the memories he has long since put away. Even in his forties he will envision it, fervently, the childhood at Stag's Crossing that he has taken pains to forget but his very skin itself has memorized; the exact method by which he would escape from this place should he find no other recourse available to him. It would be dark and there would be no other sound than that of his breathing, the sacred hollowness of the Quonset welcoming him like a freshly dug grave. Like one of the stags hung from the gambrel he would sway from the rafters. A theophany, a vision for the saints.

Xxiv.

NOW

When he closes his eyes he is in the Quonset again. On the southern wall above his father's impressive collection of guns hangs a veritable museum exhibit of flayed creatures, nailed to the metal siding with great precision. Looking up at them he comprehends neither their deaths nor the purpose of their display. Glassy-eyed, they stare down at him until he can bear it no longer. In their gaze there is only bleak emptiness, a distorted reflection of himself at forty-three floating in their black pupils. All manner of beast has perished here and been preserved in the precise moment of its death: deer, elk, waterfowl, fox.

The elk speaks. The voice rasping, unplaceable. Not the voice of his father or brother but a primordial, hollow evocation that fills him with dread.

Look at me, it says. Nick approaches and sees the missing tuft of fur on its shoulder. Where the saw had snagged as he and Joshua were taking the head off for the taxidermist. His father had sat watching with a discerning eye; when they were done they had loaded the massive elk into the truck bed. So big its hooves dangled halfway off the side.

Nick comes closer. Approaching the southern wall he must look directly upward at the animals. The essence of death thick and cloying in his throat. He bears it like a martyr bears his gaping wounds, knowing that he is at fault for this artful display of suffering. The sound of the saw against bone unforgettable. Joshua yelling at him as the elk's head fell to the ground, severed from the rest of it. Blood in the grass. The flies already gathering like visitors to a grand feast.

The elk leans down, its neck unusually long, its shoulders terribly broad. Its soft nose touches the side of his face. It whispers in his ear: Look at me—

His father's voice now. Look me in the eye, boy—

When he opens his eyes he expects to be in his bed at Stag's Crossing. The second bedroom, once his brother's, rectangular and unassuming. Instead he finds himself barefoot, walking on gravel. Wearing only his boxers and an old shirt with a loose hem, his sad attempt at pajamas. He must be halfway down the long driveway that curves sinuously like the spine of a snake down to the road north of the house, the passageway between the world of Stag's Crossing and the world of ordinary people that his father has always so despised.

He has not been sleepwalking since he was a child;

these episodes usually came with a period of bed-wetting, which Carlyle was quick to beat out of him. He bears no scars of this, though the memory lies heavy in his bones. An inexorable shame floods him before he forces it back down, forces himself to begin walking toward the bleak emptiness of the house where his brother and father sleep undisturbed. He sees a figure emerge from the Quonset and close the metal door. Only when he approaches does he realize it is Emilia in her nightgown. The fabric is a limpid white that shimmers like mother-of-pearl. She is not carrying a flashlight; the moon and stars give just enough light to see by. Her hair is unbraided and left fluttering in the night breeze.

Emilia, he says.

She turns, surprised. Nick? What are you doing out here?

I could ask the same of you. You shouldn't be out here in the dead of night, it's not safe.

His voice sounds strange to him, as though it has detached from his body. His own thoughts becoming unclear to him as she slowly strides into view. Just as the string of a fine violin is refined and tuned so is his consciousness redirected to focus entirely on Emilia. Her dark eyes, her dark hair. The lazy and unhurried arc of her eyebrows, furrowed slightly. Her face like a vision of some unnamed and unholy saint.

I'm fine, she says, flipping a strand of hair over her shoulder. Like a wild pony might toss its mane in defiance.

Does Joshua know you're out here?

Absolutely not. She smiles then, a small mischievous grin playing across her face. Nick is almost alarmed by how extraordinary it is to behold her, shining brilliantly in the light of the moon. I just wanted to get some air. Joshua has been—

Difficult?

Yes, she says, quietly. Her eyes slightly downturned as she admits this. The vulnerability of the gesture palpable to him.

He gets that way. Don't worry about it, it's not something you've done.

That's not much of a relief.

What were you doing in the Quonset?

Looking for something.

For what?

I have a small interest in taxidermy.

Nick raises an eyebrow.

Very charming, I know. I just wanted to see if you had any little animals preserved in there. Like raccoons, coyotes, maybe a fox or two—

Why do you like the little animals? The elk and deer we have are a lot more impressive.

She smiles. It's a secret.

Didn't I say I'd find all those out?

You haven't, though.

Give it time, he says.

They go up the driveway together. Nick lingering behind. Though he attempts to feign indifference he knows he is no good at it. Knows as soon as she turned her pellucid face toward him that she had him.

When they reach the front doors of the house, he says, You go in first.

Such a gentleman.

Not hardly. I just don't want Joshua to see us together.

Do you think he's a jealous man? she asks. Casually she puts her hand up and brushes a speck of dirt from the collar of his shirt. He looks down at his sternum where he briefly felt the touch of her hand. Even as he does this he can feel the blood rising in his face, against his will. He quickly covers his face with his hands as she laughs—perhaps cruelly, perhaps otherwise.

I'm not bold enough to find out, he finally says, and looks away.

Have it your way.

She turns the handle with practiced ease. Happily the doors of the house open to her, beckoning her into this palatial estate that might one day be her husband's inheritance.

When she has disappeared from view and the door has closed behind her, Nick takes a seat on the rotted porch swing. He remembers sitting out there on so many languid summer evenings with his father and brother. Catching fireflies and tumbling together in the dirt. At Stag's Crossing he learned the measure of his manhood, that he would lie forever in Joshua's shadow with the pathetic air of a beaten dog. And now he finds himself contemplating the matter of Joshua's lovely wife—how he might do nothing but contemplate her, endlessly, the appearance of his desire inconvenient and menacing to him. His past intimacies with women were nothing like it was with Henry—furtive escapades in a dormitory coat closet, so dark he could barely see the girl. No visions of the future, or the sideways present. No emotion behind the gesture at all.

Now instead he finds the air is suffused with a luxurious anticipation. He senses he could lie in bed all day talking to Emilia. Listening attentively to what she has to say as the words pour forth from her honey-drenched mouth. This seductive image coming to him unbidden, unasked for. He wonders if Joshua felt the same way, waiting for her in the bridal chamber after the wedding. Knowing or not knowing what he had just married.

He imagines Emilia sneaking carefully upstairs and into bed. Laying her slender body down next to Joshua's and pulling the covers over her shoulders. Joshua might stir, might toss beneath the sheets. She will lean over and whisper something unknowable in his ear. Running her fingers through his brilliant hair. Smiling her secret, pestilent smile.

XXV.

THEN

From the walkway ten feet above Nick sees thousands of heads of cattle bunched together in the pens. Steeped in the hideous fragrance of blood and manure they swish their tails at the gathering flies. Men of all creeds run about bellowing and hollering at the livestock: Greeks, Italians, the Irish from South Omaha. Below him Carlyle speaks to a rider on horseback wearing a suit and tie. When Carlyle waves for him to come over Nick descends from the walkway into the chaotic crush of men, cattle, insects. He ducks under swinging elbows, dodges men slamming gates and cursing each other in every possible language. These are the kind of men his father would never allow into the house; they could drive Carlyle's tractor and drink his beer on the patio but would never be permitted inside. Yet out here far from Stag's Crossing they mingle freely, as equals, covered in dirt and dust just the same.

Loping past the loading ramps he reaches his father slightly out of breath and does his best to hide it. The rider looks down at him. He is so tall Nick thinks he might be a Texan with his craggy face and cowboy hat. By his patrician bearing Nick knows this is the kind of man who would be allowed inside the house. An almost impossible privilege for a stranger. Received at the front door and invited inside, into the grand and empty chambers of Nick's childhood.

Nick, this is Jim Reynolds. He's a friend of your mother's from back when. Jim's been kind enough to help with this expedition. Jim, this is my boy Nick.

Pleased to meet you.

Likewise, Nick says. Are you one of those cattlemen from Texas?

Not hardly. I grew up in Tulsa but I came here to work for Armour. Ended up as a cattle buyer by accident. I was more of a hogman as a kid.

I'm looking to buy, Carlyle says. Next year. Wanted to browse the wares first. Got any advice?

You got the land for it?

I have a thousand acres right now. I don't want to build a ranch. Just a nice herd—maybe twenty, twenty-five.

That's plenty. You only need an acre and a half per head I'd say.

Sounds good to me.

I've seen some nice Red Angus I can show you over here. Charolais and Simmental too if that's more to your fancy. Course you won't be buying for another year so it'll just be browsing.

Carlyle says, Stay out of trouble while I take a look at these.

Nick says, I can't come with?

No. You're off school—don't ask for more.

If you leave him there they'll think he's a runner, Jim says. Probably'll put him to work.

Let them, Carlyle says. He needs the discipline.

Jim says, I'm happy to have the boy come along. It'll be a good learning experience.

Nick says, I'd like to see some of the steers.

Fine, Carlyle says. Come along then. Talking to Nick like he is no better than a dog which he is not. Jim points his horse east and they stroll past the rows of pens side by side, leisurely, like women going to church together on an early Sunday morning. Except Carlyle recognizes no God who requires the work of men for habitation, no magnificent cathedral for a home—only the God of the prairie brushfire, the Platte River nourishing him sweet as mother's milk. Merciless are Carlyle's dreams which are the same dreams of white men before him who have made their fortune reaping corn and plowing great furrows into the land. He has winnowed the softness from his sons leaving behind merely sinew, bone. In thirty years the Stockyards will smell of rust and carrion and disrepair but his sons will thrive like stubborn weeds. He raised them to live in the hostile terrain of his house and he has driven their roots deep into the soil, so deep he has bloodied his hands, bloodied the handle of the auger. With Joshua out of the house he sees a need to expand—another thousand acres, another hundred head of cattle. He could build an extra wing of the house for Joshua and his children, who will grow to be just as beautiful and forthright as their father.

Lost in conversation with Jim he barely pays attention to Nick who follows a few paces behind. Half listening to his father and Jim talking business he slowly makes his way through the crowd of people as they mill about aimless as geese. Their voices shrill to the ear as they haggle and goad each other. The air foul with decay.

Jim says, Here's a nice selection of Red Angus. Look at the calves. Lots of good fat on em.

I see, Carlyle says. Clearly unimpressed. Nick examines the calves with interest—bulky and covered in thick fat they have none of the leanness, the concision of his father's favored hounds.

Top-dollar beef, Jim says.

That so.

Nick wanders to the next pen over empty except for a man shoveling cowshit. He leans into the work with gusto, his jaw tight with effort. Sweat collecting in droplets on his neck even in the chilled winter air. He drives his shovel into the ground, stopping momentarily to catch his breath and when he looks up from his labor Nick can see he is some kind of Oriental. His face and arms are the same hue as a white man's but there is no mistaking the foreign topography of his visage—the low bridge of the nose, the dark and melancholy eyes.

His father says to Jim, too loudly, I didn't know they let Japs work here.

He's just a yardman. He shovels shit and he cleans.

No better than a gofer.

No. But he does good work. They have a good work ethic, the Japanese.

Sure. And my brother shot a lot of them during the war, too. Put up a hell of a fight.

Carlyle speaks rarely of the war though he tells himself he would have joined if he could have. With a rich father and a history of profligacy he received through bribery or subterfuge an exemption from the draft. It was his brother Frank who had gone abroad and played at blood sport in Okinawa. Had Carlyle been drafted he knows he would have committed all manner of manic atrocities so perhaps it is for the better that he waited out the war in the foyer of his father's regal plantation home. Seething with anger at having been thwarted of his rightful inheritance. The architecture of Stag's Crossing already materializing in his mind. Eden or Arcadia it would not be but a spacious estate with high ceilings and an elegant pack of perfect greyhounds. A thousand acres, a lovely house that everyone from miles around would know belonged to an important man. How rich he would be. How rich his sons would be.

With the war in Vietnam there has been talk of sending Joshua to Canada. Nick could go to the Peace Corps. Or Nick could go to war like Frank and come back a stranger—he might spend all day sleeping or drinking, or never go outside. Or he might return standing tall and unbent. Hardened by a violence that has stripped his boyhood from him he would be an entirely different man and Carlyle would embrace him in the doorway of

Stag's Crossing, this son who has reached apotheosis in a foxhole. Now carrying a godly nature within him, the charred scent of the divine.

Jim says, All right, Carlyle. Let's have a look at the Charolais.

Nick lingers at the fence. He will not go to war. Not now, not ever. Instead he watches the men coming and going. Out of the corner of his eye he sees the Japanese man put his shovel down and leave the pen. Walking briskly to the Exchange Building without so much as looking back.

Carlyle says, Can't believe he just left.

Nick knows too well how to cultivate no reaction to his father's barbarism. Carlyle's words striking the deepest parts of him, meant to injure profoundly. How else can he survive the nadir of his childhood? If he does not endure he will die.

Jim says, The Charolais just started coming in from New England last year—

Right, Carlyle says. The air has gone out of him. Like a wolf who has lost the scent he retreats, goes in circles. Lacking conventional prey he must find other ways to entertain himself. Regurgitating the same humor until all the men around him are laughing too, their laughter smug and unsophisticated, as though they have never been laughed at themselves and desire nothing more than to crush others with their petty derision. Carlyle has made it clear to Nick that relations between men are merely eternal cycles of humiliation—complex social rituals that determine who will lead and who will follow. Ravage or be ravaged in turn.

He watches the outline of the Japanese man grow smaller and smaller before finally disappearing altogether. Then he goes to join his father. To stand at his side as he has always done.

Xxvi.

NOW

So oppressive is his father's fury that all of Stag's Crossing has fallen silent in its wake. His dogs, his children quietly slinking through the hallways. Speaking only in hushed and muffled tones like visitors at a museum they hover anxiously in every room of the house. Nick walks through the fields every day, cataloguing each furrow, each shorn stalk of wheat thrown carelessly to the ground. Feeds the dogs in his father's absence. He has found that if he does not leave the house at dawn he will inevitably encounter his brother or worse he will encounter Emilia. He and Joshua may lock antlers like two stubborn bucks in rut but it is the sight of Emilia alone that courts true disaster. She grows somehow lovelier and more mysterious by the day, sitting at the kitchen table combing out her hair, singing softly to herself in the shower when she thinks no one can hear. Reverberating through the drain the sound takes on a breathless, metallic quality that is pleasing to him.

One crisp morning he lingers too long in the house and catches sight of her through a door left carelessly open. Lying asleep on what used to be Carlyle's bed—illuminated only by a tantalizing slit of light from the window he sees her long hair fanned out over the sheets, her bare shoulders. Hurrying downstairs he pushes the image from his mind though it returns to him later that night, vividly theatrical in its reappearance. Her sleeping form cradled amongst the cushions like a precious gemstone. The alluring, beatific expression on her face.

Joshua's anger mirrors his father's. A withering hostility has burrowed inside him and begins to consume him from within. Having been denied his birthright he seems content to waste away together with the fields, ever fallow. The wheat blighted by the ergot of a rainy summer. Whenever he sees Nick he always looks like he wants to say something before quickly walking away.

His father refuses to acknowledge their presence; he eats at night after everyone has gone to bed. Furtively devouring their leftovers like an unknown species of vermin he sneaks back into the little room at the end of the hallway for his nightly vigil. The only trace of him a trail of incriminating crumbs in the stairwell. Once so paranoid about outsiders in his home he has now become a prisoner within it, decaying in Nick's old bedroom that is small enough to serve as an oubliette.

Seized by a singular and fitting aestival madness they are plagued by bouts of uncontrollable melancholy, mania, agitation that rankles their limbs. Nick hears Carlyle pacing endlessly in his room. A week spent in silence at Stag's Crossing is agony but no more so than the agony of childhood. Like a sickness it lingers in the marrow; the memory of his youth spent running wild through the fields. Ivy and bramble in his hair. Joshua running after him, his face haloed by the dying light of evening. The eternal pursuer.

Catching Emilia alone in the kitchen one evening he leans against the doorway and watches her. She has pinned her hair into a fetching French twist and rolled up her sleeves. Exposing the fragile arc of her wrist, slender as the foreleg of a doe. Water boils in a pot atop the stove; she tosses in a pinch of salt. Turning to wipe her hands on a towel she sees him standing there.

Don't mind me, he says. I'm just observing.

Me making dinner isn't much of a show, she says. Her tone unusually melancholic.

Something wrong?

I'm worried about your dad. The way he's behaving.

It's probably just cabin fever.

You think so?

What else could it be?

I think he's very sick, she says. Sicker than he knows.

He's dying. Of course he's moody.

That's not what I mean, she says. The rages, the silent treatment, how he talks to you and Joshua—how he talks to me—

That's normal for him.

That doesn't make it right, she says.

He goes up to her. Standing too close as she works her knife across the cutting board with enviable swiftness.

What're you making?

Spaghetti with garlic and olive oil.

My favorite.

Joshua mentioned, she says. Stirring the pot of boiling water she begins adding the dry pasta.

He talks about me?

Sometimes. If I ask.

And he's so quick to reveal all our family secrets, I suppose.

She flashes Nick a look. He's certainly stubborn. But I think you'll find I'm *very* persuasive.

Where is he now?

Sleeping. Didn't feel like having dinner.

Interesting. He picks up a strand of hair that has fallen out of her twist and gently twirls it back and forth between his index and thumb. Black with a hint of umber. He wonders at what has changed to make him so bold as to attempt this—knowing weeks or days ago he would not have even dared to stand in her light. But now he has been thoroughly seduced by her suffering, her vulnerability. As men are attracted to a woman in pain. He envisions an affair extravagant and uncontrollable as the creek when it floods. A disastrous and untimely end to his family.

Nick, she says. Only half scolding. He could come downstairs any minute.

That would certainly be a surprise. Do you think he'd kill me? I might enjoy that.

If you're going to say ridiculous things, you could at least help me mince the garlic.

He tucks the errant strand back into her French twist and takes the knife and cutting board from her. Working in companionable silence he finds the colander on a high shelf and holds it over the sink for her as she drains the pasta water. Grates the cheese. By the time they are finished the house smells charmingly of Parmesan. An infectious, unexplainable delight suffuses him as he rolls each strand of pasta onto his fork. Emilia eats daintily, like a gourmand. Dabbing her mouth after each bite.

Looking up at him with an endearing shyness she says, Is it any good?

Delicious. Absolutely delicious.

I'm glad.

Where did you learn to cook like this?

My mom taught me. When I was growing up in Connecticut.

I thought you said you grew up in Pennsylvania.

Her gaze never wavers from his. Is that so? she says. You must be mistaken. Then her face flushes all over, as though she has been caught out—a nervous crimson tinting her cheeks. Rather than marring her complexion it somehow adds to her magnetism. Her entire face an invitation, an open door into another future. With his brother slumbering upstairs and his father unheeding, locked inside his little bedroom like a hermit, Nick cannot help but indulge in a certain recklessness not permitted to him since he was young. Seizing her by the shoulder he traces his thumb over her collarbone and pulls her to him, pressing their mouths together. He brings up his other hand to forcefully thread through her hair. Scattering her bobby pins onto the floor, the table.

She parts her mouth with hesitation. Her eyes remain locked open, fixed on some invisible point behind him. He is used to receiving something unspoken in these moments of intimacy, his unusual gift of reading people applied to their deepest and innermost selves. Ever-mysterious, she gives him nothing—no shadowed memories, no insight into her world. He clumsily presses onward, attempting to deepen the kiss before a sharp pain sends him reeling back in his chair. He instinctively touches his lip and sees fresh blood on his hand.

Fuck, he says. You bit me. The blood on his fingers wet and red.

She says, What else did you expect?

Something a little nicer.

You'll just have to try harder next time.

Try harder?

You think I'm just going to have an affair with you because I'm bored.

Here I was hoping the mutual loneliness and resentment would work in my favor, he says.

She rolls her eyes, not without affection, and gathers her bobby pins from the table and floor. Rearranging her hair until it is coiled into a perfect bun that leaves the white nape of her neck exposed. Nick watches her do this casually, like he is not even there. Then she collects her plate and silverware and starts to tidy up.

Two greyhounds, long and lean with brindle saddles come up to the door and begin barking agitatedly. Scratching and pawing at the screen.

You should probably get that, she says.

He opens the door and steps outside to see several of

the hounds chasing each other in circles. Mere horseplay. Uncoiling the green hose he refills their water bowls and checks their kennels to make sure everything is clean. Sprays a few of them with water to cool them down in the shimmering heat. Their huffing and panting appearing to him almost pathetic, even childish.

One of the dogs comes and rubs against his leg, strangely catlike. Nuzzling and licking his wrist, his hand like a desperate supplicant. He leans over to scratch between its ears and sees that its dark brown eyes, its slender gait all remind him of Emilia. The ridges of its vertebrae just visible beneath the skin like Emilia's spine through her linen blouse.

After mere weeks enduring her presence he has fallen prey to the same cataclysmic desire that once tormented Joshua and sent him into exile. And in a single, fatal action he has commenced the destruction of their family. He imagines telling Carlyle of his monumental transgression. He imagines, with delirious pleasure, Joshua killing him for what he has done.

He would be a fool to pursue this. And yet it brings him great satisfaction to conjure her moody blushes, her flirtations. Piercing her veil of careful politeness he recalls that even as she drew blood she had not denied him. He would simply have to try again.

Returning to the dining room he finds it empty. All but one of the lights turned off. Dishes and silverware cleaned and stacked in the sink. He walks through the ground floor now vacant of life. Ascending the stairs he sees all the bedroom doors save his are shut. Darkness passes over the house, passes through him as he makes his way into bed. The only memory of the kiss stained onto his fingertips like the remnant of a holy and unhealable wound.

Xxvii.

THEN

In the lobby of the Exchange Building stands a familiar figure, dark-haired and dark-eyed with the towering physique of a bricklayer. Or else he might be one of those statues Nick has seen in his schoolbooks, some svelte youth preserved perfectly in bronze.

From afar Nick perhaps recognizes him as he might recognize the face of a beloved in a haze of dreaming—at fourteen he is unacquainted with the bottomless obsession that allows one person to distinguish another at a hundred feet by their reflection in a shopwindow, their laugh three rooms over at a crowded party.

Henry's thick eyebrows wrinkle, deep in thought. He has not seen him yet; Nick lingers. Exhausted from spending the morning with his father who has decided to go drinking with Jim for the next hour or so. Likely planning to return red-faced and outraged at the asking price of cattle in this age of decadence. Carlyle is a righteous drunkard worse than any preacher for he needs no pulpit to begin his sermons. He rarely drinks outside his weekend sojourns in town so he must make it mean something, his moment of licentiousness, or else his talent for invective will be wasted. His most brilliant and inattentive son will play audience and in this way Nick will be taught how to compose his beautiful paragraphs of scathing prose. The dialect may be modern but the cadence is his father's—long, unending diatribes, filed to an impeccable sharpness.

Nick finally catches Henry's eye and gives a brief wave. Henry waves back before walking over.

Fancy seeing you here.

My dad wanted to look at cattle.

Is he buying?

Maybe next year.

I wouldn't if I were him, Henry says.

Why so?

Heard from Adam in geography class there's a wolf on the loose.

You can't be serious.

His dad has been losing calves. Even heard one was found dead last Saturday. Missing its liver.

Sounds like a person and not a wolf. Wolves eat the whole animal.

Henry says, Kearney's not known for its big population of cattle thieves.

How would you know?

Grew up in Kearney. Never stole anything bigger than a bottle of beer myself.

So why are you here? Playing hooky too?

Came with my dad to check out the goods, same as you.

Where's your dad, then?

I'm just window-shopping right now. He's got a business meeting.

There anything to do around here?

Lots. You got any money?

No.

Well, says Henry lightly, maybe we should wash up first. Then we can go find someplace around here to eat. There're some washrooms away from the bar that aren't too crowded.

Okay, Nick says. Lead the way.

Henry briskly turns on his heel, guiding Nick through a maze of hallways and doorways until they come to the men's room. Inside Nick sees the cramped row of white urinals, white sinks, stalls with their doors hanging wide open. He goes to the sink and washes his face and hands. Then he goes into one of the stalls and is about to lock the door and pull his pants down before he turns around and sees that Henry is there behind him, his expression gleaming with anticipation as he says, Don't worry, I blocked the door. Backing Nick up against the toilet seat he adds, You want this?

Nick knows the question contains the answer hidden within it—just out of reach, as though it is a riddle that must be solved. Yet he cannot parse it. Young and having barely grown his first pair of antlers he is innocent of this fatal desire to engrave himself into the body of another. Reworking and remaking the fabric of his destiny, skin against skin.

Nick nods slowly, his entire body tensed. Henry reaches out to grip his sleeve, his shoulder. With Henry's hands on him he relaxes into the soft curve of his mouth, embellishing him with kisses. Closing his eyes he imagines himself elsewhere, a succession of strange and fleeting images passing through him—on the beach, watching the sea at starlight; traveling through a forest overgrown with flowers. Henry's memories. In the absence of understanding they are merely apparitions to him. Reflections broken apart by rippling water. His nude form sprawled in the sand. From behind one of the dunes emerges a strange boy with tawny hair. His swim trunks dangling from his fist. The air is salt and sweat. Nick presses his cheek to the shoal and feels the seawater lapping at his inner thighs. Come closer, the water says. The boy says.

Someone begins banging on the door. Loud thundering strikes like the knocking of his father at his bedroom door in the morning. He catches himself in the act; pulls away. Henry rolls his eyes at the interruption and straightens his shirt. He unlocks the stall and quickly moves the coatrack leaned up against the door. Cracking open the door Henry speaks in a low voice to the stranger outside. For a moment Nick worries it is his father though surely it is not for he would not ask to come in, he would simply make his arrival known by force. Would understand immediately the meaning of his son with his shirt buttons half undone hiding behind the bathroom sink.

Henry closes the door and sees Nick hastily rearranging

his clothing. Watching him with a sly expression he says, Need some help with that?

I'm fine, Nick says. Who was that?

Some Jap I guess. Could barely speak English.

Did he see anything?

With those slanty eyes of his? Henry says, laughing. I doubt it. In the mirror his expression is artless, unstudied. He means what he says and therein fruits a rich and fertile cruelty. Nick has seen this cruelty before, in the hardened face of a dead stag. In the face of his father and his thoughtless tyranny.

He presses a fist to his mouth to catch himself from vomiting. Warm bile coming up his throat thick as rotting oatmeal.

I have to go, he says.

Go where? We were just getting started.

We were? Nick chokes out, backing away. Henry grabs him by the shoulders and pushes him up against the door. They are so close Nick can peer deeply into the milky sclera of Henry's eyes. Their breaths mingling in the cramped room. He swallows his weakness, his illness, and feels it settle deep in his stomach. When Henry touches his lips he wills them to open and receive Henry's fingers like a holy anointing. Licking at them hungrily. So thoroughly has he been starved of affection he knows he must do this or he will perish. If he does not aim to please there will be nothing left in him worthy to love.

Henry kneels.

The beach at nightfall; he and the boy wading through shallow water. A name caught between his teeth. Here in this memory they are linked, Henry and himself, both of their bodies joined to the same continuum of space. Acting in harmony they are a perfect machine in perpetual motion. Such an intimacy possible only in dreaming. Yet Nick is severed from this splendor—he lacks the proper instrument for affection. An imprecise art that is lost to him. He will never be able to name this loss though it will pursue him for years to come. The wolf of his loneliness grotesquely slavering, forever ravenous.

Henry stands up and wipes his mouth with the back of his hand. Then rubs his hand on the front of his jeans. Leaving behind only a small clear stain. As though nothing at all has happened he says, I'll come by again. Saturday night. His face is slightly flushed—pleasure, or exertion—but otherwise he is enviously unruffled by what has just transpired.

Nick says, What happened to dinner?

Oh, I think I've had my fill, Henry says, his voice smug.

Brushing Nick aside he opens the door and leaves with only a perfunctory wave goodbye. Nick stands dumbfounded for a moment, alone with himself, before going to the bathroom window and looking out. Time has moved strangely in Henry's presence—the chaos of the cattle pens has largely dissipated, the sky darkening as the clouds recede. He realizes he needs to zip up his fly and find his father before Carlyle starts looking for him. He clears the winding passageways of the Exchange Building before walking outside and checking for his father's pickup parked nearby. Wandering through rows of cars he eventually finds the white Ford and his father leaning against the driver's-side door with his mouth pulled into a furious expression.

Where've you been?

Out, says Nick. Are you going to open the door?

His father wordlessly climbs into the driver's seat. With his right hand he swings open the passenger door. Nick gets in next to him and watches the last rays of light rake across the buildings, the empty cattle pens.

Carlyle begins to head west on L Street. Homebound.

Don't do that again, he says.

Do what?

Wander off like that.

Why?

I couldn't find you when Jim and I were finished. Had to wait for you to come back like one of the dogs. Course I knew you'd come back. Nobody else would feed you.

I'm not a child, Dad. I don't have to follow you everywhere.

You're fourteen. You're a child.

And how old was Joshua when you started letting him in on the business? Nick says.

Carlyle frowns but says nothing.

Emboldened by his father's uncharacteristic silence Nick adds, Anyone can tell we don't need cattle and if you ask me we're just fine focusing on soybeans and corn. We'd have to build entirely new infrastructure for the place—hire someone to slaughter, we'd need a cattle barn, invest in hay—

You think you can run this place as good as your old man?

I'm just giving my opinion, Dad.

Your *opinion*. You mean those little comments of yours that show how superior you are to the rest of us.

I don't feel superior.

Bullshit, Carlyle says. You're exactly like I was at that age. Arrogant. Thought I knew better than my father and I know you sure as hell think so too. If you're so sure why don't you do what I did. Leave and build something elsewhere.

Maybe I'll do that, he spits back.

I'd like to see you try.

With the incandescent fervor of boyhood Nick revives an old, ancient fantasy: killing his father just as Carlyle must have fantasized about killing Edward long ago. Too young to carry out his dreams of overthrowing the Morrow patriarch instead he massacres beetles with a gardening hose. What remains of his tragic feeling is a violence bent inward, upon himself. Constantly he is pierced by the daggers of his father's disregard and in this agony he finds a clarion sense of purpose. One day he will be an authority in his own right no matter what his father says though he senses not the form his mastery will take, nor the fierceness with which he will wield it. In this way he might prove himself to be equal to his brother, in the sheer electricity of his scorn. He is a Morrow boy through and through; his violence is a paternal violence, steel perfected in the forge of Carlyle's ferocity. In the manner of his father he scorches his hand against the anvil and does not pull away.

Xxviii.

NOW

When he awakens the blood on his lip has dried. Tasting now of sweat, bitter copper. His fingertips still bearing the shameful evidence of his yearning. Stained a lascivious red where he has touched his mouth, opened himself to another. Ardor, arousal, fear mingling in the taste.

He lies in bed for another few minutes. Listening to the patter of bare feet against the wooden floors at Stag's Crossing with closed eyes. Rain whips the windows with the fervor of a jockey near the finish line, his fevered hand urging ever forward. Something thrilling in the air, in each beam of sunlight through the half-drawn shade.

He checks the clock on the nightstand. Ten in the morning—he should be out feeding the chickens by now, if they had any chickens left. He is still unused to the patterns of a gentler life, leisurely mornings reading the newspaper, lying cradled in the arms of another. Instead as cattle are taught with the goad he was taught discipline, the measure of a man. Knowing that to grow up meant carving away all externalities. His vital organs removed with the knife of his adulthood.

Resigning himself to a morning of bickering with Joshua and avoiding his father he puts on a white shirt, black pants, calfskin belt. Leather loafers that still remind him of the man who gifted them. He shaves and brushes his teeth, combs his unruly brown hair. His hands refusing to keep still. Pricked with desire he cannot help but feel wounded, made vulnerable by it. A trembling in him that was not there before.

On the desk he sees the little painting Emilia made. In the night it appears to have changed slightly. The woman's face no longer wholly hidden by her hair but turned toward the viewer, exposing a hint of her eyelashes, the edge of her lips. Though perhaps he is just imagining it. A gift as mysterious as the woman who gave it to him.

Upon going downstairs he finds Emilia standing in the foyer looking at the framed pictures of his family. The photographs yellowed and the glass smudged over. Taken with his father's Kodak Retina they are strange relics of another time. Pictures of Nick and Joshua as boys, ready for church. Carlyle standing on the patio of Stag's Crossing looking out over his domain. Nick watching Joshua horse around in the front yard. Even as a young boy Joshua steers the eye to him with his fearless gaze. Posing like he is ready to be rendered in oils by some Renaissance painter.

Nick, humorless, hovers at the edge of each photograph. His face holds no meaningful expression; he might otherwise be dead.

You look so sad in these pictures, she says.

I'm sad in all my pictures, he says. I have that kind of face.

It's a very dramatic face.

Yes, the tragic white male. Very literary.

She laughs. Joshua said you were a writer.

I'm a literary critic. If I were more handsome, I might've been an actor, but, alas.

So you enjoy reading?

When I was younger. Now it's mostly a chore.

Who's your favorite author, then?

Probably one I haven't read yet, he says. Otherwise, I suppose Hemingway will do.

The house is silent; no sound comes from the kitchen or the dining room. Normally he sees Joshua sitting at the table eating breakfast; Emilia studying her eggs on the stove. He might even glimpse the light on in his old bedroom—hidden signals from his father, whose reclusiveness has ceased to interest his sons. Now they go about their day as though Carlyle's return is inevitable, as the world might continue to turn in the absence of God.

He says, Where's everyone?

Joshua told me this morning he was going to town with your dad, she says.

I thought Dad was still giving us the silent treatment.

She shrugs. Guess he changed his mind.

You didn't go with them?

I wasn't invited, she says.

You don't think that's strange?

You're inquisitive this morning, she says. Deflecting him with uncanny efficiency. Why don't you help me make breakfast? I got up so late I didn't have anything prepared. I think there's still some pancake mix left from yesterday—we could make that.

He follows her into the kitchen. Standing behind her as she opens the fridge and digs around. He studies her minutiae closely, cataloguing every expression. The feeling of being alone with Emilia is an irresistible, nefarious agony. The compulsive magnetism of her voice, mesmeric and clear. The alarmingly attractive tilt of her mouth. He fantasizes not about having her, as he has done before, but of having never met her. Telling his father he would never speak to him again that he will never return to Stag's Crossing nor would he inform Joshua of the final destruction of their family, his father will die alone in that hollowed-out house, hollow as the sloughed shell of a dying cicada. Never to summon them back again to that place where ivy tangles in the trees like the loose hair of women. And then he would be free from this ensnarement having never set his eyes upon her—unsubtle in her premonition, harbinger of an unknown destiny.

Found it, she says, handing him a glass bowl covered in Saran Wrap. He sets it on the counter and turns on the stove. Watches the flames lick the bottom of the skillet as Emilia cuts a stick of butter.

So you don't know where they went, he says.

Mm, she demurs. No, I don't. You can pour now.

They make two perfect stacks of pancakes, lightly browned and doused in maple syrup. Nick allows himself the small thrill of sitting in his father's seat at the table while Emilia sits across from him. Where his mother would have sat had she not died at such a young and predestined age.

In another, stranger life he imagines that he and Emilia might have married. Then he would have been the one disavowed, cast out like yesterday's leftovers. His father red-faced, incandescent over his betrayal. Nick is far plainer than Joshua, not a man of many charms, but he does not think he would make a terrible husband. Perhaps he might linger too long at dinner parties filled with terribly bright-eyed young men, twentysomethings whose sylphlike air remind him of those inescapable evenings with Henry. Alone and twisted together among the sumac. But always he would return to partake in her ritual disrobing, her fertile mysteries. To bury himself in the open grave of her body.

His tower of pancakes begins to lean, sliding sideways until it is more architectural mistake than skyscraper. Emilia sips her morning coffee, her face turned away as she looks out the window at the rain. Nick watches her silently. The astonishment of her beauty rising in him like a heady perfume.

When she finishes her food she puts the knife and fork down. Smiling with the distant and peaceful air of those dark-haired beauties he saw in her book of Japanese paintings, lounging in the shade of the cherry trees.

Delicious, she says.

He has not touched his food. He says, If the rain stops soon, we could go for a walk.

I forgot to shower this morning, she says. Let me take a quick bath, and I'll come back down.

She gets up from her seat and heads through the kitchen to the stairs. As she brushes past him he feels her lightly touch his shoulder though perhaps he is merely imagining it, this covert intimacy. He does not look back to her see her ascend the staircase, the long skirt of her dress rippling behind her like a bridal train. Does not see her pause at the top of the stairs to see if he has followed before disappearing into the master bedroom to undress.

He stares at the food in front of him, uneaten. Picking up the knife he rests it gently against his wrist, the hollow of his throat. Testing its heft, the delight of its sharpness. When he was a child he used to pray for God to let him die. Now that feeling swarms him again as he hears her walking around upstairs, shedding her clothes and climbing into the tub. Wringing out her long, dark hair. Water coming down, the hissing of the showerhead nozzle. With slender fingers she reaches up and points it toward her, enveloping her body in the spray. Her face shining as oracle bone and perfection besides.

He puts the knife back and stands up. His throat still uncut—a sacrifice blessedly delayed. With deliberate leisure he makes his way through the house, up the staircase. The door to the master bedroom lies open. He enters; crossing the threshold with the knowingness of a trespasser. He catches sight of Joshua's ties, neatly arranged, wrinkled shirts hanging in the closet. Emilia's clothes strewn onto the floor, dresses for every occasion. Muslin, taffeta, woven silk. Skirts embroidered with flowers and birds. Nick turns one over in his hand, the material thin and delicate between his fingers. It seems astonishing that she had worn these, draping the fabric over her body. Fitting herself into them, folding herself neatly inside.

From inside the bathroom he hears Emilia turn off the water and splash about in the bath. He looks through the keyhole and glimpses only fragments of her body through a haze of steam—her knee, the curve of her elbow.

The metal rings slide against the rod as she pulls back the shower curtain.

Nick? she says.

He freezes. His eye still at the keyhole.

She says, You can come in if you want. It's unlocked.

He opens the door. The room is humid and smells cloyingly of shampoo, cheap bath fragrance. Emilia is sitting in the tub. Her feet dangling over the side, dripping water onto the pristine tile. Her damp hair thick as seaweed; she twists it between her fingers. He goes up to the edge of the tub and skims his fingers over the top of the water, not touching her, only the water's surface, feeling like he is a boy again waiting with his father at the riverside where he must concentrate on the bobber, his consciousness narrowing to a single point before he is pulled completely, utterly under.

Are you waiting for something? she says.

He takes her face in his hands. Her brown eyes are wet; her lip trembles slightly. When he leans down to kiss her he feels her mouth curve into a smile. Not a smile of pleasure but of triumph, victorious at last. Over him, the grand fool. Over Joshua, viciously humiliated by his own brother, in the house that will one day be his, atop the thousand acres that will be his final resting place. Over Carlyle, who said that she would not marry his favored son—and now she has eaten the elder for breakfast and devoured the younger for dinner. Picking her white teeth with their bones.

Pulling her from the tub he lays her down on the old polyester bath mat. Examining her naked body like a fisherman who has caught a rare pearl in his net, though who is the fisherman and who is the fish he is not entirely sure—so terribly he is drawn to her, the stringer threaded through his gills as he thrashes in the shallows. Unable to escape he must surrender, sink to the bottom of the riverbed, fill his dying mouth with silt. She will kill him later, slit him open belly first and he cannot protest as she slides her hand down and begins to unbuckle his belt, her fingers still slippery with bathwater.

Once he gets his fly unzipped he takes her right there on the bathroom floor. Not as Joshua has made love with her long ago in their wedding bed but a coupling born from a frenetic impulse. His visions of her arrive with thrilling clarity, at last: the sight of her standing in the airport waiting lounge, the image of her lying naked next to a pool of wine. Surrounded by a garden in symphonic bloom. A man feeds her fresh apricots by hand. From each tree branch dangles roasted meats, delicacies of all kinds. Burying his face in her neck Nick can smell the fragrant perfume she once wore. Sweat and salt mingling in the same breath.

She gasps; rakes her nails against his neck, his shoulders. As if to tear away at him, to peel his skin from his flesh like a ripened fruit. He sees her left hand up close as it cradles his face—it is covered in scars. A surgery, an old injury, a bite from a large creature. He cannot tell.

When he finishes he says nothing. Afraid to look her in the eye, to truly face what he has done. Loose-limbed and spent he lies on the tile as Emilia carefully pours bathwater onto the floor, washing away all evidence of their crime. He cannot bring himself to break the silence though they are alone, the house deserted and vacant. No witnesses to their furtive wrongdoing, hidden as they are by the walls of his father's slaughterhouse, Stag's Crossing nothing more than an experiment in raising young boys into beasts of prey though in truth they have emerged hooved and foolish fit only to be fed on grain and sliced into the tenderest cuts of veal. As he walked from the dining room to the bath he envisioned with each step what was to come. What he would find beneath her clothing, the body of a woman or else a convincing illusion, enough to satisfy his wild imagination.

Nick says, Emilia—

Yes?

Was I any good? he asks. Almost ashamed. Like he is fourteen again, nervous and callow. Revisiting an encounter with Henry in his mind. The lover's lane darkly beckoning. Only this time it is not Henry's face that comes into view but Emilia's, as she lifts her head and rests it on his shoulder.

In what way? she asks.

He fails to answer. Hearing first the dogs tearing from their kennels and running up the driveway. Their long legs jackknifing against gravel, their stride a unified, elegant motion. The car wheels churning, crackling. His brother, his father sitting side by side in the truck. Joshua getting out, unlocking the gate, letting it swing wide as Carlyle pulls the car through. The buck's head staring with its mouth agape. Nick feels with a wrenching terror that it has seen them, it knows, such a betrayal cannot go unpunished, can never be forgiven—

Emilia says, Leave. They're here.

Xxix.

THEN

Nick's renewed obsession with the fox, childlike in its intensity, has led to an even greater understanding of what his father requires of him. Lying in his small bed after a day of endless and grueling work his mind falls upon the five or six or seven hens left living. How they gaze upon him with suspicion as he collects their eggs every few days. Sheepish in the knowledge that he cannot save them. Having fixed the fencing round the coop once already he knows the fox will only devise some casual subterfuge to avoid it. Its cunning far stronger than that of any man's. His father is correct in all ways that matter—as soon as a fox has found a place for its feasting, it will return until it is killed.

One of the greyhounds slinks into his room and lies asleep at the foot of his bed. Carlyle must be in a good mood today. Rarely does he let them come upstairs lest they dirty his furniture, the grandness of his design. Yet still he dotes on them. This one blue all over, an exceedingly rare color, and Carlyle delighted to see it. Even fed it with a bottle when it was a puppy. How strange for Nick to witness this as a child, this clandestine gentleness as his father warmed evaporated milk on the stove and set out a pile of blankets near the fireplace. Even when the dog chewed up a pair of beautiful leather shoes, marvelously stippled, he only laughed and said he would buy new ones.

Nick has rarely seen his father strike one of the dogs, though this detail is irrelevant to him. They have no relationship to each other, dogs and children, except a shared master. The terror of his brilliance apparent to both.

Unable to sleep Nick goes downstairs for a glass of water. The light of his father's study still turned on. He can see the top of Carlyle's head poking out over the tall wingback chair as he does his monthly accounting. Surrounded by shelves filled with beautiful books he does not read but displays to show his mastery, as though he could claim dominance over language itself. Determined that his sons be more learned than he ever was he intends to send them to colleges both prestigious and thousands of miles away. Joshua returning with the keen intelligence needed to run Stag's Crossing, to expand and secure a future for himself. Nick might change not at all—he has always been far more stubborn than his brother. But at least he would read thoroughly, and write incisively, and speak deceptively, all things considered. Carlyle would be satisfied with this. The markers of a man well-made.

Couldn't sleep? he says, hearing Nick's quiet steps on the stairs.

Been thinking about the fox, Nick says.

Good. Come here.

Nick approaches his father's study with hesitation. He is not often permitted to set foot inside while Carlyle is working.

His father gestures to a piece of paper. Tell me what this is, he says.

Nick picks it up and reads it. It is a receipt for seed, sold to one Carlyle Morrow in the last year.

Seed receipt, he says, and puts it back down.

Do you see anything wrong with it? Carlyle leans back in his chair and appraises Nick carefully.

Nick has never thought much about the business of Stag's Crossing. He knows that whether the soil is gorged with so much water it floods or if there is famine their thousand acres will continue to prosper regardless. Their true wealth lies elsewhere, properties and machinations that lie so far back in his lineage they appear uncountably ancient. Though compared to the woods and the dry creek near the house they are very recent indeed. He is reminded of his mother's gnawing absence; she appears to him only in memories, in pictures. In the signature line of oil-field deeds.

He remembers his friend Kenny telling him about how his father was mad about the price of seed this year. Seems like mild bullshit but he has no other answer. He knows he will not oversee these matters in five years or ten.

The price has gone up this year, he offers. Maybe you're getting ripped off.

Just what I was thinking, Carlyle says. He puts the piece of paper under a stack of other identical-looking papers on his desk. Turning his face toward Nick, he looks at him directly. Nick forces himself not to shy away.

How's school?

Fine, Nick says.

Joshua called again today. Said things were going well for him.

That's good.

He barely phones home anymore.

It's expensive, Nick offers. Maybe he's trying to save you money.

Well, in a couple of years you won't be calling me either, Carlyle says. I'm sure you'll be glad to be rid of your old man.

Nick has nothing to say to this. His father has him dead to rights. How many nights has he lain awake stoking his anger like coals in a furnace. Collecting the injuries he has suffered as though he might one day bring them to his father and tell him, Remember everything you did to me.

Carlyle opens the top drawer of his desk and pulls out a small Bible. Tiny enough to fit in his pocket. Nick does not think of his father as a particularly churchgoing man so much as he is a man who has set foot in a church a few times in his life. His wedding. A funeral. Dragging his sons with him on those fitful occasions where he develops a concern for his immortal soul, before lapsing back into his old habits.

You ever read this?

A little. In church.

Interesting stuff, Carlyle says. Maybe not so many

things appropriate for a boy of your age. My pops used to read this to me all the time. There's one part that says when Jesus comes he'll be here to turn sons against their fathers. Brother against brother. I thought it was so strange. That's something the Devil does, no?

He puts the Bible back into the drawer and closes it. Resting his clasped hands on his left knee.

But then I realized it was only natural. I turned away from my father. That's how Stag's Crossing came to be. I know Joshua is turning away from me. You, I already know you've decided on some other path for yourself. I tried to raise my sons the way I wanted but you turned out to be a bunch of Midwesterners.

When you're grown, Carlyle says, I'm curious to see what you'll do.

I'd never leave you, Dad, Nick says. Half of him means it. The other half remains unsure, vague in his promises. Having been birthed at Stag's Crossing means a part of him will always remain there. The section of his life he has apportioned to these limitless fields of yellow grain, the cloudy thunderstorms that seem to choke the very life out of the dogs.

Bullshit. I know you're fixing to do it as we speak. Carlyle retrieves a sheet of wrinkled paper from the pile in front of him and smooths it onto the flat surface of his desk.

You know, he says, there was a time where I thought it might be you that would be the one to take over. You're clearly smarter than Joshua. Got a better head for numbers than him. Use bigger words than him, even though I don't even think you've read more than half a book in your life. But you've got too much of your mother in you. She hated it here. She didn't belong. And now look at her.

Nick says, quietly, so quietly he can hardly believe he is saying it, Don't talk about her like that.

Go back to bed, he says. I've got business to take care of.

Nick takes the glass of water upstairs and lies down with the window open and the glass of water on his bedside table. Not drinking it. He is no longer thirsty. Emptied of all desire, he hungers for nothing. Like one of the dogs lolling happily in the snow. Perfectly satisfied.

Xxx.

NOW

In bed he lies boneless and unmoving. Having tossed aside his wrinkled clothes he feels his damp skin sticking to the sheets, an unpleasant sensation. The scent of Emilia lingering in the empty room. He turns her over in his mind, recalling what of herself she has hidden from him, what she dares not let him see. He senses if he cut her open like a felled doe he would find within something inhuman, even diseased. How else might he explain her casual devouring, the acrid delight of her allure? Her possession of him so complete he is entirely engulfed. The heart, having dived to such a depth, has no other choice than to drown.

At last Nick comprehends Carlyle's words as he had not before. *You brought that bitch into this house.* Each impeccably Southern vowel tinged with poison, as if to hide the profundity of his helplessness. He must have known she would return one day and upon her return she would reap what Carlyle had sowed driving her husband from the house while Emilia watched unflinching. All of Carlyle's prejudice, his fruitless bellowing through the halls of Stag's Crossing has been for nothing; he has failed to prevent the contamination of their bloodline. The blight upon the wheat. Desire like a sickness in the air.

Would that he had sired daughters—for women in Carlyle's mind never run feverish in the summertime. Their violence is particular, internal, unmysterious. But the wretchedness of sons is unforgivable. Inevitably they will turn against the father and after succeeding in killing him, they will tear at the walls of the house until there is nothing left but splinters.

Through the opening at the bottom of his door Nick sees a shadow flit down the hallway. Emilia, barefoot. He listens for her as she walks to the edge of the stairwell where she waits in silence. He can hear the car coming up the driveway, his father and brother emerging, talking avidly about nothing as they enter the house where Emilia stands at the top of the stairs.

Emilia! Joshua says.

Welcome back, she says. Where've you been all this time?

Nick gets up and walks slowly to the door. Puts his ear against it.

Carlyle says, Didn't Joshua tell you? We went fishing.

He said you were going to town and would be back in half an hour, Emilia says.

That's funny. I must've gotten mixed up, Joshua says.

You didn't get mixed up, she says. You lied to me.

Carlyle claps Joshua on the shoulder. All right, he says, who's ready to cook up some trout?

Joshua says, Emilia, where's Nick?

She says, In his room. He's been sleeping all day.

Can you get him? We need to get ready for lunch. Everybody together, the whole family.

It's too early for lunch, she says. It's only eleven-thirty.

Joshua says, I wasn't asking for your opinion, Emilia.

Slowly Emilia turns around and walks back down to Nick's room. Knocks twice, very softly each time.

One second, he says. He throws on a striped long-sleeve shirt and dark gray jeans.

When he opens the door she says, You should come downstairs.

He looks at her, standing in the doorway. She is wearing one of the more striking pieces he saw scattered on the floor of the master bedroom—a cream-colored silk sundress embroidered with leaves. He notices that she does not at all appear to have just emerged from the shower. Her presence is wrapped in the throes of yet another exotic and unplaceable perfume; her face, turned slightly away from him, bears the faintest hint of blush.

Downstairs he hears Carlyle and Joshua enter the kitchen. The antic jangling of pots and pans, porcelain dishes. The hiss of water from the faucet, splashing in the metal basin.

Emilia says, Joshua's making everyone lunch. Truly a historical event. I wonder what it'll be this time, given his utter lack of culinary imagination. Lukewarm artichokes?

He reaches for her arm and grabs her by the elbow. Pulling her close to him, holding her in his arms. She does not move for several moments. Her breathing slow and measured. Then she wrenches herself from him, breaking his grasp.

Nick, she hisses. Quickly moving the strap of her dress back into place. Stop being so sentimental.

He follows her down the staircase without another word. A mere supplicant trailing behind her. In the kitchen he sees someone has cleared the table and thrown away his unfinished breakfast. Now Carlyle sits there, drinking a glass of water while Joshua brandishes a glittering knife and commences his bloody work. Beginning by cutting the head off, he slits open the belly and disposes of the entrails. Finally he scrapes away the bloodline and gives the headless, gutless body a good rinse before setting it aside. There are three more trout in the open bag on the countertop. One still has a hook stuck in its mouth. Blood trickling out the gills.

Panfrying them? Nick says.

Sure will, Joshua says. Nice to see you up at this hour.

It was an exciting day, Nick says.

I'll bet. Take a seat. I'll have everything ready in twenty.

He sits across from his father. Emilia sits next to him. They glance at each other but not for too long in case Carlyle notices, though he seemingly does not. So absorbed is he watching his son clean the trout. Joshua who knows instinctively the exact measure of his knife and wields it with an enviable decisiveness. He finishes by holding the headless fish by the tail and scraping the scales away from the flesh, leaving only bare and leathery skin. Then he heats a little butter in a pan and fries them, before depositing each trout onto a separate plate.

Emilia, he says, can you help pass these out?

She gets up from her seat in one fluid, elegant motion. Carefully she picks up two plates and carries them back to the table while Joshua brings the other two plates and the silverware. In silent unison they all brandish their glittering pair of fork and knife, cutting into the fish and taking a middling bite of it.

Carlyle says, Joshua, how wonderful.

Emilia says, You should have added lemon. And green beans.

Joshua—ignoring her—says, Nick? How is it?

It's good, he replies. His mouth full of mediocre and tasteless flesh. He chews; swallows without grimacing.

See? Even Nick thinks it's good.

Emilia says nothing; wipes her mouth with the back of her hand. Leaving the rest of her food uneaten she says, You seem excited today.

Big news, Carlyle says.

I've decided to stay on, Joshua chimes in. I'll be taking over after Dad. Just like he wanted.

Emilia turns her eyes downward. Joshua, she says. You didn't ask me.

Joshua says, Why does it matter? You were going to say no anyway.

You didn't want to come here, and now you're taking over? Nick says.

So I'm not allowed to change my mind?

You're allowed to change your mind; you're just not allowed to be a jackass.

Joshua's face is luminous with fury. An all-destroying anger consumes the perfect symmetry of his features like a wildfire. His handsomeness turned to pure grotesquerie.

Just say you've always been jealous of me, Nick, he snarls. Go ahead. It was never planned for you to have this place. Dad just made a mistake—

A *mistake*? Dad disowned you, and let's not even get into why—

Don't tell me what Dad did, I know what the fuck Dad did—

Carlyle slams his fists on the table so hard the silverware jumps. Will you two stop fighting for once in your goddamn lives?

They both fall silent. Nick stabs another piece of fish and moves it around on his plate. Feels the metal of the fork scratching against the ceramic, making parallel grooves in the glaze. Through the kitchen window he sees a pair of greyhounds frolicking with wild abandon in the grass. No other living souls as far as he can see. The swathe of land carved out by his father seeming inestimably vast, beyond comprehension. After some weeks the isolation of Stag's Crossing that has shaped his family has also driven them all into a state of reckless mania, possessed them with the seeds of their destruction. The passage of a torturous affair—his father's undying anger—and now Joshua, once so devoted to the lovely Emilia, turning from her as Hosea turned from his unfaithful wife. None of them will be spared by the corruption that lies beneath the house, inflamed like a savage wound. The anguish of their shared histories.

Emilia says, And what am I supposed to do? Quit my job and stay here? Do we even have enough money for this harebrained scheme of yours?

Why don't we discuss this some other time? Carlyle suggests. I'm sure planning can wait.

You're the same, the two of you, she says. Exactly the same.

Now listen here, you stubborn bitch, he says. Goddamn— Jap—

Emilia looks at him like she is looking through him. There is no expression on her face. Nick expects something—anger, shock—but there is only a chilling blankness, a sense that she has predicted this scene from the moment she stepped onto the wet earth of his ancestral home, that first night at Stag's Crossing where Nick lay awake listening to the cries of the mole crickets, filled with bloodless dread.

Know this, Carlyle, she says. You'll die soon. But not in the way you expect. And I look forward to seeing it.

He watches her get up from the table. Walking down the long hallway to the foyer she ascends the stairs without another word.

Jesus Christ, Nick says.

Joshua says, You could stand to be more polite, Dad.

I don't take orders from you, says Carlyle. His face tinted an unpleasant red as he works himself into this frenzy. I've known something was completely wrong with that woman from the day I met her. You're just too much of a fool to see it. She's like a siren. She'll kill you if she can. Did you hear what she said to me? That crazy bitch. Tell me again, why did you marry her?

Nick rolls his eyes and says nothing.

Are you rolling your eyes at me?

Yes, because clearly nothing's changed, Nick says. You're the same as you've always been.

Carlyle turns on him with a familiar ferocity. You better drop this if you know what's good for you, he snaps. Spittle leaks from the corner of his mouth. His left eye twitches, then spasms monstrously. Pinkish foam emerges from beneath his tongue, sliding down his chin. His face contorts into a repulsive rictus. Still he tries to get the words out, his teeth grinding together as he struggles. His entire body wracked with small tremors.

Dad! Joshua says, rushing to his side.

Carlyle moans and then begins to seize. Nick gets up from his chair and with Joshua's help together they lay their father flat onto the kitchen tile. As he cradles Carlyle's frail body in his arms he wonders at how light his father has become. Remembering how his spiderlike limbs were once wiry with muscle, every strike like a thunderclap. He pushes the memory from his mind, telling himself that he has already forgiven his father, that he himself is the one who will remain forever unforgiven. Brazen enough to begin an affair under the same roof as his brother. Foolish enough to think anything good will come of this, his doomed obsession. Once stoked, never sated.

Dad, stay with us, Joshua says.

Carlyle stares at him. His eyes moving back and forth without focusing.

Nick says, I'll call an ambulance. It's probably a stroke.

Joshua nods. Nick walks to the study and dials 911. Holding the plastic handset up against his ear he says, My father has collapsed. Please hurry.

The dispatcher says something that does not register to him as language. He repeats the address though no one from the surrounding area knows this place by the street number but by the name of Stag's Crossing, its impossibly primordial nature evident upon the first glimpse of the house through the tree line.

Are they coming? Joshua asks. His voice unusually panicked.

Yes, Nick says, covering the receiver with his hand. The dispatcher is still speaking to him, perhaps offering words of comfort. From beneath his palm the words appear distorted, the Midwestern accent unplaceable. The ambulance could be there in three minutes or twenty-five. Unlike his brother, Nick feels no panic. He is cool as the glass of water still sitting on the kitchen table. He knows his father will survive, because a worse fate awaits him. One Nick can sense only vaguely, the amorphous outline of it taking shape at some indeterminate future moment.

The dispatcher is silent. Nick realizes he is waiting for him to respond and finds that he has no desire to. He pulls on the long cord and successfully untangles it. He hands the phone to Joshua, still kneeling, disconsolate. What has he been hoping for, all his pathetic life? For his father to turn to him and apologize, for once? He knows now it will never happen. Carlyle's all-consuming paranoia is too great to give way to contrition.

Here, he says. Joshua takes the handset from him and

begins speaking, though Nick is no longer listening. He is dazed, seeing the faint rise and fall of his father's chest. The summer light streaking across the wooden table, the tile, Carlyle's garish plaid shirt. Any moment now there would be a frantic knocking on the door, the blaring of sirens interrupting his fever dream. With Joshua thoroughly occupied and his father staring determinedly at the ceiling, he knows he will not be missed. He ascends the spiral staircase and goes into the master bedroom, where he sees Emilia sitting on the bed. She is clothed anew, a red dress like silken fire.

He kneels by the bed and puts his head in her lap, a supplicant. She lazily strokes his hair.

You did this, he whispers. As though he is murmuring to himself. For once in this house: the truth.

How could I? she says.

Her uncanny, moonlit beauty. Untouched by age. The nonexistent reflection. The shadow that writhes, that torments him so. The scars on her left hand.

Somewhere, from deep within him, a memory emerges and is then shut away. Six of his father's greyhounds surround him, a shining retinue. Tumbling eagerly behind the white Ford that lazily winds its way back to the house. On his hands and knees, he crawls through the golden grass back to Stag's Crossing. His face bruised and bleeding.

Tell me what you are, he begs. Please.

Now where's the fun in that? she says, as he begins to weep.

Xxxi.

THEN

At midnight exactly Nick opens his bedroom window and looks out onto Stag's Crossing. The yard illuminated only by a mysterious starlight. Snow covers the grass thick and soft as cake frosting. His father snores two rooms over, the great snores of a slumbering bear. Nick knows in a way he is utterly alone now. Trapped by desire and anticipation he waits to see headlights at the gate. Yet he perceives nothing in the dim blackness beyond the line of barren trees at the front of the house. Slowly realizing he will have to go down to the gate and wait there, alone. He gets out of bed and changes into a blue button-up and his cleanest jeans. Pulling on his brother's old goose down coat, no longer so big, he navigates the treacherous winding staircase. Leaping barefoot over the final creaking step. He puts on his socks and snow boots before taking the keys that hang from a hook in the entryway. Bracing himself against the wind he swings open the grand double doors and invites in the dark and chilling vastness of the plains. The sky like a funeral shroud sequined with pinpoints of light. Coming through the trees he feels the boreal wind bearing down, heavy as a sledgehammer. Staggering backward he is nearly felled by it. After a moment he rights himself and trundles onward. Making his way through the sinister throng of trees he watches a barn owl look toward him then turn its head all the way around to look back at nothing.

At last he encounters the gate, its jagged silhouette. The buck's dead eyes, dead expression, staring eternally outward. Corona of antlers casting strange shadows across the gravel. Stag's Crossing, the ashen tomb in which he has interred his childhood. Unmistakable even beneath the half-light of the waning moon, the faraway stars.

A dark shape comes up the hill. He goes through the gate and closes it behind him. Turning his face toward the road Nick watches the rough contour of a car emerge from the darkness. The headlights of a lean and handsome Chevy El Camino bathe him in an unsettling yellow aura. He can just make out the visage of the driver through the frosted-over window, a face he will recall nearly thirty years from their final meeting with perfect, painful lucidity.

Henry rolls down the window. His hair is neatly combed and his face scrubbed clean. Freckles dust the bridge of his nose, his cheekbones, the mark of a haphazard God. Idling outside the driveway of Stag's Crossing just after midnight his appearance is like that of a phantasm. Something Nick imagined in the strange winter haze, spectral and obscure. Yet he has imagined their meeting so often he knows it cannot come to pass in any other way. Shivering outside the gates of his home as he waits for his beloved like a character in a poem he read once and forgot the name of.

Why hello there, Nick says.

Told you I'd come.

Sure did.

Well hop in then.

Nick climbs into the passenger seat and Henry turns up the heater. After he is done fiddling with the dial he swings his arm over Nick's shoulder. His hand tracing abstract patterns through the fabric of Nick's sleeve. The gesture so casually intimate Nick feels he must remain silent. Bearing witness to this act of tenderness without comment.

Where to?

Nowhere, Nick says. Anywhere.

I know just the place. It's close. Right near the Anderson farm.

Henry drives east, then north for a little while. Nick watches the sides of the road for signs of deer though they have likely retreated to the depths of the forest to weather the harsh winter. Not for nothing is his father's thousand acres called Stag's Crossing—in the summer they commit suicide by the handfuls, dashing themselves against windshields with wild abandon. Magnificent, exquisite bucks lying bleeding in the gravel like common roadkill. Carlyle finds it a terrible shame. Thinks the only good way for a deer to go out is gunshot or wolves.

Looking for something? Henry says.

I wonder if my dad knows I snuck out.

Do you sneak out a lot?

No, Nick says.

Funny. You look like the kind of guy who sneaks out a lot.

You think? Nick says. He turns his head to the side in an indecisive motion, pink embarrassment coloring his face.

My dad's pretty clueless. Barely knows what I'm up to half the time if I'm not at the store.

My dad's a different breed than that. He watches me like a hawk.

Didn't watch you too closely last week, Henry says. Careful with his allusions, not naming what they are both thinking. Almost absent-mindedly he slips his hand beneath the collar of Nick's shirt where it presses hot against his skin. The calculating look in Henry's eyes betraying his true intentions though what other intentions could he have. Midnight on one of the coldest days in the winter and here he is pulling onto a side road wedged between two adjacent farms, a clandestine lover's lane. In summer Nick imagines this place could be glorious, overgrown with splendid weeds disguising the entrance from the main road. Now the dirt is barren and icy, almost too slippery to drive. Heather withered and frozen underfoot.

Henry parks in between two bowed trees. From where Nick sits beneath them it is like they are leaning down to greet them. Naked and shorn of all leaves their thin branches are tangled together in a kind of latticed canopy that shrouds them from passersby. Without warning Henry turns off his headlights and now Nick can only see by the moonglow, the outline of Henry's hair that curls gently at the back of his head. In the semidarkness he sees that Henry has left the heater running though now it is almost unbearably hot inside the car, suffused with the cloying air of a fever dream.

Removing his hand from beneath Nick's shirt Henry reaches out to caress his face. Like Carlyle tenderly petting the face of one of his favored greyhounds. The same agonizing softness in Henry's expression as he leans in for a chaste kiss.

An uncommon, unnamable hunger quickly ruptures all civility in the proceedings—Nick is rapidly stripped of his jacket, his shirt, his pants and shoes. He closes his eyes and feels Henry's hands roaming, grasping and peeling away at him. Pulling his bare skin apart at the seams. Henry climbs over his legs and gets on top of him. Nick clutches at the lapels of Henry's jacket as Henry loosens his belt and undoes his jeans. The world constricts around him until it is all sensation, the feeling of Henry rhythmically panting in his ear, the warmth of his body on top of him, a pleasant heaviness to it.

When they are finished Henry helps Nick clean up, wiping away any wet spots with a rag he finds in the glove box. He even holds up Nick's shirt for him so he can slide his arms into it. Brushing aside a piece of Nick's hair that has flopped in his face, ungainly as a foal's first mane.

On the drive back they are mostly silent, awkward in the moments afterward. Henry turns on the radio but finds only meaningless noise before turning it back off again.

Henry says, I had fun tonight. But it seems strange coming out of his mouth, in this moment. More like something he'd say to a girl after feeling her up in a movie theater.

Nick frowns and Henry sees him frowning.

Did you not like it? Henry says.

No, I did. Why're you asking?

It's hard to tell with you sometimes, Henry says.

Nick is silent.

So—is this—

What? Nick says.

I mean, do you do this often.

No. Do you?

Some, Henry says. Deliberately he keeps his eyes on the road. His fingers drumming anxiously against the steering wheel.

Jealousy and ecstasy mingle inside Nick. Sharp as brine. Without thinking he says, So I'm not the only one, then.

For God's sake, Henry says. When has this ever been about that?

Nick says, Fine. Forget I said anything. A saltwater edge creeping into his voice, the bitterness of the tide forever throwing itself against the shoal, listless and futile. The boy with his swim shorts walking down the beach, Henry's boy, the inamorato of another. As the young man emerges from the water in a graceful seallike movement Nick feels desire wash over him anew. He focuses on the vision like he is looking through a camera lens, rewinding and reliving it in slow motion. Seared down to sinew and bone by longing.

Are you jealous?

I'm not jealous, Nick says. He realizes he is gripping his left wrist so hard he might draw blood; let's go.

Henry sighs. Look, he says. I like you, I really do, but this can't go on forever. You have to know that. Be practical.

Nick says, I'm not a very practical person, I'm afraid.

Never has he been more relieved to see the familiar antlers, the wrought-iron gate that will ferment with rust twenty years from now. Pulling up to Stag's Crossing at last Henry says, all business, Got a call from our supplier in Minnesota. The traps should be here in a week. Come to the store anytime.

Without a word Nick exits the car and makes sure to slam the door. Stalking through the trees he hears the snapping of branches beneath his heavy boots. Henry revs the engine, his Chevy peeling away, tires churning over the gravel. The wind has quieted down and as Nick enters the house he is greeted only by the grandfather clock in the entryway, ticking relentlessly. He sheds his jacket like a dried cocoon and is pulling off his left boot when his father appears in the doorway. Still in his nightshirt he carries his belt held loosely in his right hand.

I was just getting ready for bed, Nick says. Realizing as he says it how absurd it appears to be saying this, having tracked snow into the house, clearly up to no good.

His father says, Explain to me why I shouldn't make you sleep outside.

Like you never snuck out when you were my age, Nick says.

Sure, I snuck out. Never got caught. That's the difference.

Bullshit.

Don't use that tone with me.

Or what?

The belt uncoils, the buckle dropping to the floor. He rubs his fingers over his leather boot and breathes silently through his nose as his father approaches. The belt slapping on the ground. He listens without flinching. Too old to shy away as a well-whipped colt might, once broken in.

They have gone through this surreal display of dominance before—always ending with Nick snarling like a wounded animal as his father straps him bloody. Yet this time something is different. He is nearly as tall as his father, nearly fifteen and in fine form. In another few years he knows he will be out of the house and there is nothing his father can do to stop this, and once he has left behind his purgatorial adolescence he will rise, matchless, far above the milieu of Stag's Crossing.

Nick says, Good night, Dad. I'm going to bed. The sight of his father with the belt no longer holding its power, its inexorable menace. Putting down his boots in the doorway he turns away from his father and walks up the stairs to his little bedroom at the end of the hall. Carlyle says nothing, watching him. This act of defiance passing without comment.

Lying in bed that night Nick wonders if he has miscalculated the depths of his father's vindictiveness. Surely his father will make him pay for this injury. Rage illuminating Carlyle's face as Nick turned away from him, turned away from his punishment like he was shunning the unwritten law of God.

He pulls the blanket over his head. Decides to deal with the old bear in the morning. As he closes his eyes he hears a scream slice through the house, unwavering in its ferocity. High-pitched, tantalizingly wild.

He imagines the chickens in the coop, crowded together before the slaughter. A flash of russet fur scaling the fence, leaping into the henhouse. That scream again, now rousing his father who opens the window of the master bedroom to yell at nothing.

Fox! his father crows back. Goddamn you, motherfucking fox!

Xxxii.

NOW

Gathered uncomfortably in the hospital waiting room they are an absurd mimicry of a sitcom family; one Nick might have been permitted to watch on a Sunday morning when his father was feeling particularly indulgent. The wife and husband, the unmarried hanger-on. The father, slowly dying, though he rages against it, comedic and pathetic in turn.

Nick has bundled himself into an overcoat and reads from a small paperback copy of Pu Songling, no larger than his palm, though it cannot save him now. Joshua lounges with his arm possessively wrapped around Emilia. He checks his watch at different intervals. Sometimes it is an hour, sometimes fifteen minutes. Death has embedded itself in every crevice of this place. It smells of it, like a slaughterhouse might.

Nick rubs his eyes and concentrates on the small text in front of him, printed on what appears to be flimsy cigarette paper. The ceiling lights are far too bright; everything outside of his immediate view appears shapeless and indistinct.

A doctor is walking toward them, a clipboard in hand. The doctors in this hospital all seem to be carrying clipboards and stethoscopes. Nick imagines a warehouse next door with clipboards, stethoscopes, records of the living and the dead piled to the ceiling.

Joshua Morrow? Nick Morrow?

Joshua rises from his seat. Emilia grips his sleeve, hesitantly, not unlike a child. He says, No, stay. I'll go with Nick. Get some rest.

In the white hospital sheets, his father lies suspended in time. Up close, Nick marvels at how aged Carlyle is, how unlike himself he looks. Frail as a stillborn calf, lifeless in the grass.

He does not open his eyes when they approach the edge of the bed, nor when the doctor shuffles his pieces of paper together and tells them that it appears to be a stroke, but luckily for Carlyle and unluckily for them, he will recover. Five to seven days in the hospital and they can take him home. Joshua discusses the finer points of poststroke recovery with the self-assurance of a man who knows absolutely nothing; Nick does not listen. Instead he gnaws on his knuckle, absent-minded. Like a horse scraping its teeth over a carrot, held in an outstretched hand.

The doctor leaves and shuts the door behind him.

After a moment, Nick says, Dad. Not really meaning it, wanting only to fill the silence.

Joshua shoots him a look. Don't wake him up, you idiot. He needs to rest. Didn't you hear what the doctor said?

Not really, Nick says.

Carlyle stirs. His breath quickens; he wheezes through his nose with the ferocity of a charging bull. His eyes are still clamped shut, as though he cannot bear to open them. Cannot look upon his two sons, the last of the Morrow dynasty. Both failures in their own way—half-formed men. They are all he has.

Go back to sleep, Dad. Joshua says. You should rest. With a stroke, and the cancer, you must be worn out.

Cancer, Carlyle mumbles. He opens one eye and closes it. His hands, as he gestures, tremble. What cancer?

Dad, Nick says, you said you had bone cancer.

Lie. All a lie.

Why did you lie to us?

Joshua says, Let him rest, Nick. This isn't an interrogation.

Coming almost as a whisper, a faint whistle of air through his throat: Get her out. No other way. My boys. Come back. Get out.

Don't worry about it, Dad, Joshua says.

Did it for you.

I know, says Joshua.

Nick is already out the door. Joshua quickly follows. As always the pursuer, swift-footed, splendid to look upon.

I can't believe this, Nick says, slightly too loud. He stops in the waiting room, where Emilia is reading from a women's magazine. The fucking liar. He'll never change. Why did I think he would change?

Nick, says Joshua.

We were both fooled. And now look. Look at us.

He's an old man. He's going senile. I'm sure there's an explanation.

You're always making excuses for him. Of course, you'll get most of it anyway. When he's dead. Soon enough now.

Joshua looks at him like he might kill him but has thought better of it. His arms rigid at his sides as he edges away while Nick leans up close, right in his face.

Emilia says, Go home, you two. Her tone is sweet and light as whipped cream, but there is poison there too. Just beneath the surface.

Joshua hisses, Take her back to Stag's Crossing. I'm staying here.

To do what?

To finish what you couldn't, Joshua says, and tosses him the keys.

Let's go, Nick says.

People are staring, Emilia whispers, as they walk side by side down the hallway. You really made a scene.

Has he always been like that?

Like what?

The glass doors slide open; his father's bloodred Cadillac is parked in the second row of the lot outside. After Joshua had gone into exile and Nick to college he had taken up a half-hearted hobby of collecting cars. One of many classic models, once loved and then discarded, that normally sit half-rusted and lifeless in some barn at Stag's Crossing. Commandeered for the sole purpose of driving to and from the hospital, it still steers well. It will take them where they need to go, a single destination.

Nick says, When you married him, was he this stubborn?

We met at an art museum. He asked for my number five times until I gave it to him. So yes.

Nick adjusts the rearview mirror. Do you still love him, then?

Absolutely, she says. And I know you didn't want him to marry me.

I didn't—

My husband tells me everything. Including why you left the wedding early.

He begins to drive. If that's the case, it seems strange that you would—

I wouldn't expect you to understand, she says. Sometimes I love him so much I think I might die from it. It's alarming. Other times, I find him insufferable.

So then what? You go and destroy his whole family?

I think your father is mostly to blame for the recent disastrous series of events, she says.

Or maybe it's just me.

What do you mean?

This. Us.

I can't blame you for making poor decisions in stressful times, she says. Not even mentioning her own culpability in the affair. And why would she? For women like Emilia, attraction is as natural as the weather. Emilia will always be exactly as beautiful as she is now, fixed in his mind, a loveliness that was given to her as her inheritance and has no logical end.

With a childhood like that, it's only normal to have some mixed feelings, she adds.

This again? You make it sound like a medieval torture chamber.

Why can't you admit that it was wrong for him to treat you that way?

Ahead he sees nothing except an endless stretch of road. Emilia in the passenger's seat, her eyes fixed on him. Like she is scrutinizing every aspect of him, carving him open and peering inside.

Because, he says, if I say it's wrong, then I'll have to admit to myself it was all for nothing.

You didn't deserve it.

I deserved it. I was a bad kid.

Oh, Nick, she says, sighing. You still don't understand, do you?

What is there to understand? The past is over. There's no going back. No matter what you say, it won't change anything. The regret—that's just weakness.

It's not a weakness to care about someone else, she says. When she touches his shoulder he recoils as though she has touched him with a branding iron. He sees a slight frown mar her face as she puts her hand back into her lap. Unused to the bitter sting of rejection.

Are you finished? he says.

With you? she says. Not at all.

He says, You know, he lied about his cancer. It was just a ploy to get Joshua to come back. To kick you out of the family.

I knew when you called that it was a lie.

How?

He'll die of something else, she says, and then is silent. The rest of the ride is filled with the insistent murmuring of locusts. Nick tapping the steering wheel with the fingers of his left hand in a nervous motion. They do not speak as he drives through the unlatched gate and up to the front of the house, walking with her across the patio covered in peeling paint, up the staircase and into the master bedroom, that soundless place of death's dominion, where like the cicadas perishing in droves they shed their skins and furiously thrill against each other. Nick knows that disaster is imminent but finds he can do nothing else except bask in the strange shadow Emilia casts over the bed, the shadow that moves when he is not looking at it. Afterward they lie apart, not touching. Emilia propped up on her right arm as she looks out the window with a pensive air. Barefoot she wears only her nightgown. Premonition raising gooseflesh in his skin as he remembers her cold gaze at the dinner table, how she had told his father how and when he would die, as though she meant it, as though her knowing came from someplace else beyond comprehension. In the dark bedroom he can see only the contours of Emilia's pellucid face which he senses some men have looked upon once and could never bring themselves to look away. Her breath warm and seductive in his ear as she whispers, What are you thinking about?

You, he says.

He is silent for a while. Recalling the events of the last few weeks, cloaked in febrile agony. The strange things he has noticed about her, imperfectly arranged into an unfinished portrait. Although he has fucked her he knows very little about her; she appears determined to make a mystery of herself. He wonders how she has aged twenty days in twenty years while he and his father have rotted from the inside out. How quickly his interest in her became an inescapable obsession. How he is the only one in his doomed, idiotic family to see that she merely inhabits the shape of a woman and knowing this he will be the only witness to the corrosive destruction she will wreak upon them.

He closes his eyes. There is still light out, enough light to see by though they have turned off the bedside lamp. Hiding in the semidarkness like they have committed a terrible crime.

We could leave, he says.

What?

We could just go. Together. You don't have to stay here. Neither of us do. There are cabs—there's a way back. The airport isn't that far.

Go to sleep, Nick. She gently runs her hand through his hair.

I don't understand, he says, almost like a child. He realizes with irritation how lost he seems. Some greater purpose unfolding before him and he cannot comprehend.

My work is not yet finished, Emilia says. You'll see.

He is tired all over, powerless against her. Watching her eyelashes flutter as he is dragged beneath the surface. The utter lightness of her body astonishing to behold. Her dark hair falling in looping cursive across the pillow, framing her face in the half-light. To conclude that a woman like this, so delicate and finely made, could have brought Joshua to heel is almost unthinkable. But she had married him, separated him from the herd with calculated finesse. And now here Nick lies, cut down by the same hand as his brother, the hand that now plays with his hair, combing through it with careful fingers. This small token of affection more painful than any beating he has ever endured.

Relaxing into the bed as she lightly presses his eyelids closed. The scent of her perfume overwhelming him. As he drifts he recalls the eerie and relentless dread he once felt upon seeing the crucifix in church, lacking all comprehension for what he has witnessed. The death of Christ. Emilia nude, eating at the kitchen table though it is not cow's liver that she feasts so hungrily upon, it is his own that he has cut out himself. His father, his brother turned grotesquely into deer and then hunted by their own dogs. Emilia watching on her splendid throne as a man Nick does not recognize walks on a cylinder of heated metal that burns his soles. He is crying and singing, crying out like an animal. While she watches she paints on a sheet of rice paper, hardly larger than her palm. A woman without a face, with nine furred tails. The low baying of the dogs, the buzzing of the horseflies that swarm him, growing louder and louder to an unrelenting drone that strikes him with a perfect and cultivated horror.

He dreams of Emilia taking his hand and walking with him to the edge of the weald that borders their property. Walking deep inside that dark place with only Emilia as his guide. Without a flashlight he is completely in darkness. Near a hidden place that smells of blood and death she stops by a hollow at the base of a tree and reaches inside. From within she retrieves a pelt of utmost beauty—carnelian in color, shining like a flame in her hands.

Now comes into view the doe he killed years ago. His

hand steady on the rifle. Joshua darting down the hillside. His father coming behind them with a killing look. Nick scrambles to follow, has his knife out before he even comes upon the doe lying gasping and weeping in the verdant grass. This time he cannot find a good angle for the cut so he grasps the doe by the ears and pulls it back to reveal the pale column of Henry's throat. A young man in his prime, utterly still. Ready for slaughter.

Nick looks at his knife. He has sharpened and polished it so much that he can see his cloudy reflection in the metal. Can see his father standing behind him, his arms crossed.

What're you waiting for? Carlyle says. Just as God must have spoken to Abraham before he made a burnt offering of his son, all he could fashion from his wretched progeny.

Nick points the tip of the knife downward and stabs once, twice. Henry's body spasming as Nick fists his hand in his hair and finds a better angle turning his knife so the sharpest edge meets the soft flesh below the chin—Henry at last attempting to speak, but it is a high-pitched whine, inhuman, and Nick pays it no heed. Like a butcher at his table of stone he is committed with purpose to his fatal work. No longer absorbed by the scent of fresh blood but the familiar aroma of Emilia's day-old perfume that now possesses no aroma but the air of nostalgia. A longing that can drive an image of Emilia into his mind as decisively as a stake through his eye.

Xxxiii.

THEN

He is alone in the house when Joshua calls. It has been hours since Carlyle finished his morning cigar and departed, leaving Nick with a half-eaten plate of biscuits and the last of the milk for breakfast. A note with his expected time of return and instructions to feed the dogs and take care of the house. With the reverence of an acolyte Nick carefully finishes his father's leftovers and stacks the dirty dishes in the sink for a later scrubbing. From the refrigerator he takes a parcel of bones and loose meat wrapped in butcher paper. It is too early for him to put on his boots and winter coat so he instead opens the kitchen window and throws each piece to the waiting dogs. Wincing to hear the crack of their teeth against the marrow. The eagerness of their feasting is foreign to him, a boy who has subsisted on scraps his entire life.

The telephone rings. It echoes strangely in the empty house—a whiny, rattling noise that makes Nick jump to hear it. He goes into his father's study and picks up the handset.

Hello, Dad? Joshua says.

It's Nick.

Oh. Hi Nick.

You can call back later. He should be back soon.

No, it's okay, says Joshua, in a way that suggests he does not really mean it. When have they ever talked amongst themselves, as brothers? Most of their childhood has been spent, like two bucks with locked antlers, in eternal strife. An endless rivalry that will not cease—not now, not thirty years from now when Joshua returns at last to Stag's Crossing with his lovely wife in tow and Nick will wonder at how perfect they seem, and how thoroughly he might destroy such a beautiful thing.

Okay then, Nick says. How's college?

Good. Got lots of classes.

What're you studying?

Not much at the moment. Getting the basics out of the way. Composition, math, literature. I live in a dorm with a bunch of other guys. My room's a lot smaller than at home.

So you're on your own, then.

Yup. I'm my own man.

That must be nice.

It's okay. A lot of responsibility. You'll see when you've got your own place.

What do you think you'll do once you graduate?

Not sure. Maybe more school. Maybe work at a bank for a little while. Then come home and apply my knowledge to our business.

You think it'll be that easy?

Why wouldn't it be?

Dad's just going to leave the whole thing to you?

Joshua's voice turns slightly acrid. The tone of a lecture, a sermon Nick has heard several times over the years. Come on, Nick. Don't be silly. You don't want it anyway. You'll be well taken care of—you can do whatever it is you want to do, without the responsibility of running the place. It's the better deal.

Nobody asked me what I want, Nick says.

See, this is why I can't hardly talk to you. I know Dad hasn't always been the easiest on you, but you've got to grow up and learn to live with it.

Is that what you've done?

Yes, Joshua says.

Nick scours his mind for what he might do with himself when he is as old as Joshua and ready to fly from the nest. What dilettantism he could engage in when his entire life has been dedicated to working at Stag's Crossing, observing quietly as his father lords over the farmhands and obsesses over the price of grain. Feeding the dogs and lingering in the shadow of his brother. On the rare occasion he is allowed to listen to whatever he likes on the radio he will listen to classical music, envisioning a world and a life so far from Stag's Crossing they might as well be fictional. The announcers speaking of names that suggest only the most exotic locales, seen through a rain-speckled window: Debussy, Prokofiev, Puccini. A small, hidden part of him is perhaps delighted by the elegance of literature, though some days his only material is fly fishing articles two years out of date that he has stuffed under his mattress for later. He has no consciousness of what an education outside of the one he has received at Stag's Crossing might do for him, or to him. Other than what Carlyle has warned him about, a transformation into the type of man who would disdain their thousand acres. At dinner parties he might say, I'm from Nebraska, and you? with the smug self-indulgence of a man who is *from* somewhere but no longer inhabits it, has no longer any need of that place called Stag's Crossing that his father so carefully constructed for his sons.

Nick hears the sound of the Ford pulling into the driveway, gravel beneath its tires. Carlyle comes in, his face pink with cold.

You're back early, Nick says.

Carlyle does not answer him. Seeing Nick standing in his study with the telephone in hand he says, Who is it?

Joshua.

He does not even take his boots and coat off before stomping past the foyer and yanking the phone from Nick's hand. Carlyle waves him off, dismissively.

Joshua! Carlyle says. My son, how are you?

They begin talking; what is uttered is not of interest. Nick does not eavesdrop on their conversation having long put aside the jealousy he feels when he sees his father addressing his brother in familiar and familial terms. Carlyle's affection for Joshua has no binding clauses, no prerequisites. It simply exists. It is Nick that has been burdened with the knowledge that he is forever the son who has stayed at his mother's bedside, clinging to her lifeless hand. The one who is left behind.

He sits at the kitchen table and reads his latest wrinkled copy of *Field & Stream.* An hour passes, then two. The distant murmuring of his father's voice fading into the background as he studies each sentence, each word before him. Concentrating so hard on the illustrations and the shape of the writing, sterile as it is, that he hardly perceives his father coming up behind him.

Doesn't look like you got much done today, he says.

Not much to do besides feed the dogs.

Carlyle nods and sits down next to him. Tapping his fingers on the table as he speaks, low and steady. Do you remember that neighbor girl?

Melissa Rasmussen?

No, the little one. Uglier.

Peggy?

Her father says she's missing. He was talking about it all over town. Even interrupted my poker game to ask me about it. Have you seen her?

Nick remembers greeting Peggy at the gate. The tattered fox pelt dangling in her hand. Skinned so inelegantly and amateurishly his father would have beaten him for ruining such a good piece of fur. A tremor of unease in the exchange; the sense that he was witnessing her commit some disastrous act, one whose consequences he could not foresee.

The doe in the forest. The ribbon in his hand.

Last I saw her was a while ago. She had some kind of

fox fur with her and was walking back to her house. Not much else to say. I sent her on her way.

Carlyle looks at him, then out the window. Scratching his face with his index finger as he thinks. And now we have a fox prowling our land. One that won't leave.

Maybe it's just a coincidence, Nick says. She could've run off with a boy maybe. She'll probably be back when she gets bored and runs out of money.

How can you be so sure? This is a dangerous place. I went down to the university in Lincoln and saw they were giving talks on the intelligence of animals. Saying they're smarter than you or I might think. Knew a man in Wyoming who was killed by a pack of wild dogs. Hunted him down like he was just another deer.

Then maybe we shouldn't have killed those pups, Nick says, quietly. Thinking of the hollow in the woods that he revisits in his nightmares, plunging his hand into the darkness and pulling it out covered in blood. The little foxes. The terrible things he has done, with his father's hand lying heavy on his shoulder.

Or maybe we should've done a better job and wiped them all out before they came back here to bother us, Carlyle says. He gets up from his chair and walks back to his study, where he goes when he does not want to be disturbed. To be alone with his paranoiac delights, his half-imagined specters and intruders that have never come to Stag's Crossing in all the years he has predicted them. They are alone in their thousand acres, so hopelessly vast that Stag's Crossing has taken on the timeless and unassailable quality of memory itself.

Xxxiv.

NOW

Who's Henry? Emilia asks.

If Nick was not awake yet he is now. The clock on the wall tells him it is nearly noon. He has slept so profoundly it was like death, and in his dream there was such a cacophony of visions that he can hardly fix his mind on any specific image. Henry's face, his nude body covered in inexplicable wounds. The deaths of his family and of himself. He is silent, ruminating on these tormented thoughts. The various failures of his life, returning as apparitions in his sleep.

He can feel the faint touch of steam emanating from the open bathroom door. The persistent drip of the shower that has only just stopped running. Emilia puts her glass of water on the nightstand and climbs into bed next to him. She is wearing a loose nightgown the color of nacre. It shimmers as she walks.

Who? he says. Willing his body to be completely still. His face to have no emotion at all.

Emilia smiles, very slowly, an expression he finds both charming and mildly terrifying. She leans in close and says, You talk in your sleep.

He's a boy I knew back in high school, he offers. Hoping it is enough to put her off the topic; already he can feel a slight alarm building in him at the very mention of excavating these numerous memories he has not touched in years. They gather dust in the museum of his mind, neglected exhibits of his failed attempts at intimacy, such a long and distinguished history preserved in painful, pristine marble. Nudes of men and women alike, equally miserable in their carved expressions.

But that's not all of it, is it?

He stares straight up at the ceiling. Has it really been so long since he has told anyone of his life in the wake of Henry, the before and after? He struggles to recall the exact outline of Henry's face, distorted by age and tender memory—he marvels at the swiftness of each decade that has passed, faster than he might have expected. He pushes himself up onto his elbows and leans against the headboard; Emilia shifts to put her head in his lap. She looks up at him expectantly. Her mouth slightly parted.

He gently strokes her neck. Her dark hair half covering her eyes like a veil. Thinking idly of how he could encircle her delicate throat with his fingers and crush it at any moment, though he would never do such a thing. Only considering it, every so often, an idle fantasy.

Henry and I had a short relationship, he says. I was fourteen and he would've been fifteen or sixteen, I suppose. He was the son of the family that owned the general store in town. That's all been torn down now, years ago. There's a mini-mart there instead.

And did you love him?

Maybe a little bit, he admits. But it wasn't the same for him. It was just—something fun, I suppose.

Have you spoken to him since?

No, I moved away, and he died years ago. A terrible accident with one of his sons. The family moved to Iowa after. Why are you so curious about this?

Her eyes move over his face. Like she is looking for something. Finally, she says, No reason. Thank you for sharing that with me.

What about you, then? Any great loves?

She laughs unexpectedly, the sound brilliant and effervescent as champagne. Not hardly, she says. But I'll tell you a story. You told me such a good one, so it's only fair.

Is it about love?

It depends on your interpretation. It's an old story my mother used to tell me.

My interest is certainly piqued.

She laughs again. Only you would say something like that.

Once there was a handsome and prideful ruler, Di Xin. He was a tyrant who enjoyed conquering. He eventually took a concubine from one of the many places he vanquished, a beautiful woman named Daji. Daji was so devastatingly beautiful, it was difficult to look at her directly. She was like the sun. But she had an evil soul. She seduced

Di Xin and convinced him to torture his subjects for her pleasure. Once she cut out a man's heart just to look at it. Eventually, Di Xin's subjects were so fed up with her behavior, they rebelled. His dynasty eventually collapsed.

What happened to Daji?

She was too beautiful to die. Instead, she vanished. Nobody knows what happened to her. She could only be killed in a special way. With a magical weapon.

That seems more than a little far-fetched. She's so beautiful, she can't be killed? When has that worked for anyone in real life?

Emilia rolls her eyes. You really have no imagination, she says. Daji is no ordinary woman. She is possessed by a thousand-year-old *huli jing.*

A what?

A *huli jing.* A nine-tailed fox with a woman's face. They are said to have magic powers. So the spirit possesses her, and kills her, taking over her original body.

And what do you make of that? Historical allegory?

She shrugs. Probably. My mother said it was only a cautionary tale. About falling in love with the wrong woman.

Wise advice. My mother never told me any stories like that. Before she died.

Not even fairy tales?

No. We didn't have time for them.

You must have really cared for her, though.

I don't really know about that. I was just a child.

Emilia opens her mouth as if to reply, then falls silent. Contemplating. With her right hand she runs her thumb over the grooved scars on her left hand, which Nick has never thought to examine up close before. The skin looks as though it has been torn and then healed over, with several deeper puncture wounds that have forever ruptured what once was smooth, pliant skin.

He looks at her, really looks at her. She seems to notice him looking and with the calculated slipperiness of an eel tries to escape him, but he grabs her by the shoulders and holds her still. She lifts her chin and looks up at him, first seductive in her mien but then Nick perceives something else entirely—a violent contempt, a yearning for a mythical past where she could transform her destiny with her own hands, bloodied as they are, and was not merely languishing in the shadow of her arcane power as she does now. He understands more clearly now that Emilia is Carlyle's reflection though his father would do everything possible to abjure her.

He thinks to himself of the possibilities. Had he shot the doe clean through the neck and not had to watch it die. Had they not started this torturous, doomed affair. Had his father not feuded with a vixen on their land, and everything that had spiraled from the moment his father shouted from the top floor of Stag's Crossing—*Goddamn you, motherfucking fox—You brought that bitch into this house—*

With aching tenderness he takes her left hand in his. Willing himself to see beyond her veil of incomprehensible beauty, which is forever delightful to the eye. Up close he notices that her hand bears three distinct scars, three puncture wounds laid in a pattern like a semicircle. Nick traces the arc with his finger. A shape that is strangely familiar to him.

Years ago, on a rainy afternoon—huddling with his brother over a wrinkled mail-order catalogue they had taken from their father's office and hidden in the Quonset. Page after glossy page of guns, bait, fishing lures. Then finally the section for fur traders. For sale: all manner of snares, fleshing knives, metal cages. Traps with steel jaws and serrated teeth arranged in a semicircle. Meant to hold the leg of an animal in its merciless grip. The big ones are for bears, Joshua had said. But these smaller ones, they're good for coyotes. Or foxes.

Emilia says, What is it?

The scar on her hand. The way she seems lovelier by the day, while the rest of them continue to age and wither. Even now he can see that she does not cast a reflection in the bedroom window, that her shadow seen out of the corner of his eye does not always hold its shape.

A nine-tailed fox with a woman's face. The little painting she gave him, so carefully folded into a cream envelope. A woman in a Chinese dress with nine beautiful tails. Turning, always turning toward him. Her face superimposed on the woman's face in his mind—a coy self-portrait.

You, he says, at last. It's you.

He practically shoves her off him. He is faster to the door than she is, though not by much. Pulling the door shut behind him he hears her nails scraping against the doorframe, her panicked cries—Nick! Nick!—before he slams the door into her hand and sends her retreating into the bedroom with a shriek of malevolent anger.

Half-undressed, he attempts to recall where he put the car keys. Yet as soon as he remembers that he set them on the kitchen counter, next to the stove, he feels his limbs slacken. With a slow-rising horror, he realizes he cannot stop himself as he stumbles forward onto the staircase that spirals downward to the ground floor of the house. Diving into an inelegant free fall, his arms flailing uselessly, unable to muster even the slightest movement.

He feels the impact of each stair like the decisive strike of a hammer against the skull of a cow. He lies at the bottom unmoving, thoroughly dazed. The double doors at the front of the house are closed, too late to bar entry to the most terrible of strangers—the woman in the shining dress at the top of the stairs who watches this scene unfold with distinct pleasure.

At last, Emilia descends. As she does so Nick summons all his strength and begins to crawl toward the foyer, leaving behind what is surely a bloody streak on the wooden floors that his father once forced him to polish for an entire afternoon. He feels one of his molars come loose. His mouth half-open as he lies on the floor gasping for air, like a fish that is slowly being gutted while it is still alive.

She kneels beside him and says, When your father's father was young, younger than you are now, there were shrines of me in Shandong. And they worshiped me there. But you'll never understand that, will you?

A trickle of blood comes out of his mouth. He tries not to choke on it.

Over twenty years, he says. Twenty years you've been in this family. Why now?

These things take time, she says. Di Xin wasn't seduced in a single day. And neither were you. I wanted to see if you would really do it. Leave all this behind. Leave your father behind. Just like Joshua did, for me. It wouldn't have spared you—but at least you would've died your own man.

He turns his head to look up at her face. She smiles down at him, almost beatific, but her eyes are shining with hatred. Nick can hardly perceive these pains—of utter betrayal, of his rapidly impending death—anymore. Much like the wound he was dealt by Henry he simply chooses not to acknowledge it. So deeply felt is his agony that it is completely sublimated, pulsating just beneath his skin.

Here they are: two boys tangled in the sand. Henry, standing on a shoal with his arms outstretched. Preparing to dive in. The water is dark and inviting. How far can he wade in, he wonders, as he feels Emilia taking hold of his wrist and dragging him into the kitchen. How deep can he submerge himself, never again to resurface.

XXXV.

THEN

Fresh as newly wept tears comes the morning snowfall. Cascading from the roof in torrents each pearlescent flake is glistering with sorrow. Nick cranks open his casement window and marvels at the hanging icicle that has formed there. Reaching out with his hand to grasp it. The ice clear and painful against his bare skin. He takes pleasure in this, a return to incisiveness, to ecstasy, to suffering.

Shutting the window at last he rummages in his room for his towel, which he wraps around himself like a mystic's shawl. Opening the door to creep out into the hallway in his loose striped boxers. The bathroom door left ajar. Fiendishly cold this Saturday he has for once risen before his father. Perhaps he has twenty precious minutes to himself, minutes he must now waste making himself presentable. His body and his soul perpetually in disarray, an impurity within him he cannot place but which has always been his disfigurement.

He grimaces as he lathers the thin bar of soap between his fingers. Disrobing he shirks from the evidence of his morning wood though there is no one there to see it. He has not laid eyes upon Henry for more than a week; he has not dreamed of him either. He turns the water shamelessly hot, then cold again. Taking care to wash his face, between his toes. Nick notices his brother's razor and tube of Brylcreem still lying on the bathroom countertop. Stag's Crossing will not give up its heir so easily—like the bones of the hounds buried in their pet cemetery his father has preserved these mementoes. Witnesses to the arrival and departure of their chosen son they molder beneath the dirty mirror, awaiting his glorious return.

Toweling himself off he thinks of Henry's hands upon him, opening him up with the skill of a sculptor. The same fatal artistry as the man who had taken the eyes from the buck at Stag's Crossing and kept them as a trophy. To the taxidermist the spoils. Now Nick, headless and bereft, is one of Henry's trophies. Mounted on a wall for all to see he is eternally marked by this. The earnest thrill of a first love, a first buck taken down in the woods by his own decisive shot.

As he leaves the bathroom he feels the door jamming. Tries it twice with his better throwing arm before realizing the snow must be weighing down the roof, must have fallen so thick and wet in the night that the whole house is sodden with it. Before Carlyle comes down for breakfast he knows he needs to clear the roof because Carlyle's expectation is that each morning he will awaken to a Stag's

Crossing as pristine as the one he envisioned before he even laid the foundation. Laid his hands upon his sons, growing underfoot with the ferocity of unruly ryegrass.

Nick dresses himself efficiently. Downstairs he finds the metal shovel, his coat. Swinging open the back door he feels a cold front coming through, chilling him through the thick goose down. He finds the ladder out back frozen in place near the green hose lying coiled silent as a garden snake. He ties the ladder down on both sides and climbs it. Upon reaching the roof he takes the shovel, his divine instrument, and begins to shave off the top layer of snow. Watches with satisfaction as it falls to the ground. Like a ritual executioner he slices; he carves. Moving across the roof with exquisite slowness.

Leaning against the chimney he sights the red streak in the snow out by the henhouse. From afar he can even see the blurry outline of the coop with its chicken wire torn, flapping uselessly in the bitter air.

He climbs down the ladder and kicks the last of the snow off the shovel. Going back inside he hangs up the shovel. His father has just come down the stairs and is making himself breakfast. Still wearing his bathrobe and indoor slippers. Carlyle has not yet stoked the fireplace and has even opened one of the windows in the dining room despite the fiendish weather. Too early for warmth; Nick will not receive succor from his father of all men.

Carlyle says, Good morning. Lying unwrapped on the countertop are raw sausages from the butcher. Freshly delivered from Wahoo.

Morning, Dad.

Did you clear the roof?

I'm finished.

Good. Come and sit.

Can't, Nick says.

You seem in a hurry.

I need the car.

What for?

McFarlane's. Traps finally came in.

Putting an end to this nonsense once and for all, are you?

Yes.

How many chickens we got left? Two? Three?

At least five, Nick says.

Can't say you'd make much of a farmer, Carlyle says. Letting a fox run the place like this.

Can I have the car or not?

Carlyle looks over his shoulder at him and shrugs. Take it. Run it into a ditch for all I care.

Thanks, Nick says.

His father says nothing; watches the pork fat sizzle in the oil. Turning the sausages over with a pair of tongs. He does not offer his son anything to eat having not made food for Nick since he was a child.

The double doors are unlocked; they would swing open if the wind was high. Through the frosted glass Nick sees the Ford parked out front. The windshield lovingly wiped clean of ice and debris. The chassis misshapen in places, having borne more than once the burden of Carlyle's erratic charioteering. The scratches on its exterior, the dents in the bumper, all indications of a particular fondness, a manner of affection sparing none from its savage intensity. The things of Carlyle's—that which he owns, which he has made manifest—his dogs, his sons, all are warped by years spent in his orbit. The hounds with their ears perked just so, their muzzles flecked with the gore of rabbits. One frolicking in the snow opens his jaws to yawn, licks his face clean. His aristocratic sneer revealing gums stained red as cranberries, the color richly vulgar, the aroma of blood in the air unmistakable.

Nick like one of his father's dogs will be sapling-thin when he is fully grown. His sharpness tempered only by the anguish of adulthood, the realization that a childhood spent lying at the bottom of the staircase where he is knocked down by his own brother, his nose smeared with blood, has all been for nothing. His suffering rendered meaningless by the voice of his father tinny and distorted through the phone. Ordering him back to Stag's Crossing where history must repeat until there is no more history left.

With the cold air knifelike against his face he shuffles over to the car and clambers quickly inside. Turning the heater on he rubs his gloved hands together and grabs the steering wheel. In his rearview mirror he sees his father calling the greyhounds into the house, throwing them the leftover sausages. Reaching down to lightly rub their ears as they enter the house one by one, stepping delicately inside. An unbearable gentleness to his touch.

Nick carefully guides the Ford through the snow, down the driveway where the dead weeds are snarled among the crushed limestone. Passing the severed buck's head he drives too fast like he is fleeing his own shadow. Then west onto the main road, the radio playing loudly, too loudly, shutting out the insistent thrumming in his skull.

He is perspiring slightly though he has kept the heater just warm enough to keep himself from getting frostbite. Every part of him is ill at ease, pulled apart in silent agony. His brother's hand-me-down coat now too tight in the shoulders, his gloves rubbing uncomfortably against his callused palms. An exasperating, nameless pain tearing its way up his spine, gouging into his eye sockets.

Arriving in town he parks outside the dressmaker's shop. The three blocks to McFarlane's seem to take no time at all, despite the cutting wind, the air so heavy and frigid it foretells a snowstorm. He walks with purpose, his arms grabbing at the flapping hem of his jacket. By the time he reaches the store the wind has turned ravenous. Whipped in all directions the snow sticks to every surface, lodging itself in the crevices of the street, dashing itself uselessly against the glass windowfronts.

Outside the store stands a boy of around fifteen. Up close Nick can see the softness of his fragile features, the long eyelashes, an unspoken radiance that appears not unlike his brother's once did. At this age Joshua exulted in his handsomeness, was set alight by it. The boy outside McFarlane's is no different and when he looks at Nick his stare is almost violently arresting. He is not the boy on the beach but he must be his likeness, one of Henry's naïve gallants well-met by the riverside, shedding his clothes as easily as a dandelion might shed its delicate petals. In the summer heat they writhe together, the boy's upturned mouth a promise, an evocation.

Looking for Henry? he says. A touch of satisfaction in his voice.

Nick wills his chattering teeth to be still, his tone unflinching. Got a fox situation, he says. Eating all our hens.

Tricky things, foxes.

You bet, he says, and goes inside.

Xxxvi.

NOW

The course of an affair runs swift and wild. And how swift, how wildly off course this one has gone. When Nick opens his eyes it is early afternoon. In his dreamless agony he hardly recognized the turning of the moon on its celestial hinge nor the bright corona of dawn rising in the east, illuminating the empty house. Against his cheek he feels the familiar and evenly polished surface of the dinner table. The southern-facing window of the house slowly coming into focus. The fields and the trees beyond it also, seeming more menacing with each day he has spent at Stag's Crossing. Ruminating upon the slow decay of his memories.

Like a marionette bereft of wires he struggles to right himself, closing and opening his hands in a faint grasping motion until he can get his elbows underneath him. From the kitchen comes the unmistakable hiss of the gas stove. The smell of meat, tenderly seared, the faint humming that seems to come from far away.

His mouth is dry; he is feverish, mildly delusional. Running his tongue over his teeth he finds none to be missing. He examines his extremities, which are all surprisingly intact. No blood, no bruises. Someone has dressed him and even combed his hair. The events of the last few hours return to his mind slowly, in fragments. Emilia's expressions lingering—desire, shock, anticipation. The eager spark in her eyes as she watched him crawling pathetically before her, clawing his way across the floorboards.

Nick reaches back into his memory and tries to understand how these events came to pass. Emilia in the shower, smiling as she lets down her curtain of wet hair. Emilia lazily tapping her finger against the dinner table, beckoning to him. All things between them unspoken. Beneath this haze of sensual entanglement he finds something far darker, far more dangerous than love. Obsession. Self-destruction. A calamitous desire for a woman his brother has long possessed and Nick can never have.

A strange weariness overcomes him when he tries to stand. Almost immediately he sinks back into the chair, his head cradled in his hands. Racked by a splintering pain that emanates from somewhere just above his left eye.

Emilia approaches. She carries a white plate and a glass of water. Bacon, eggs, a fork and a steak knife. These items are placed carefully in front of him, like an offering. He pushes them away with trembling fingers. Unable to look her in the eye.

At least drink something, she says. Looking back over her shoulder at the skillet still on the stove.

No, he says.

Okay. Have it your way.

She sits down next to him. He is repulsed by this. In trying to pull away, he finds his arms are useless to him.

Your father and brother will be here soon.

How do you know?

I just do, she says. Casually reaching toward him to run her index finger over his exposed wrist. His open palm. A studious look on her face, like she is reading his future from the grooves of his skin.

No lasting injuries, she says. You didn't even thank me for fixing you. You were pretty beat up after falling down the stairs.

You were the one who pushed me.

Oh, Nick. You're so funny. How could I possibly push you?

He struggles to form the words. You made my dad have a stroke. You pushed me down the stairs. Who knows what else you're capable of.

She smiles at him. Do you know how crazy you sound right now?

I'll tell Joshua. I'll tell everyone what you've done.

She leans in very close to him and says, Di Xin tried that too. Go ahead. I think you'll find I'm *very* persuasive.

With boyhood clarity he hears the creaking of the gate, the gravel crackling upon the approach of a vehicle. Voices, men's voices. His father and his brother, returning at last. Emilia turns her head to look toward the front of the house where any moment now the doors will open and when they do she will rise to greet them, husband and father-in-law, boundless in her radiance, the splendor of her destruction.

Joshua comes in first. Then after him—Carlyle, trembling and frail. Struggling to walk even with a metal cane he grips Joshua's elbow like a drowning man. Not a triumphal procession but a funeral march.

You're early.

Look, he insisted on coming back, Joshua says. I know he was supposed to stay for a few days, but he wanted to come home.

Carlyle grunts his approval but says nothing. Swaying slightly, his feet unsteady beneath him.

Emilia ushers them forward into the dining room and pulls out a chair for Carlyle at the head of the table. A chair for Joshua, at the right hand of his father. Nick at the other end of the table lets out a long groan, rubbing his forehead with sweaty and pallid fingers.

What's wrong with him?

Nick's not feeling well.

That's a shame, Joshua says. Maybe it's the flu. Hardly turning his gaze away from his father, who half slumbers in his chair. Carlyle's skin drawn tight over his bones is so thin and translucent it resembles rice paper. Wrinkled and distended he is frail as an infant.

Emilia, can you go upstairs and get some Tylenol for Dad? It should be in the medicine cabinet.

Of course, she says.

Nick watches her as she leaves the room. Feeling the

tendrils of his paralysis loosening slightly as she vanishes from his presence. Listening to her walk up the stairs as he reaches toward the knife on the table. Joshua's back is turned; he attends to Carlyle, who is mumbling something too soft to hear. Nick grips the knife with his fingers and slowly, very slowly, coaxes it into his sleeve. Almost cutting himself on the tip he conceals it successfully just as Emilia returns, proffering a little red tablet in her outstretched hand. Joshua carefully feeds it to his father. Gentle as a mother bird with her children.

At the back door several of the dogs have crowded, as if to watch the afternoon's proceedings. Some of them now beginning to whine and scratch at the screen door.

Joshua says, We should let some of them in. They must be hungry.

Oh, don't, Emilia says, already walking to the back door. I'll handle it.

Nick says, Joshua. His voice quiet, barely audible over the huffing of the dogs, the tremulous cry of the summer cicadas that circle outside.

What?

We need to leave, he says.

Why?

Joshua, you have to believe me. Emilia isn't what she seems—

I don't want to hear about it, Joshua interrupts. His face rigid with anger. I'm just here to take care of Dad. I don't care to hear whatever lies you're making up about my wife. All this time, you've been conspiring against me, because you wanted Stag's Crossing for yourself—

I don't care about Stag's Crossing. Nobody except our

family cares about Stag's Crossing. It's a thousand acres in the middle of nowhere. Have you ever wondered why she looks the same as she did twenty years ago? Have you ever seen her in front of a mirror?

What does that have to do with anything? Joshua says. Beneath his bristling anger lies a fundamental ignorance—men like Joshua are not expected to understand things. No deeper knowledge is required of them to move through the world as though everything they touch might one day be their possession.

I think I've figured it out. Finally. He is almost manic now, explaining this to his brother. Threatening to vibrate out of his own skin. The grand mystery of Emilia. Don't you remember, right before you went off to college, a fox came here? Dad asked me to kill it, but I didn't, and he took me into the woods and he made me—

The dogs have started barking now, cacophonous and uncontrollable. He hears Emilia saying, Quiet, before they all fall silent in unison. A few of them slinking away, their ears drawn back, defeated.

Nick sees his father's eyes half-open as Emilia returns. Though Carlyle's speech is halting and disjointed the tongue remains sharp as ever.

Why is she still here.

Dad, Joshua says. Let's talk about this later.

We should go, Nick says, although no one hears him. No one cares to hear him. Joshua and Carlyle are both turned toward Emilia, reappearing in the doorway of the dining room.

Don't worry, Carlyle, she says. You'll be rid of me soon enough.

Joshua says, He doesn't mean it.

Nick says, Oh, he means it.

What're you going to do? Carlyle rasps. His speech slurred, uneven, but the meaning is clear. Run off with his brother?

You can't be serious, Joshua says.

You should see the way he looks at her, if you weren't blind—

Is this true? Joshua says. He rounds on Nick, his hands already balled into fists. Ready for a fight.

Joshua, I— he begins, before Joshua hits him. Forceful and sudden as a thunderclap. He feels part of his nose crushed beneath the blow. Blood pouring from his left nostril as he looks up at his brother who readies himself for a second strike.

Fuck, Nick says. His head pounding; his vision blurring.

The cicadas outside have commenced their afternoon sinfonietta. Rising to an anxious crescendo the scraping of their wings strident and percussive they fill the southern part of the house with relentless noise.

That's enough, Emilia says.

Nick watches feverishly as she makes a gesture with her right hand and stops Joshua mid-swing. The born pugilist halted by some unknown power. He struggles to move, struggles to speak. The muscles of his arm twitching furiously.

Joshua says, Emilia, what are you—

I've waited so long for this, she says.

Joshua is frozen where he stands. Nick sees the twitching of his fingers, his eyebrows. A small panic flickering in his eyes as Emilia comes toward him and reaches up to brush a strand of golden hair from his forehead. Then she takes his head in both of her hands and wrenches it free.

Thin strands of bloody flesh dangle from Joshua's neck. It is a clean cut like the paintings Nick has seen of guillotined men. The lips twitching and spasming as if to form speech. The face still so lifelike and full of vigor that he thinks it might open its eyes and speak to him again, in a voice familiar and primordial. Known to him always.

Xxxvii.

THEN

When he comes in Linda is cleaning the counter with a dirty cloth that smells pungently of Lysol. The walls are lined with racks of winter hunting gear, ice fishing implements. Last summer Nick came here and bought his beautiful split-cane fly rod that still resides in his closet, tended to as carefully as the most precious of stringed instruments. With the exactitude of a luthier he polishes the wood with a soft cloth and oils the cassette reel. He so rarely owns things of his own. Long used to a life of Joshua's castoffs he is like a sad facsimile of his father and brother—made in their image but irrevocably set apart.

Linda's long brown hair falls in her face as she cleans; she brushes it back behind her ear with one hand. At the sound of the door chime she looks up at him and says, Oh, hi Nick.

Hey Linda, he says. He puts his hands in his pockets, almost sheepish. I'm looking for Henry.

He's gone out, she says, too quickly. I can give you the trap if you want. Just got here this morning in fact. She gestures to a package wrapped in twine and brown paper on the shelf behind the counter. Labeled in achingly precise handwriting that is not Linda's—*Nick Morrow.*

Henry told me he'd show me how to set it up, he says.

I told you, he's not here.

Nick looks over Linda's shoulder at the entrance to the back room, which is closed. The telltale shadow that creeps out from beneath the door.

Why doesn't he want to see me? he says. Wincing at the sound of his own voice, shrill and pathetic.

Linda acts as though she has not heard him, as though he might be some madman shouting at the wind. There are instructions from the manufacturer inside, she says, placing the package on the counter. If you run into any problems you should call them.

After some time he settles on, Thanks. He takes the package from her, the contents tightly bound with twine. Carrying it out to the Ford he sees that the boy idling by the front of the shop has disappeared, leaving only his tracks in the snow. Leading round the back of McFarlane's, where the boy's suitor waits beneath the shaded eaves of the store. His face obscured in shadow. And there, at last, Henry can no longer conceal a fragrant and richly wrought affection. The reckless savor of sea salt in the air. The boy in the water, the boy on the beach, writhing like a hooked fish, gutless, the image of him consuming Nick's mind with the fervor of quicksand. Scattered all around him are the beach-pebbles, the vespertine moonlight. The litanies of the breaking waves that say, This is not for you.

To this Nick does not have to listen. He already knows; he has known his entire life what it is like to go without.

He drops his package in the passenger's seat of the truck and closes the door behind him. The windshield reflects his face back to him, almost mocking, and in it he sees a glimpse of the man he will become: knowing passion but not its true name, repeating forever the indiscretions of his childhood. By forty-three there will be an impressive catalogue of men, and women besides—but the memory of Henry will remain forever buried inside him, like a seed that has failed to sprout.

He takes his right glove off with his teeth and drops it in his lap. Holding the car keys in his hand so tightly he can feel the metal warming between his fingers. Without thinking he turns the key over and pushes it into his palm. Willing himself to be still as the sharpest point digs into his skin, cutting open his hand. Willing it to leave a scar, or else to remain forever open, festering with disease until it finally kills him as he so often desires.

After a little while he finds the feeling has left him. He is empty of it, like a broken jug. When he opens his hand the key is speckled with blood. He hastily wipes his hand on his jeans. The wetness of the stain seeping through the fabric, settling against his thigh. He takes an old car rag out of the glove box and wraps up his hand before beginning the drive home. Slowly he guides the Ford past the edge of town. Down the long road he has traversed before, sitting next to his father in perfect silence. So familiar he will find it again nearly thirty years later with neither map nor compass, only the starlight of dreams to guide him.

What his Southerner father considered mere unrelenting flatland he knows with an intimacy granted only to the progeny of this chthonic birthplace. Each hillock and riverbank catalogued precisely in his mind. On these never-ending drives with Carlyle he would look out the window and allow his mind to depart from his body with practiced ease. As efficiently as he had once seen his mother use her sewing scissors to trim an errant thread from her embroidery. He must have been exceptionally young then, no older than five years of age, to remember his mother still alive. Or perhaps this memory was one that Joshua had relayed to him and he had simply imagined it for himself. Always taking what was not his, the indefatigable magpie of his childhood.

Easing the Ford into a right turn he finds himself just down the road from Stag's Crossing. The blood in his palm drying to a dark maroon. Pulling up alongside the edge of the farm he sees his father has left the gate open for him. At the end of the driveway he notices Carlyle pulling weeds without his gloves on.

Nick rolls down the window. Dad, he says, where are your gloves?

You took my good pair, Carlyle says. I just had a couple of old ones and one of em tore. Not worth it to fix.

Nick parks and gets out. With both his gloves in his left hand he goes up to his father and offers them. C'mon, Dad, he says. Don't want you to get frostbite.

You keep them, he says. I'm used to it. He sees the rag tied over Nick's palm, the mottled bloodstain. You get into a fight while you were out?

Nick puts the gloves back on. No, he says. I slipped and cut myself on some ice.

Well, be more careful, Carlyle says.

Okay, Dad.

I mean it.

Nick nods, very slowly. He is somehow conscious that his hand hurts, though when he injured himself he barely felt it. Just as he barely felt it when Henry dropped him off without so much as a goodbye. As he imagines the fish might barely feel it upon seizing the lure in its mouth. Only a mild surprise, a sharp pinch, before being reeled ashore.

Carlyle tosses a handful of lifeless weeds aside and marches to the truck. Opening the passenger-side door he picks up the package and snaps apart the twine. Peeling the wrapping from the items inside like the layers of an onion he reveals a metal trap with a sleekly menacing jaw and two small glass bottles inside.

Did good, he says, mostly to himself. Trap, bait, and lure. Could use some urine but this'll do fine.

Nick nods again, hoping to convey that he understands his father though he barely does even on the best days.

Your friend Henry's a smart boy.

He's not my friend.

You get into it over some girl?

For lack of anything better to say, Nick responds, Yeah.

Well that'll happen. Just don't come crying to me about it.

Sure, Dad.

Carlyle gestures behind him, vaguely indicating the Quonset. Go in there and get me the hand auger, a trowel, and a stake. We're gonna set this up right outside the coop. Meet me there.

Nick walks past his father and loops around the house. Out back he sees the coop with the chicken wire all torn up. A fresh humiliation every day. Once the fox has eaten every chicken in the coop he half thinks he will discover it sneaking into the house, raiding the meat freezer, perching in Carlyle's bed and licking its paws clean with unsubtle smugness.

Opening the door of the Quonset he fumbles for the chain that hangs to his left before switching on the light. The uncovered bulb swings overhead in a hypnotic, circular motion. Hallowed is this place of slaughter, where he and Joshua would hang deer from the ceiling and process the carcasses, cut the flesh from the hides. Joshua perfect and gleaming in his boyhood verve. The killing of animals their only shared language, the language of their youth.

His father's shelves are stuffed with all manner of dangerous things—long-toothed tree saws; axes; the occasional hunting knife, sharp as thorn, gleaming bitterly. He finds a hand auger leaning against a workbench and tucks it under his arm. The metal body shaped like a question mark. He picks up a trowel peeking out from behind a few shovels arranged carelessly in a corner. Buried beneath a dozen other knickknacks are several eighteen-inch rebar stakes; he takes one and goes back outside. Closing the doors behind him, shutting the image of his childhood inside.

His father leans against the coop with his arms crossed. When Nick comes up to him with the items Carlyle looks at him with something like delight in his eyes.

Got everything?

Yep.

Watch carefully, Carlyle says, taking the items from Nick and setting them carefully onto the top of the coop. Back in South Carolina we used to hunt foxes on horseback with dogs.

That sounds fun, Nick says, though it does not sound fun at all.

Carlyle nods, clearly pleased. He squats in the snow and begins to hack at the dirt with his trowel.

Hard as hell, Nick says.

That's the winter for you, Carlyle says. At last he gains some purchase in the soil and soon chunks of dirt are flying everywhere as he digs a hole right in front of the torn spot in the chicken wire. Picking up the trap he fiddles with it until the jaws are wide open and it lies flat inside the hole. He takes the hand auger out and drills a hole into the ground with alarming swiftness then threads the rebar through the trap chain and plunges it into the hole he has made. Bait and lure in hand he adds, Don't put these directly onto the trap. Put em in the back of the hole so the animal comes right up looking for prey. He deposits a small amount of bait and lure into the hole just behind the trap. Finally he uses his trowel to break up some of the dirt into fine pieces. Carefully scattering it over the wide-open jaws, the pan, filling in the trap bed. When he is finished Nick can barely see the metal glinting beneath the dirt so skillfully his father has disguised it.

With any luck it'll snow tonight and you won't even be able to tell we dug here, Carlyle says.

What if the fox never comes back?

Carlyle shrugs. It'll be here. Just like you and me.

They walk back to the house together. For once his father does not force him to trail behind. Inside Carlyle puts his tools in the pockets of his coat and hangs it up. Leaning the auger against the wall the same place he will lean his cane in thirty years' time. Nick takes off his jacket and boots as well. With Carlyle's back turned and briefly distracted Nick sneaks his gloves back into his father's coat pocket.

After dinner I'll take everything back to the Quonset so you don't have to.

Don't bother. Let me get a look at your hand, Carlyle says.

They go into the kitchen and Nick unwraps the rag. The blood has dried in streaks across his palm. His father grasps his arm and puts it under a stream of hot water from the faucet and begins rubbing at it with a bar of soap. He presses the bar into Nick's hand and says, Keep going til it's clean. Don't want it to get infected.

While his father rummages in the cupboards for his tin of bandages Nick scrubs the wound without any real conviction. Thinking idly of killing himself as he sometimes does when the afternoon light is unbearable to witness as it almost always is.

Found it, Carlyle says. He reaches up to the highest shelf and retrieves a tin of bandages. Nick finishes rinsing his hand and wipes it on a nearby towel.

Open your palm, Carlyle says.

Nick obeys. His father presses the Band-Aid onto his hand. Smoothing it over with his callused fingers. His touch forceful yet nurturing.

Good as new, Nick says.

Reminds me of that book your mother would read to you when you were little. *Doctor Dan the Bandage Man.* Course I thought it was stupid. If it had been me I would've raised you on something with a little more meat to it. A little more blood.

He looks away from Nick, still holding on to his wrist. It was real hard when she died. Getting up the next morning was like agony. But I had to take care of you two, had to take care of my boys. After a while it faded. Wasn't so bad. You've got all that's left of her. Her hair and her eyes.

After a moment he lets go and moves to sit in the large recliner near the window. One of the dogs coming up to him, resting its head in his lap. Carlyle picks up one of his many books stacked on the windowsill and begins thumbing through it.

Nick goes and sits in the love seat opposite his father. His boldness evades him, breaks free like a front-running hound from the pack. Once his father let him tumble with the dogs in the wide-open stretch of land between the fields and the house and when he came back to the house muddied with a manic glint in his eye his father squeezed his shoulder and Nick knew the words before they even took shape in his mouth, before he formed them so painstakingly with a half-paralyzed tongue: I love you.

I love you too, Carlyle says, without looking up from the page. He expresses it with an envious matter-of-factness, as though he has no idea that Nick will receive this utterance like an edict. If Stag's Crossing were to burn entirely to the ground, its foundations collapsing in a charred wreck, Nick would still carry this knowledge within him—that his father loved him once, in his own way, even if only for a single moment. It would have to be enough.

Xxxviii.

NOW

What remains of Joshua crumples onto the floor. Spilling its viscera all over the tile. The dining room at Stag's Crossing taking on the unmistakably inelegant air of an abattoir. Never has Stag's Crossing entertained any number of steers. Now it is the men of the house who must come and be broken in, be beaten down into their undignified deaths.

Carlyle groans. Joshua, he wheezes. Joshua—my son—

With pointed disgust, Emilia discards the rest of him, tossing the head to the ground where it rolls under the table and rests at Nick's feet. Bloodying his shoes. Nick wills himself to move his knees, his legs. Finding that he can raise his arms just a little, can push himself from his chair ever so slightly.

What are you doing to my family? Carlyle says. His voice rendered pathetic by the horrific scene before him.

Only what is deserved, she says. Advancing on Carlyle she turns her back to Nick for a brief moment. Her face is bright with pleasure, delighting in her cruelties. Without the need to hide it any longer he can see that they are as succulent to her as a rich meal.

Nick takes the knife from his sleeve and stabs her in the shoulder. Straight through her white blouse, her soft and pliant body. Almost to the hilt. A wound forms, a strange gaping thing that oozes blood; yet she does not even flinch.

When she turns to look at him with a feigned expression of shock he understands now, truly, the contemptuous brilliance that she must have artfully concealed from him as Emilia the imitationist, Emilia with the shadow that writhes, that twists and shape-changes before his very eyes. Di Xin must have tried this too, and what came of it? He realizes now that she is too beautiful to be killed, as the sun falls upon her thick hair, her dark and pulsing wound.

Nick, she says. Her voice half-scolding, half-seductive. You should know better than that. Heroism is a young man's game.

Before he can reply she has pulled the knife from her body and holding it downward at an angle just as his brother taught him to mercy kill a fish that he once caught and left dying on the shore of Lake McConaughy she puts her arm into it, puts her entire body into the downward motion that pierces his chest as precisely as a lepidopterist pins a dying butterfly to a mounting board. The blade embedded so deeply he can hardly dislodge it. If he cries out in pain he does not hear it; if his father says anything he does not hear it. He watches the bloodstain slowly bloom across his shirt, shading it a deep red.

Goddamn, he says.

He falls to his knees, waiting for Emilia to strike him dead. To pluck out his eyes, or his intestines, or to feast on his heart. Far beyond Stag's Crossing, the thousand acres that are his father's demesne, Nick hears the caterwaul of the sea wind. The rush and roar of the waves. In the sand there are two figures: the recollection of himself as a boy and Henry, aged, in his forties. As he would be now.

How much could he be wounded by one person? To die ignominiously, here, in the kitchen of Stag's Crossing could hardly hurt him more than the memory of the tender intimacy they might have shared, had they been allowed to grow old together. Had they had more time, and had Nick not once phoned home out of nostalgia, only for his father to tell him: Remember that McFarlane boy? Died just last year. Only a few years since he got married, left her with two kids. Such a shame.

Of what?

Was out teaching one of his sons how to hunt. The boy shot him. An accident.

That's sad.

I know. I remembered he went to your school. You were friends.

We weren't close.

Mm-hmm, Carlyle said, quickly moving to another topic. Leaving Nick standing in his living room, unable to say anything. He would retreat to his bedroom afterward to cry, alone, for someone he had not spoken to in years. For a loss that was not his to lose in the first place.

He can smell Emilia's perfume so near she stands to him. So often he has imagined his own death that he feels relief in this waiting. Knowing that any moment Emilia might destroy him as she has so desired upon setting foot into the house for the first time.

Instead he watches Emilia go into the kitchen. Leaving him there on his hands and knees next to his brother's corpse, already attracting flies. Joshua's severed head has rolled several feet away. Its eyes still open, its mouth still agape.

She turns on the gas stove. The house completely silent except for the wind striking the patio, rattling the shades. The flame of the stove hissing violently as it alights. His father moaning where he is slumped in his chair, like a skeleton with the skin pulled over him tight as hide on a tanning rack.

Emilia pulls out the silverware drawer and tosses its contents onto the floor. It shatters into pieces. The wood softened by age. Nick watches as his mother's wedding cutlery is scattered across the tile, her precious silverware that he would polish by hand once a month. Taking from this collection a wooden splinter Emilia places it into the flame of the stove and waits for it to catch fire.

In seconds the splinter is engulfed in flame before she uses it to light the cabinets on fire. Before long the southeastern section of the house smells of embers, smoke, and ash. Gray-and-black clouds pouring from the window, from every possible orifice of Stag's Crossing. Nick can hardly see what lies right in front of him. Can only witness Emilia, unperturbed, surveying this ghastly tableau.

Goodbye, Nicholas, she says, before walking away.

The knife lodged in his chest seems heavier by the moment. He thinks of lying down and dying there. Burning to death as Stag's Crossing falls into ruins around him.

He can hear his father muttering to himself, a muttering that becomes louder and more frenzied as the tendrils of flame threaten to overcome him. From behind him he hears Carlyle: Look at me, boy! Look— And turning his head he catches sight of Carlyle slowly burning to death, his flesh bubbling and roasting like rendered fat on a fresh cut of venison. Nothing can reduce the sickening pleasure that fills him to hear Carlyle now, helpless and impotent, shouting for him and not Joshua who lies at their feet as useless as a dead dog; instead he calls for his second son, his only son, and Nick turns away from him and begins to crawl toward the front doors of the house.

The fire consumes much of the southern wing of Stag's Crossing before it turns its attention to the staircase, engorged and aflame. The second floor of the house burns as easily. It will be some time before the fire station is called and many more hours before any police arrive.

He reaches the doorway and throws open the double doors. Half falling down the white steps of the patio before he reaches the gravel driveway. The bed of soft green clover where many a greyhound has sunned itself on an afternoon such as this. In the driveway he stands, a witness and accomplice in this destruction. Had he not seen Emilia at the wedding and been so enchanted by her—had he stayed away—had he not allowed his father to invite her back to Stag's Crossing which now collapses before him, folding in on itself like a piece of blackened origami. Having saved himself instead of dying with dignity he knows what comes after will be inglorious. He should have died with his father; he should have hung himself in the Quonset as he so often fantasized as a child, before all this came to pass.

Pressing his hands to his chest to stop the bleeding—the bitch missed his heart and went through his lung instead—he walks down to the gate where he knows he will find no hope of rescue or salvation. Finding Emilia standing at the edge of the path instead. She leans casually against the gate. Her loose skirt swaying in the breeze. A smile gracing her pert mouth.

What is this? he says.

Justice, she says.

This isn't justice.

My vindication, then, she says.

Xxxix.

THEN

His father bids him goodbye that morning and tells him, Be good. The white Ford idling in front of the open gate covered in snow. That night it had fallen in sheets over the darkened house, the thousand acres surrounding it. His father no longer goes to church on Sundays; he goes into town instead, leaving Nick to his own errant devices.

First he makes himself some food, misshapen sausages from yesterday that sear deliciously on the stove. Then he reads the newspaper like a big man in his father's armchair. None of the words make much sense to him—premonitions of violence in vague locales overseas, complex economic analyses that have little to do with life at Stag's Crossing. He will discover the pleasure of sentences and paragraphs only later, at college, left to wander through the library shelves that appear to stretch endlessly into the horizon. The words on the page arranging themselves into a hypnotic spiral.

Having grown bored of this playing at his father, always Joshua's preferred game, Nick puts on his snow boots and goes outside. Determined to survey Stag's Crossing, as he has done many times before. Every inch of it his father's holy demesne. He starts at the Quonset, traipses inside and clears away the cobwebs beneath the workbench. On the wall his father has displayed his killing tools: hammers, an axe, a saw that might cut through bone. Here they have hung many stags from the rafters and butchered them, slitting open their bellies with practiced ease. Joshua with his even hand, wiping it across his brow, bloodying his fine golden hair.

Above this hangs his father's collection of hunting rifles. Carlyle keeps a few in the house for protection, but these have a singular purpose—the hares that startle from their burrows, chased by a pack of frenzied greyhounds, or else an ill-fated buck that might stare proudly at its own death. Nick knows which one is his and takes it from the wall. The walnut of the stock scratched and weathered by the generations. Carrying it with the assuredness of a young man who has nothing to entertain him except perhaps shooting at the squirrels that gather in the trees. A perfect and aimless winter afternoon.

He takes the westward route, loping round the side of the house to the back where he can see the coop, covered in light snow. The hens cluck at his approach. One leans forward, puffing herself up like a balloon.

There is something lying next to the coop, covered

in snow. From afar it could be another dead hen. Nick unslings the rifle and approaches with caution. Keeping his stance low, the barrel pointed straight ahead.

When he is less than six feet away the shape finally stirs. The hens are whipped to a frenzy of clucking and squawking. They peck at the fencing that keeps them in the coop, pacing back and forth like condemned prisoners. They have seen the hangman. They know it by the russet red tail that pops free from the snow. The white teeth, displayed in a fierce grimace. With its ears pulled back and its eyes full of hatred Nick knows—this is the fox.

He circles the scene, examining it from all angles. The fox's left paw is smashed thoroughly between the jaws of the steel trap. Just like his father had said would happen. The ground is undisturbed after the recent snowfall. It must have been caught in the trap all night, fuming silently beneath the snow.

The rage of a predator is far different from the rage of a prey animal. A steer might hate, might long to gore you with his horns, but it is the passionless hatred of an animal that knows it will one day be felled by another, walking on two legs or otherwise. The hate of a predator is pure and unchanging, for it is the greatest humiliation to be bested at its own game.

He approaches with caution. Watching the tongue loll from the fox's mouth as it widens into a lazy grimace. Seemingly unhurried, unbothered by the scene before it. Blood coming out of its paw, crusting around the metal jaws of the trap. In trying to escape it has yanked the trap out from beneath the snow. Nick can see the edge of his face reflected in the glinting metal. The frost on the ground almost blinding him.

He knows what he must do. What his father and brother have done before him. Kill the fox with a single bullet. Carlyle had always deemed it unmanly, to prolong an animal's misery. No use hunting with a bow and arrow. One shot between the eyes would do. Then he would take the body from the trap and bring it to the Quonset where he could skin it and make something from the fur. A lady's stole. A collar for his jacket, fiery red.

Raising the rifle he points it at the fox who stands unmoving next to the coop. Looking straight down at it he sees its dark pupils and almost hesitates, though there is no time for hesitation, he must kill the fox and in this act kill what is left of his kindness, his tender mercy that was bestowed upon him by an uncaring God. Only then will he take his rightful place in the Morrow family, one meted out to him by fate, a seat at the right hand of the throne.

The fox opens its mouth and emits a violent scream. Like the scream he heard first from within the depths of his father's house, the bowels of Stag's Crossing, that womanlike scream that echoed through the halls and woke Joshua and Carlyle both. That scream that might torment him, thirty years from now, chilling in its mimicry.

The widow-wail. The cry of bitter and perpetual grief. He has killed its children and it has returned, now, to face him. All his useless guilt. But it is too late now. The little foxes are dead; he and his father have committed a crime for which he can never atone. And so begins the slow decline of the Morrow family, the crumbling of the foundation at Stag's Crossing, where his father has seeded the fields with fox-bones.

He lowers the rifle. A faint shiver runs through him. Destiny, long foretold, has come to Stag's Crossing at last. He cannot kill—not like the long-legged hounds that traipse through the house, slavering at the mere thought of rabbits. Nor like his brother, who has shot and felled young deer by the hundreds. He is not a boy made for this work, though death follows swiftly at his heels, a pursuer he will not soon forget.

He kneels until his face is almost level with the fox. So close he can see the russet etching of its fur, vivid in the snow. There is no understanding in its eyes as he reaches toward the trap and carefully pulls it forward. No sense that it knows beyond an animal cunning what this act represents. Defiance, forgiveness, all things Nick will never extend to himself. Unlike himself this fox has never known shame or the clawing fear of abandonment, the self-disgust that consumes him at every waking hour.

Are you going to hurt me? he says. Knowing the fox will not respond. Knowing full well the ramifications of his actions may not come today nor tomorrow, but at some strange point in the future when the alfalfa has risen strong and high, untouched by the plains wind, and his father stoops to examine the soil, his back bent with age. A future he can hardly envision, its distance unfathomable, the span of years appearing to him like millennia.

The fox retreats, its paw still out. Gently he takes the trap in hand and pushes down on the springs holding the jaws of the trap together. With great effort—he knows acutely that this is far more effort than Joshua would have ever taken—he finally opens the trap and allows the fox to pull away from him. The snow is red with dried blood. It stands there and looks at him, licking its paw almost contemplatively.

Go on, Nick says. He waves his hand as if to dismiss it from his sight.

The fox sits and continues licking its paw until it is clean of blood. It cares nothing for his concerns. The underlying dread of what his father will do if he finds out that he has let loose the fox upon the henhouse. The impostor at Stag's Crossing.

Finally it gets up and begins to limp away. Leaving a light speckling of blood in its wake. Nick watches it break into a run as it reaches the tree line. None of his father's menacing greyhounds willing to chase after it, lolling as they do in the grand foyer of the house where the biting cold cannot reach them.

The fox disappears beyond the next hill, its red tail flashing crimson before it dives into the shadow of the woods. Nick hastily covers its tracks with his boot prints. Dusting another layer of snow over the trap like no one had been there before, the jaws ready and open to receive to the flesh of another unsuspecting animal. The rest of the day he entertains himself with the dogs, within the warm rib cage of the house where he stokes the fireplace and makes dinner from scraps.

His father returns that evening. He takes his boots off in the foyer and hangs up his coat. Nick looks at him from the couch where one of the dogs is sleeping at his feet before rising and bringing his father a plate of sausages. Carlyle sits at the table and begins tearing into the sausages like a starving man. Nick knows his friends' fathers often come home from town smelling of alcohol or worse, but Carlyle reeks of nothing but the singular urge to destroy. He watches his father rip the casing apart with his bare hands and stuff himself like some terrifying giant from a children's book he was never read, and though they are almost the same height his father might terrify him still.

See anything interesting while I was out? Carlyle says. Wiping his hands clean on the napkin Nick proffers.

No, Nick says. Wondering if his father can see the shame on his face. How he quickly turns away to take the dirty dishes to the sink for a good scrubbing.

Carlyle says, Let's go take a look at the coop.

Now? It's dark.

Yes, now. Get your coat on.

Nick grabs his coat from the rack and puts it on. His hands do not shake but he is a little paler when he comes to the back porch to join his father, who has found one of his rifles and is waiting by the screen door. Out they go into the chilling wind, toward the wooden coop where the chickens have huddled together on their roost.

You put petroleum jelly on the wattles? Carlyle asks, shining his flashlight on the brood.

Yeah, Nick says. He shoves his hands into his coat pockets.

Good. Let's have a look at the trap.

In the darkness it is hard to see more than a few feet away, until his father points the beam at the ground and sees the edge of the trap sticking out of the snow. The surrounding ground marked by Nick's footprints, chicken tracks, a few dead leaves curling sullenly in on themselves.

You come out here?

Came to check. Didn't see anything.

His father turns and shines the light directly in his face. It's been moved, he says. His voice soft but ungentle, the cold rasp of it clear to Nick. There's no more bait.

Kenny told me some of those foxes are clever. Cleverer than you and I might think. They've escaped him many times before. Just have to keep trying.

Carlyle moves the beam onto the trap and then back onto Nick's face. Nick wills himself to look straight ahead, into Carlyle's eyes. His hands clenched in his pockets he stands rigid as an elm. They are almost the same height now—Nick might grow a little taller still. Surpassing his father in one way, or all ways. His morals that of a compassionate and forgiving almighty. One he might have prayed to as a child, to kill him where he stood because he could bear it no more.

Carlyle flicks the flashlight downward and says, Fine. You'll reset the trap in the morning then. Just like I showed you. Don't want any more dead hens.

Nick does not allow relief to show on his face. He feels only the shearing of the cold night air whipping against his nose.

Yes, Dad, he says.

Go back in the house, Carlyle says. Nick obeys. Beginning the walk back to his room alone, he turns only once to see his father kneeling by the trap with the little light in his hand. Reading the past, the future from the marks in the snow.

He has covered his deception well. He knows this. He knows the mien of his father, that it is likely he is believed.

Still he finds it difficult to concentrate on finishing the dishwashing. Changing into his pajamas in his little room he wonders at how much he is grown. The notches in the doorway stopped weeks ago, but he has surpassed this. Filling his empty body with the soft loam of Stag's Crossing he has rooted and flowered into such a young man as this. Poisonous to behold.

Come morning he sees his father in the doorway. A dark, towering shadow that stretches across the ceiling. He rises from the bed but not before his father says, I know you think you're clever. Resetting the trap, he says. Hiding what you did from me. But I saw the blood. Any fool would know just by looking at it that it had been sprung. You think I was born yesterday?

Nick has no reply to this. The mastery, the sheer force of Carlyle's anger apparent to him. In the confines of his small bedroom he has nowhere to hide. He is worse off than the fox with its butchered paw, waiting near the henhouse for its inevitable death.

Dad, Nick begins, feebly.

His father comes right up next to his bed. Normally he does not care to ever come into Nick's room but now he is so close Nick can feel Carlyle's spittle on his face. His father grabbing him by the collar, near-choking him with it like one of the dogs. The fabric so tight in his fist he tears open a seam as Nick gasps and tries to wriggle away.

Shouldn't have been Christopher who died with her, Carlyle says. Should've been you.

He has doomed his family. Nick knows this now; has always known this. Will know this in thirty years when Emilia sets foot in the grand foyer of the house, that it is not his brother but himself who has ruined them all. He has let the fox out of the trap and through their front door, he has invited the beasts of the woods into the civilized manor at Stag's Crossing where only men were meant to tread and in doing so he has allowed the first outsider in decades to water their blighted fields with his family's blood.

Carlyle storms downstairs, slamming the door behind him. Leaving Nick alone in the semidarkness, wrapped in the blanket his mother sewed for him. The last witness to the distinct and totalizing pleasure of Carlyle's cruelty.

Ten, maybe fifteen brittle years from now Nick will be confronted by a man professing his love and find that he cannot reciprocate. Not because he does not want to, but because all he has been taught about love—that strange emotion that forever ties him to his father, that will link him to Henry until both of their deaths—was taught to him on a spring evening. Dragging himself from a ditch, his sleeves covered with dirt. The little foxes and their pleading eyes. A precious thing, once residing within him, that has now been utterly destroyed.

XI.

THEN & NOW

Emilia is nearly two thousand years out of practice in destroying men, but it is as easy as it ever was. She marvels at herself, her magnificent handiwork. The locusts swarming overhead in agony. Stag's Crossing ablaze. Nick falling to his knees before her. Unable to even beg her for a reprieve, knowing that there will be none.

That morning she had risen early and listened to the birds, their secret language. In the mirror that cast no reflection she cultivated her face as a gardener might cultivate a precious flower—she had always been so beautiful in this form, striking down even emperors with her allure. In her other permutations she has no need for her long black hair, her painted visage. Instead she might glow brilliantly as an ember, sloughing off the ridiculousness of her human body. She finds her skin particularly frustrating—how bare and shaven it is. Unhelpful in the deep winter. Fantasizing often about crawling beneath the roots of a willow tree and lying in the damp soil for hours before emerging newly born, monstrous to behold.

With Nick sleeping soundly in the master bedroom, she sat on the bed next to him and remembered. The darkness of the forest that had once sheltered her. There she had mated during a sun-shower, lying in the hollow beneath a fallen tree. Then came the birthing, bloody and painful. In another age she would have raised them with her magic, taught them sorcery, and sent them to the capital for their education. Instead they were dead; her fool of a fox-husband also, who had lain down in the middle of a dirt road and waited to die.

Her attentions have long turned to the fond pleasures of deceit and revenge. As delicious as a well-played game of go. She of all creatures knows that a human shape is temporary, and all animals that can turn one way can turn another—that little stripling who cut her husband into pieces—how delicious it was to watch the hooves burst from her body, her face taking the mien of a sorrowful doe.

Centuries ago she had possessed a very beautiful young woman named Daji and wreaked havoc on an entire dynasty. Now the world had a different shape, a different path for its stars; her creator was a goddess both lovely and fickle, and her favor departed as quickly as it came. When the boy freed her she was no better than the lowest insect, spared by the hand that had torn her children to pieces. She would have wept for them if she could have. But a fox does not weep.

And so she waited. Observing the house from afar for years, until the eldest son was old enough to put her teeth in him, all forty-two of them. Shedding her skin by moonlight, a distasteful ritual, but necessary. The first night she stole a dress and fed on a man she met near a hotel in Pennsylvania. He might have deserved it, but she doubted it. She removed his liver in the bathtub and ate it raw while he watched.

A bus ticket east brought her to the doorstep of Joshua's favored haunts. She waited there, in strange bars, on park benches, until she finally found him at one of the grand museums that still displayed pictures of her. Better days, halcyon days. She reminisced while waiting to cross paths with him. Looking at one of the white museum placards with feigned interest. There it was written that she had been killed, but of course she had not—she had simply crossed the sea, and never returned. Perhaps she had been banished from her homeland by a minor goddess in a fit of pique; perhaps she had traveled to these distant plains with the first Chinese immigrants who settled there, who opened laundries and had their shops vandalized with bricks. Or perhaps she had left for better hunting grounds, centuries ago, in search of men who had not yet learned from their grandmothers to check for fox-fur in the wedding bed.

She remembered very little of their first conversation. Her charm inescapable, she waited patiently for him to ask for her name, her occupation. She had read the name Emilia in a play and liked it; the girl whose body she had brutally parasitized so many years ago had been a painter, so she said that she, too, was a painter. She had always found conversations with men to be acts of gamesmanship—volleying speech back and forth until she obtained what she truly desired.

He took her to a restaurant for their first date. She wore her best dress that shone like flames and by eight o'clock she knew that she had him. She could have carved out his heart that very night. Returning to her apartment, which was entirely empty of all furniture, she saw in the bathroom mirror not her face but a future in which he would marry her and disdain his father. Premonitions of what was to come—twenty years of waiting, folding her body up into this grotesque shell, a *human woman*, that she had always despised.

He never asked about the scars on her left hand, nor why she preferred to make love in the pitch black—lest he see something that might reveal her to be anything other than the most enchanting of women. She spoke to him often, with her voice of silver and whipped cream, so he would learn to obey. At the wedding her dress had a long train, long enough to obscure the flash of russet, the improperly shaped feet that might alarm even the most enamored husband.

When Joshua brought her back to Stag's Crossing for the first time, she waited in the car as Carlyle raged furiously, meaninglessly. Casting her from the house with the futility of a man who has just attempted to disregard his own death. From the second floor Joshua's younger brother watched in the window—she noted him, the curiosity with which he regarded her. In twenty years, what then? Her husband would be older, and she would be young and beautiful as ever. Age had never held dominion over her, no more than disease or death. Perhaps she could make something of it.

She ran her fingers through Nick's hair and contemplated the possibility of strangling him in his sleep. She could drag his body to the second bedroom that no one enters and carve out his heart and liver. *Raw eater* had once been her epithet—another time, another country. Were she a real woman she might feel real affection for him, but she is a *huli jing.* Living only for the ferocious hunt, the glorious betrayal. The suffering of others is its own delicacy, more pleasurable than that of even raw flesh.

In the bathroom she washed her face and found that the lovely Nüwa favored her, returning the ecstasy of the hunt to her bones. She told Nick of her truest self. Relishing in how quickly he ran from her, how easily he was cut down. How she longed to slit him open and look inside, to lie on the kitchen tile with him and slowly feed herself pieces of his intestine as he died.

But then again, she thought, he would be so handsomely adorned with antlers.

The arrival of Joshua and his near-dying father put an end to these considerations. She watched without emotion as Joshua, jealous as ever, enacted his last act of vengeance on his younger brother. The family allegiances as tangled as thorned sweetbrier. Carlyle with his half-paralyzed face, witnessing the breakdown of his house. She could have healed him then and there. Returned him to his sons the picture of health—a miracle, Joshua would say. But the season of forgiveness was long past. The flowers in the garden were sprouting again, rich and vibrantly colored. She had not lived decades in this shell of a body to turn back now.

Joshua had never understood the true nature of his predicament. What man could? To think that his wife was conspiring against him, every minute of every hour, plotting his demise? A part of her had thought to tear his heart out as soon as she set eyes on him. But she could be patient. She had been lonely in the woods for so many years. She had great affection for him, despite everything. The only affection she might ever feel for a mortal man was reliant on how well he could serve her, and Joshua had served her very well. She might like to play with her food a little while longer. And twenty years, thirty even, was not such a long time.

When his head finally came free from his body she wondered if she might return later and gnaw on his exposed sinews, delicately aged, a delightful anticipation. Interrupted in her thoughts only by Nick's final attempt to rescue himself from an undoing of his own making. When he put the knife in her it was like so many other men who had tried to kill her and failed, who had not read the books that would tell them nothing less than a peach-wood sword would fell her, the *huli jing* that had taken the name of Daji, the body of Daji, but was herself an enigma in a woman's skin.

The fox set loose, at last, upon the henhouse. Just as she had burned alive those chattering ministers who had opposed her seductive hold on Di Xin, so she would not be satisfied until the Morrow house and all it contained was turned to ash. The fire gorging itself on the house until the walls were blackened, licked clean by the flames. She listened as Carlyle immolated. Vacating his skin as an insect might discard its exoskeleton except this time it was his burned body sloughing off piecemeal, until all that lingered was the memory of him.

Now only Nick remains. He who supplicates her on his knees like he is supplicating an unknown God. Just down the path the flames and smoke have risen so high it is like a blessed conflagration at the end of days.

Get up, she says.

He stands to look at her, clutching at the wound in his chest where the knife is still lodged inside. The fear in his eyes mixed with a disturbed resignation. Six lean greyhounds that escaped the blaze have started the walk down from the back of the house. They make no noise.

Nick coughs—bile rises from his throat and splashes into his hand. He recalls his sickness upon seeing the parasitic innards of the doe he had failed to shoot so many years ago on that ill-fated hunting trip. The memory burned in his mind like a brand.

A death deferred has come to Stag's Crossing. It is his own, and he has let it into the henhouse himself. Released it from the trap that snowy afternoon where the dogs could not keep still for hours at a time. A restlessness in the winter air. The wind so cold it hurt his throat to breathe it in. How could he have not seen it earlier? When he heard the fox screaming it was the wailing of a woman; he and his father had killed her children. Tore one's head off and threw the other to the dogs. It is only fitting to be repaid exactly in return.

Closer come the greyhounds—some loping, others

picking up the pace. It is startling to see them all take flight at once, their slender legs jackknifing across gravel.

When they are here, he wonders if he will run on four legs or two. If he will possess the sixteen points of a monarch stag, woven elaborately above his head. He imagines the gossip: Stag's Crossing burned to the ground—one son found decapitated, the other missing. A magnificent buck lying dead in the weald behind the house, coursed down by six fleet-footed greyhounds.

Emilia, he says. Please—

That's not my name, she says.

Then what is it?

She gently grasps his head in her hands. Smoothing over the skin of his face with her fingers, pushing back an unruly strand of hair. Leaning close, he can feel her breath hot in his ear. Her lips barely seeming to move. She speaks her name, like fire, like an incantation. A spell so powerful that he knows when she leaves this place, shorn of her humanity, she will have utterly erased the Morrows from the earth. The charred wreck that is Stag's Crossing will be bulldozed within a year. The family that once lived there, falling into nameless obscurity. The story will be told and retold again until there is no truth left in the telling.

Emilia takes his hand. Her touch is gentle. The dogs are almost upon them now. Slowly, carefully she extends her tongue. Licking the dried blood from his palm, until it is clean and white as the day he was born.

ACKNOWLEDGMENTS

The writing of this novel would not have been possible without the encouragement and perceptive edits of my fantastic agent, Paul Lucas. Thank you for seeing the potential in this book and guiding me through revisions and every step of the publishing process. Additional thanks to Eloy Bleifuss for his thoughtful contributions, and to everyone at Janklow & Nesbit.

Thank you to all the incredible people at St. Martin's Press who supported this book on its journey to publication. Many thanks especially to my editor, Michael Homler, for championing the novel and providing editorial guidance that helped shape it into a great read.

Thank you to the many wonderful teachers who I've had over the years who encouraged me to write: to Dutch Fichthorn, my high school English teacher and forensics coach, who molded me into a serious artist. To Collomia Charles, my ancient-Greek instructor, who introduced me to a language that genuinely changed my life, and taught me so much beyond conjugating the aorist.

Thank you to my parents, Jon and Conni, for reading an early draft of this novel and supporting my work, as well as for the helpful comments on authentically rendering Nebraska farm life.

Thank you to Tim Fowler, for over a decade of friendship and over a decade of listening to my weird novel ideas. I also thank my friends Garfio, Grace, Jason, Ryan, Wilton, and York for their kind support. Special thanks to my old friend Constantinos, who was one of the first people to encourage me as a writer. I hope you're enjoying this book in the afterlife, my friend.